# FRETTED AND MOANING

## ANDY SUMMERS

First published 2021 by Rocket 88 Books
an imprint of Essential Works Limited,
40 Bowling Green Lane,
London EC1R ONE
United Kingdom

Printed in Malta by Gutenberg Press

ISBN: 9781910978665

andysummersbook.com

rocket88books.com

## ACKNOWLEDGEMENTS

Deep thanks to all the dear friends, travelling companions, work mates, inspirers, writers and musicians and fellow shufflers on the mortal coil. I thank you because without you there would be no ink in the well...

Kate, Layla, Mo, Anton, Enzo, and Gia Summers. Laura Josephson for the fabulous cover, Paul Slansky for great editing advice, Liz Dubelman for belief and encouragement. Dennis Smith, Tarquin Gotch, Manfred Seipt, Gilles Mora, Stijn Huijts, Cecilia Miniucchi, Jeffrey Coulter, Zoot Money, Peter Alan Roberts, Emily Bauer, Sting, Stewart Copeland, John Dearman, Ralph Gibson, Mary Jane Marcasiano, Norman Moore, Francie Moore, Bradley Bambarger, Ben Verdery, John Etheridge, Jerome Laperrousaz, Cathy Colman, Luiz Paulo Assunção – Man! Let's play...! Roberto Menescal, Hideyuki Taguchi, Lenny Breau, Julian Bream, Bill Borden, Count Ian Blair, Lawrence Impey, Kevin Coyne, Brian Cinadr, Rodrigo Santos, Joa Barone, Dittany Lang, John Silva, Miguel Senovilla, Michael Luevano, et al...

# CONTENTS

# INTRODUCTION

I've played the guitar since I was about eleven. My first was a shabby little Spanish number with one string missing, passed on to me by an uncle who had strummed it all over the place in South Africa. He told me he had also used it to ward off lions. I was immediately entranced (gobsmacked) with this wondrous thing and obsession lit up my prepubescent soul and I disappeared into my bedroom, sat on the edge of my bed and confronted the mystery of strings and frets for the first time. And well … since that glorious and innocent moment, I haven't been seen much, basically, because after entering the labyrinth I never thought of ever doing anything else, like … forever! Although, I did have a brief flirtation with ornithology and indulged a vague interest in theoretical physics. But in the end the guitar and music are what got me through. At times it's been a faith-testing relationship, but the romance continues.

I started writing these stories a little while back and showed them to a few musician friends, who encouraged me to keep at it. I also read them in front of a live audience – it seemed to go well, someone laughed – so indeed I kept at it. Most of these tales are drawn from real life or are things I have heard about in the dark corners of various backstage dressing rooms. It's hard to be a musician, but for some of us there is simply no choice. Meanwhile, there's writing about it. Let me know what you think …

*Andy Summers*
*Los Angeles, 2021*

# CARTER AND LEWIS

"Goddam Rhonda, she's done it again."

Carter Lewis slumped heavily on the dark mahogany counter at the Pig in Skirts saloon and wiped his mouth with the sleeve of his shirt, almost cutting his lip open with a rhinestone. "She just smashed the fuckin' headstock off my Gibson J-00. That belonged to my granddaddy, Goddammit! He even had a hit using it – 'I'll Scream When It's Over'. Goddammit! They don't make 'em like that anymore. Takes a long time for a guitar to get that way, sound that good, get that soul. I should kill her and be done with it. Probably a song in there somewhere. Hmm… gotta think about that. Something in dropped D, maybe."

"Bet'cha could come up with one." Curly, Carter's buddy, stared over the bar and blew out a long stream of smoke. "Whad'ya gonna do? Women – fuckin' hopeless. Write it out, man, sing it out. Make some Benjamins off it."

"Fuckin' A," said Busta, Carter's other buddy, tossing back a shot of whiskey and rye and nodding slowly, the wisdom of a long-derailed life oozing from his pitted features.

"This is it," said Carter. "I swear today it gets real and you clowns are going to bear witness."

"You swear what?" ventured Busta. "C'mon, Carter, we all seen ya go through this before and you wrote a lot of fuckin' songs off the back of it. She's a source of inspiration, man. A muse or whatever they call it."

"Don't make me puke. She's on the sauce," Carter snorted. "Can't get another guitar like that and she's cheatin', been cheatin', *is* cheatin' on me right now and with you know who. This is it. Here's the plan."

"Uh-oh," said Curly.

"Fuck," said Busta.

Rhonda, Carter's wife, was involved with a no-longer mystery man who happened to be the nemesis of Carter's life, another country singer named – unbelievably – Lewis Carter. A piss-awful truth that Carter had to live with every day.

Carter Lewis had been the first on the scene, but had been followed not much later by Lewis Carter, who had a song almost identical to Carter's first hit. It became confusing for a while. Carter was really pissed off about it, while Lewis just laughed his ass off. Promoters weren't sure of who they were booking and radio DJs got mixed up, and sometimes the fans turned up at the wrong concert until it became a great public joke, but one which the public really enjoyed.

Carter Lewis started putting 'The Original' on his posters and records for a while, but the public didn't like it. It was as if he was spoiling the fun, so he quietly let it go, even as people reversed the name in spray paint over his name on the posters.

Their rivalry was intense. They hated each other's guts and tried to outsing, outplay, outgun each other, although Lewis Carter seemed to have a perverse sense of humour about it. Carter Lewis started bringing in slick LA session musicians to shine up his recordings, while his rival went the other way and got real old-time and authentic with his stuff, showing the fans that he was more real, more sincere and more in direct contact with the lives of the people. He *was* country. He even came out with a song called 'I'm More Country Than You'. That went down very well with the locals, once again to Carter's screaming frustration.

Then it was cars. Carter Lewis got the biggest, longest-finned blue, cream and gold Caddy you could buy anywhere, thinking that would shut Lewis Carter the fuck up. But then the bastard drove into town with a gleaming vintage red and silver Buick with guitars painted on the wings. Grinding his teeth, Carter ordered a giant ten-gallon papiermaché cowboy hat, which he had fixed to the roof of his Cadillac. *That* would prove that he was still king in these parts. But sadly, very soon after getting the hat in position, bad weather hit town. The rain was Biblical and the hat collapsed into a pathetic heap of soggy paper and glue which ruined the Caddy's paintwork.

Lewis Carter immediately came out with a new song about hats and cars and it became a local hit. It seemed like everyone in town could sing it, knew all the words and even knew the guitar chords. Lewis Carter then topped that off by riding through town on a golden palomino.

Carter Lewis was at his wits end, now almost out of everything he could think of to beat his opponent to the ground. Then he had an idea. Rhinestones. Yes, he could outdo Lewis Carter with the sheer number of rhinestones he wore. He knew in his heart of hearts that rhinestones were probably a bit passé in this modern era of country, where it was almost rock, but he felt sure in his Tennessee heart that his sentiment was right. There were plenty of folks around who would remember the Grand Ole Opry, with stars like Porter Wagoner, Lefty Frizzell, Ernest Tubb, Gene Autry, Hank Williams, Kitty Wells, Tammy Wynette and Loretta Lynn. That memory, plus simple heartfelt songs about life's tribulations and a shitload of rhinestones, would tug at their heartstrings. That should put Lewis Carter away once and for all and he, Carter Lewis, would be back on top.

Carter went to his local tailor and described what he wanted. It was demanding even by a rhinestone tailor's standards, as it involved many thousands of the little fake stones and long, *long* nights of sewing. But it was Carter Lewis doing the asking so the tailor, cursing his luck, agreed to the unreasonable demands.

About a month later the tailor, with ravaged fingers, presented the suit to Carter. It was magnificent, even if extremely heavy with the phenomenal number of rhinestones sewn into the suit fabric, which was now no longer even visible. Carter, in the confines of a tiny dressing room and struggling to get the suit on, got his pants snagged in the spurs attached to his boots and fell with a mighty crash, smashing through the dressing room wall and breaking his wrist as he hit the floor in a cloud of plaster and cheap sheetrock.

He lay there in a crumpled heap for a few minutes and then, shouting various expletives with religious overtones, eventually got back up on his feet, pulled on the suit and, through a blurred wall of pain, actually liked what he saw – a god in pure rhinestone. Once this vision had passed, he realized that something was wrong. His left wrist hurt like hell and surely was busted – Goddammit.

Broken wrist, feeling pissed – once again there was a song in there somewhere, like 'rhinestone suit,' 'tripped on my boot,' 'no more loot,' or something.

The immediate problem was that Carter was due on stage to-night at the Opry and it was sold out. Sure, he could still sing, but his guitar playing was also part of the Carter Lewis legend. He had a new record out. He couldn't miss the show. What to do? He needed a substitute guitar player, someone who could carry the songs in the Carter Lewis style.

Carter sat in his motel room and, through his drugged pain, thought long and hard about who could come in at the last minute and play all those signature guitar parts. He mentally went through the list of the local guitar slingers who could cover it but kept coming back to the one horrendous thought. It was Lewis Carter, Goddammit. He who had copied Carter all the way and sometimes outdone him with his own stylings would now play guitar.

In a twisted way, Carter liked the idea. His new backup guitar player would shut the fuck up and Carter would do the singing. It would finally show the people who the real star was. Lewis would just be some guitar player in his backing band. Now, *that* would be justice. Carter, presuming that Lewis would of course take the gig, made a call to his manager. Twenty minutes passed and then the phone rang. Carter's manager confirmed that Lewis would do the gig. He'd even said it was an honour for him. Slightly befuddled by this word from his arch-enemy, Carter mumbled, "Well, alright, but no rehearsal. Just know the Goddamn songs."

At 9pm the band walked out onto the stage at the Grand Ole Opry. The audience gasped as they recognized Lewis Carter, and not Carter Lewis as advertised. Had they got it wrong again or had the promoter made a mistake again? Whatever, it was going to be good. And then, just as they were getting used to that idea, out walked Carter Lewis, dazzling in rhinestone and smiling at his fans with his arm in a sling. The audience gasped again. This was a first. Impossible. Two titans and sworn rivals on the stage together. Awesome!

With a brief nod at the band Carter started into the first song. All went well. The band was in good shape, possibly slightly better with the addition of Lewis Carter on guitar.

Carter carried on with his usual routine and patter but began to feel irritated by how good the guitar playing was tonight. With each new song the guitar solos started to get louder and flashier and increase in bar length from sixteen to thirty-two, and then to sixty-four, until Carter realized he was merely mouthing the lyrics and getting out of the way for the onslaught of another brilliant solo. He saw his life passing, fading in a sea of tarnished rhinestones. He was losing this battle, as well as the audience. He looked back over his good shoulder at the band and saw that Lewis Carter was playing his Telecaster with his teeth, the audience hanging off every note.

In a last desperate attempt to get the upper hand, he invited Rhonda on stage to sing a duet with him. The usual show-stopper, a fast-paced country tune with a story about chickens. The audience picked up on it and howled along until once again it was time for the guitar solo. Lewis Carter stepped into the spotlight and, doing a little jig as he played, ripped out another incendiary solo. Rhonda sashayed over to him and stroked his shoulder and then, looking at the crowd, winked at them and slowly ran her hand down the guitar player's thigh. The crowd screamed back, wanting more, but Rhonda made another suggestive wink and skedaddled back to her husband. Carter, now in a seething fury, ended the song, shrugged at the crowd and stomped off the stage.

Back in his dressing room Carter slumped on his couch and reached for a bottle of Jack Daniel's – anything to ease the pain. His wrist was aching and the unbearable weight of the rhinestone suit was killing him. What a piece of shit. He angrily waited for Rhonda so that they could have a total brawl about her antics tonight. "What the fuck?"

The door opened and his manager Pete walked in, nodding. "Never thought I'd see that," he drawled.

"And you will never fuckin' see it again," snarled Carter. "Well, I dunno," said Pete, pulling out a Marlboro. "There might be something there. The fuckin' act was dynamite. Really might wanna think about it… Where's Rhonda?"

"Ain't seen her," said Carter morosely, taking another slug of Jack. As he said this, he and Pete heard a roar of laughter from the next dressing room – the backing band's dressing room. It sounded like they were having a great time, a fantastic party, and it also sounded like most of the audience was in there. Carter wanted to go in and be the star finally making an entrance, but he hesitated. He was the star, Goddammit. He couldn't go down to that level, blow his cool, his mystique. And where the fuck was Rhonda?

And then he got it. She was in there with him, sticking her surgical enhancements in his face, no doubt. It was the final insult. Carter reached for his pistol, which he was never without. But as his hands touched the cold steel a song title sprang into his head: 'Crime of Passion'. Yeah, could be worth it. Cover – lover, gotta die – alibi, deceiver – meat cleaver. Country-style lyrics flooded his head. Took my wife – took his life, gotta pay – you're dead today, heaven above – died for love. Hmm...

That night, after they got back to the mansion, he and Rhonda had one of their standard knock-down drag-out fights, only worse than usual. Rhonda smashed Carter's favourite guitar, along with a couple of gold records, and in the ensuing wrestling match managed to unleash millions of rhinestones from his new suit. She then stomped off into the night.

Carter, hung over, woke up in a sea of rhinestones that stuck into him and burrowed in his flesh like an army of red ants. But through the blur and fog, the lyrics to the possible new song, 'Crime of Passion', were still passing through his head. They all seemed to fit this particular moment. After a life of making this shit up, the shit was now going to get real.

Carter hauled his ass out of bed, took a look in the mirror and set off to meet Busta and Curly.

After several drinks and confirmation of their lifelong friendship, and a laying out of his plan, Carter staggered out of the Pig in Skirts, piled into Busta's crapmobile and directed Busta over to where he knew for sure that Rhonda and Lewis Carter were shacking up. The Longhorn Love Motel, to be exact. How did he know that? Because Carter was working off animal instinct and a cowboy sense of justice. Also, it was where Lewis lived.

They pulled up at the Longhorn. Carter told his buddies to stay in the car and keep the engine revving – they might have to make a fast getaway. He strode into the lobby and, seeing that the receptionist was out like a light, quickly looked into the hotel entry book and saw a fancy signature that was unmistakable: Lewis Carter, room 101. Carter strode up the stairs like the Grim Reaper, country lyrics howling in his head. Outside room 101 he knocked lightly on the door and squeaked out in his best Dolly Parton falsetto, "Maid…"

No answer. He rapped on the door again. There was a faint "What the fuck?" and a female voice muttering something like "Ah, poor baby," then a shuffling of feet and the door opened. Lewis Carter and Carter Lewis stood facing each other.

"Oh, shit," said Lewis.

"What is it, honey?" Rhonda called out from back on the bed. Carter stomped into the room waving his gun as Lewis slid back between the sheets. Carter tried a tricky finger-twirling thing with his revolver but it didn't quite work. So he just gripped it in a John Wayne style and levelled it at Lewis's head.

"Carter?" said Lewis.

"Lewis?" said Carter.

The two men stared at each other and then Carter snarled, "This is it" and he squeezed the trigger. But nothing happened.

"What the fuck?" he snorted. He held the gun upside down, shook it and spun the chamber. A number of rhinestones fell out.

Lewis burst into laughter and that sent Carter into a hyena hoot so hard that he fell over sideways and shot off his kneecap.

# NO VALUE

We were out in West Virginia one time, playing in a coal-mining town. We were about three-quarters of the way through our set, which had been filled with jeering, booing and shouts along the lines of Thirsty's mother having had sex with every man in the room, plus calls for Dolly Parton songs and a few simple "Get off the f…n' stage!" Then the culmination of this hell's brew happened when a fat-assed bearded trucker guy came to the edge of the stage, took the headstock of my bass guitar in his mouth, bit clean through the wood and spat it out on the floor.

But let me backtrack a bit – well, quite a bit, actually. Our band is/was called the Deaf Mutes. We got together in downtown New York ages ago. There was a great scene going on then. Anybody could be in a band. You still used the minimal props – guitar, bass, drums and a mic. But what you did with them was beside the point as long as you had, you know, 'tude. That counted far more than a gift for music, which we regarded as an artistic lie.

We were a weird band because we all came from different parts of the US, had nothing in common, and didn't like each other, or music, come to think of it. My boyfriend Thirsty Need at just under seven feet tall, was the guitarist. He was our leader and really was a brilliant conceptual artist. In truth, he regarded his guitar as a paintbrush, while I thought of my bass guitar as a toothbrush. The drums were a place on which to rest your beer. Having given up all attempts at learning the guitar, Thirsty would hit any random six notes on a keyboard and tune his guitar strings to those pitches. This often involved dangerous snapping of strings and severe slashing of Thirsty's cheeks. But he took it well, receiving those scars as a tribute to real art. Not knowing any actual guitar chords, but getting the general idea, Thirsty would make up geometric shapes, anything from a simple parallelogram to a ten-pointed dodecahedron, and just stick that shape anywhere on the neck of the guitar. Once he had that in place, we would try to fit ourselves around it. Thirsty, of course, could not let go of the configuration as he manfully gripped the strings like a sailor in a gale-force wind, while I plodded away on the bass and moaned a one-note dirge. Thirsty always set his guitar amp at full-on everything and faced his guitar right into the cone of the speaker, so the only sound we knew was howling feedback. It was effective.

We did an early gig at ggbbggbb's and wowed the crowd. No one asked for their two dollars admission back, either because their minds were blown by us or they were on drugs, or both. We felt it was a triumph and also a high point in the history of the movement we started calling 'No Value'. I stuck to one note for the whole show and fixed the crowd with a zombie stare. It killed 'em, and I knew I had found my place in the universe, if not the road to Hollywood.

Well, after that we thought the world was ours. We felt a surge of interest and we responded. I guess it was our general weirdness, a sexy chick (me) with a giant guitarist and a wall of feedback. I was the visual point of interest, so I responded by cutting up my clothes with a small pair of nail scissors and doing crazy shit with my hair and strapping an M16 across my back. It worked beautifully and a couple of deconstructivist critiques on our band were published, notably in France.

We actually started to make a living as a band. Thirsty gave up his job at the One Hung Low Laundromat and I stopped being a waitress at the Vomitorium.

Several years later things changed in an unexpected way. It was when, one day, Thirsty played a sound on his guitar that was ultra-weird.

"What the fuck is that?" we all cried out in unison.

Thirsty turned his back to us and played the strange sound again. Then he whispered over his shoulder, "This is 'C'."

"What's that?" we all yelled in bewilderment. "It's a chord," said Thirsty in an even huskier voice.

Well, there was much discussion and argument over this desolate new sound. It was disturbing and challenging but there was no turning back. Thirsty kept coming up with these weird new chords; 'C' was followed by 'F' then by 'G'. When he said one sound was called 'G seventh' we were ready to call it a day.

Then he came up with an actual melody and that just about finished us off. But he was the leader and we had to follow him. We ended up making a record with songs that had verses, choruses and melodies that you could sing along to. I couldn't find my place in it, the zombie stare was no longer working. I found it so hard to put on a smile. I knew my cover was blown. I longed for the old days when what we did was pure art and not something as banal as music.

The result was that we became extremely popular and broke up forever.

# COME TOGETHER

Floyd's career was finally winding down, after almost thirty years of it – the gypsy life, the deathly tarmac, the ceaseless and self-perpetuating freeway, the graffiti, the drugs, the sex, the rock 'n' roll, well, not really rock 'n' roll, more like his own version of country rock. Floyd Perkins style, he called it. But anyway, he was sick of it all and needed a rest, repose and time to mellow out, kick back and be with his wife. He made the decision. It was a big one. "Ain't doin' this no more," he said one Thursday night to the filthy mirror in his dressing room. Of course his interest and enthusiasm for music would never die – that's who he was and who he always would be. No denying it, and for that reason even after all these years he kept his guitar playing up, worked at it and made sure that didn't slip away. But he was a singer with a good voice, even if a little raspy these days, and a pretty decent songwriter. But still he played his guitar every day, listened to some of the latest hits, although they weren't much to his taste, and checked out what the younger guys were doing. Things were changing for sure and Floyd was not going to just fade away and disappear after all this time. No sir, he would keep the edge. Maybe he would just write songs for other people now and then, play guitar on a track here and there. It would be enough. So, despite his general tendency toward the dissolute, Floyd did impose a little discipline upon himself with various little practices, like putting a small drum machine in his dressing rooms and jamming along with it – he didn't want to lose his chops, even if he didn't intend to go out there any more. He practised improvising over unfamiliar non-country chord changes in an effort to sound more modern, just to see if he could do it, played the blues and even tried some Bach once, but always returned to his own country rock, which was his musical home. He had a lot of guitars, too many really, but they were all catalogued and he knew that they would be worth something one day, as he had purchased them way before they all became a big deal – the vintage thing and all that. So he now had enough to retire on and stop for a while. Maybe write an autobiography. And then there was the other thing. He was married. That was another deal altogether. His wife Rita was emphatically stating that she was fed up with the endless road life and by implication the benefits that went along with it, and had been urging him to quit for a while or else. And the truth was that Floyd, despite all the guitars and women, liked having someone to come home to after all that travel in the company of men. Someone to get back with, someone familiar, someone warm who knew his needs. They were a family of sorts even if they had no kids. She took care of him, they shared a gentle humour and she was sexy with it, still a looker. He didn't see bustin' it up so he agreed – he'd open a guitar shop or something and drink beer on the porch. It was like giving up a drug but what the hell, he reckoned, I had a great run. Time to git down and mow the lawn, take the dog for a walk or whatever people do, I guess. Rita worked a lot and was often out in the afternoon and sometimes at night. Private clients, she said, portfolio advice. She was trained in all that financial stuff, had a mind for it. Her career had always been in banking and she talked about things like fiduciary responsibilities, but that stuff was beyond him and he just took it for granted that she was an expert. They were an odd couple, alright. She had a brain, no question, but deep down in there somewhere she had the heart of a country girl. Floyd often thought she could have been anything, could have got anyone. So… why me? Some sort of roots connection maybe, or the music, I guess. She brought in a substantial amount of money on a regular basis, so between the two of them they lived a comfortable existence. Floyd wondered how she did it, working so hard and still in great physical, not to mention, sexy shape. I've got it better than most of those suckers out there, he thought, so who am I to argue? I'm gonna ride this train out. He thought about writing a lyric that went, 'You've got the beauty and I've got the brains,' but the brains *and* the beauty belonged to her. So what am I? Floyd wondered … A lucky S-O-B, you dumbass, just keep playin' that guitar and mind your manners. Out she went on business, and if it was not business it was a yoga class or some sort of workout session, which left Floyd noodling away on his guitar while he was watching a football match or some old TV series re-run. One thing that had seemed to dry up, though, was their sex life. It drove Floyd a little bit crazy. She still had a sexy body, and with all the yoga and workouts she was in serious sporting shape. But she didn't seem interested in him in that way any more. Maybe she sensed all the infidelity, the scent of other women still lingering on him, but Floyd just thought, well, that shit ain't happening no more, and she ain't left me. Lucky. So he plugged in his famous Gibson Melody Maker and hacked away at a blues, thinking of all the chicks he had bedded, the tight jeans peeling off, the skimpy tank tops unfurling, the lips, the mouths, the eyes. Oh my God, he thought, I lived a man's life, or am I just an undeserving swine after all? He had always been able to get them. He and Rita never spoke about this sort of thing, as he kept up the pretence of an innocent musician who never strayed from the fold, he was in it purely for the music, he said, that was his contribution, that was why he was here on the planet, money be damned. Feeling sex-starved and a tad morose, along with a tingling sensation and an urge to get back out there again, Floyd stared at the TV screen. "I guess we have been living a lie all these years," he said to a player in the Red Sox as the player raced across a small TV screen. "Shit!" said Floyd as he stroked an F chord. He felt a brief moment of compassion for his old lady. He had been a lying sack of shit the whole time – the cheater of Rita. But as he meditated and saw it as a possible song title his mind drifted back over all the nubile bodies that had bounced underneath him. Had, had, had … He groaned, sure will miss that, maybe I should get back out there and get me some more of that poontang, Goddammit! Probably need a load of Viagra now, but whatever. He worked himself up into a fever pitch thinking about all those good old days and then a neon sign went on in his head, blinking rapidly, saying "Floyd Perkins ain't getting none," over and over. Floyd strummed his guitar furiously and growled, "Ain't getting none – ain't right." And he stood there for a minute with his guitar around his neck like a hangman's noose. He could set up some shows and it would happen right away, he knew it for sure. But how about all the promises he'd made to Rita? It was difficult. He couldn't say they needed the money, really, because of Rita and her earning power. He couldn't pull a line like my fans need me – that would be the road to divorce. And then it popped into his head. It was so simple. How about I get one of those escort girls and fix this little problem? Can't hurt, can it? A little help on the side, she ain't never gonna know. He looked through an ancient Yellow Pages phone book and saw the name of a local escort service. That's it, he said to himself, I'm calling them. But it has to be somewhere private she don't know about. There was a motel on the edge of town close to the I-45. That's the place, he thought – not too romantic, but I'm paying so it will be where I want it to be. Later that night as usual, Rita drove him crazy as she stripped down to her underwear in the bathroom and made ready for bed. He casually asked her about her plans for the coming week.

"Out on Thursday night and Friday night," she replied, before pulling a dowdy nightgown over her hot body. They went to bed and Rita went straight to sleep. Floyd lay there wide awake going over his plan. It would have to be a Thursday night, that would give him time and space to do the deed. If he played it right it would all be over and done with before he was at home with Rita, just another notch on the belt, forgotten already. He drifted off to sleep with a smile on his face.

Thursday afternoon came and after some anxiety and a slug of Jack he called the Come Together Escort Agency. A brief minute of The Beatles' 'Come Together' floated down the line and then a sexy girl's voice said huskily, "Come Together," and then a pause, finally adding the word "Agency," and "Betsy speaking."

"Hi!" said Floyd, trying to sound like it was just another day and this was mere routine. "I, um, I wanted, um, would like to, um, hire an escort tonight to, um, take to dinner."

"Where would you like to meet your personal angel?" asked Betsy.

"I, um, the Six Stars Motel," breathed Floyd.

"We have Anastasia available," said the girl. "She is one of our best escorts, very beautiful. I think you will get all you want."

Floyd gulped. "Okay, Anastasia," he said, aware that he had just crossed a line.

"That will be two hundred dollars now," said Betsy. "Which credit card will you be using?"

"Does it have to be on credit card?" gasped Floyd, thinking about the shit he would get if Rita saw the card statement.

"Yes, it's a down payment," said Betsy. "There will be another two hundred at the end of the service."

"Anastasia will call us after you are finished and don't worry, we don't put escort service on the bill. It will be something quite neutral."

"Okay, okay," said Floyd, his erotic impulse now rapidly diminishing on account of this business transaction, and feeling an overwhelming urge to call the whole thing off, not to mention the bleeding wallet price. Later that afternoon, and a little freaked out that he was actually doing this, he drove out to the motel at the edge of the freeway and checked in for one night. Not wanting any more suspicious charges on his credit card bill he paid cash up front, went to the room and chucked his small bag and guitar on the bed. He didn't know why he had brought the bag with its change of clothes and all, but there it was. It seemed to make him more substantial, like some sort of travelling salesman or something. And he brought his guitar because he had a few ideas for his next album, *The Lyin' Years*. He sat on the bed for a while with his guitar, almost feeling like he was in the confession box as he tried out lines like, 'Here comes little Suzy and here comes Carol Jane / here I am a blind man, between the sheets again'. Simple chords G D C with the ending line over an E minor. Sounds like a hit, he thought. And then these ideas and songs began to depress him, so he stopped and watched the motel TV for a while and the bad shit happening all over the world and knew that there was a song in there somewhere, something that rhymed with chump. Around 6:30pm he took a shower, shaved and patted some Old Spice on his cheeks, beneath his underarms and below decks and said to the mirror, "You are going to get it big time, baby, seriously big time." He picked up his guitar and played a couple of his own songs, 'Draggin' My Ass', which had been a local hit, and 'Short and Curly', which made it to number three on a Birmingham, Alabama station. The songs reinforced his sense of self, why not take a ride, it didn't mean anything, where's

the harm? He took another slug of Jack and started into 'You Callin'
Me a Liar' when there was a knock at the door. He took one last look
in the mirror, undid one more button on his shirt and walked over
to the door. Before he opened it he cooed out in his famous singing
voice, "Who's there?"

"Anastasia," a low, sexy voice replied.

He pulled the door open.

… "Floyd!"

# THE LOTUS POSITION

"What would you like to eat tonight?" Valery asked, trying to keep the despair out of her voice.

"Chicken and fries," Dawson replied.

Yeah, right, she thought, what an imagination. Just like the last three hundred and sixty-five nights.

Her grandmother had warned her about this. "Good luck with one of them," she said. "You'll never get it right with a man and the older they get, the weirder they get. They still think there's a future, they go to the grave thinking it." Her grandmother – the only rebel in the family, married and divorced three times – was right.

She stared at the chicken thighs. She – Valery – had sexy thighs. She knew it. Men stared at her like she was lunch; it was obvious what they wanted. But he didn't want it. She wondered what was wrong with him. It was because his hands were on that tinny-sounding solid body guitar, forever twiddling away like a man trying to get to a place he would never reach. It was weird. He was a computer salesman, but he thought he was in a rock band – a Duane Allman wannabe.

Her parents had pushed her into the marriage when she was still too young and brainwashed to get out of their Bible class idea of life. Getting married was the convention, but life with this guy was mediocre, boring, *average*. She churned inside. She knew she was better than crappy suburban lawns, shit television, the local bowling alley and building for the future. What was next – prescription drugs? That's what happened in places like this.

I'm young, she thought, I have to do something. I need to fly. I need something or someone that will take me over body and soul. She started looking around, reading, searching for a way out.

She noticed an ad in a local paper for a yoga studio. It was a place called The Aleph, with a couple of lines about ultimate health of mind and body. It caught her imagination, and anyway she needed to do something physical, something hard and fierce that would break her out of the mould. A few mornings later she found the building and went to the studio on the second floor. A nymph-like girl in tie-dye workout clothes greeted her at the reception desk and asked her if she wanted to sign up for a few classes, adding with a smile that it was a hot yoga class. Valery signed and entered the steamy atmosphere.

At the front of the class, demonstrating an impossible pose, was an exotic-looking man of indeterminate age who was ripped in all the right places, spoke with a soft, intoxicating purr and exuded sex on a higher plane. He bathed in the light of adoration as he walked around the room putting his hands on their bodies, correcting spinal alignment and sometimes whispering in the ear of the particular beauty he was hovering over. It was all incredibly seductive. Valery was struck dumb that there could be a man like that – a universe apart from her obsessive, guitar-fiddling and apparently asexual husband. She immediately fell in love with the teacher – or The Aleph, as he was known – as she also fell in love with all the women in the class and this ancient mind-body practice known as yoga.

At first she felt awkward and embarrassed by her lack of physical skill and stayed back in the corner of the room, trying so very hard to bend into whatever pretzel shape was being called out. She wanted to be like them – the assertive, back-bending and clear-eyed young women who always and only referred to the poses with their incomprehensible but original Indian names.

She bought a book on yoga, and while her husband fumbled and botched guitar chords down in the basement, she tried to memorize the names of the poses, Utthitya Parshvakon-asana, Dhanur-asana, Uttuan-asana. She kept going to the classes, she was addicted. The weeks passed and she felt her body changing, as if moving into a new space. She stared at the mirror and saw a woman who was becoming stronger, taller and clearer, as if a cloud was being blown out of her life. Victim no more. She could see it in her own eyes. She purchased more books and read about self-actualization, personal growth, the inner child and the butterfly emerging from the chrysalis. The old wounds were dissolving. She did the tree pose in front of the mirror and said to herself, "I am fantastic, desirable, beautiful – everyone wants me." When her husband emerged from the basement, she had already eaten her own nutritional Ayurvedic dinner and merely pointed him toward the oven, where he could find the invariable chicken and French fries.

Why had she married him? What was the attraction? He was just a lousy businessman who wanted to be a guitar player but had no real talent for it. Times were changing. It was time to abandon the conventions of her dull, safe parents and let her freak flag fly, and maybe it was time to leave the sexless asshole she had married at seventeen. She was still young, getting more attractive and could perform a mean Nataraj-asana that would drive most men wild. The path ahead was becoming clear. She studied more poses in her favourite book on yoga and kept it underneath her pillow in a vague hope that some of the Indian names would float up into her brain while she dreamed of life in an ashram.

Back at the yoga studio she moved out of the dark corner at the back of the class and into the centre of the room. She smiled at the other girls feeling like she was one of them, or even one with them. They smiled back and, in unison, went into Extended Side Angle pose. And then it happened. He came to her, put his hand on her hips, moved them seductively and then whispered huskily into her ear, "You have a beautiful body – use it." The remainder of the class was like a dream. She went through the rest of the poses but it was more like she was levitating, floating and drifting as her mind took her to various *Kama Sutra* positions with him, The Aleph.

At home her husband hacked away at 'Sunshine of Your Love' before morphing badly into 'Purple Haze'. Standing in the kitchen, she winced at his efforts and felt mixed emotions at what she was about to do.

And then out of nowhere came a terrible smashing sound accompanied by horrible cursing and then a muffled sobbing. She stood there transfixed. It was him, in the basement; Dawson came up the stairs and into the kitchen. Tears were streaming down his face.

"I can't do it any more," he choked out. "I'll never get it. I'm done. I hate the guitar."

"Oh my God," she said. She went to him and embraced him with her well-toned arms, remembering that Yoginis were full of compassion which she could practise now, although she had not been near this guy for months and regarded him as a stranger. So she hugged him, stroked his hair and thought of it as a spiritual lesson.

From somewhere deep in her young bosom he asked if he could sleep with her tonight. She mumbled a sound as if in confirmation but was confused at the thought. She was a different person now, not the girl he married. The marriage was a failure – should never have happened. She shared the bed that night with him but stayed away from physical contact as her mind teemed with thoughts about her new resolve, the path forward and how she might even become a yoga instructor.

She slipped out of bed early in the morning to avoid the sleeping ex-guitarist and, after a latte and a non-Ayurvedic croissant at Pete's, went to the class. She was one of the first there. It was strange to see the room empty, but she laid out her designer yoga mat and put herself into a full Lotus with eyes closed, trying to process the scenes of the night before. Her breathing became slow and even and she came to the beautiful place of meditation. Just as she was merging with a fluffy white cloud, a voice whispered in her ear. "Namaste, nice to see you this morning. How does your body feel?" It was him. She looked up into his eyes. They were a deep Himalayan blue that radiated an otherworldly spirit. They seemed to be saying "I choose you."

"I've been watching you in our session," he murmured. "You are doing very well, you're a natural. I would like to be alone with you and give you a higher teaching; can you come to me tonight?"

"Well, yes," she exhaled, as if doing a Ujjayi yoga breath. She looked up at him adoringly and almost added "Master."

"I will tell you where and when after our class." He smiled at her beatifically, and then moved like a panther to the front of the room that was now swollen with devotees.

At seven that night she left home nervously, making sure to avoid her soon-to-be-gone husband. She arrived at the guru's door and knocked, trying to slow her breathing, affect a casual smile and act as if this happened every day. But a different movie was playing inside her hot yoga body. The Aleph opened the door and greeted her with a thousand-year-old smile and said, "You have come. Please enter."

From this point, time and space unfolded like a magic carpet, wine flowed, spiritual wisdom took wing and culminated with the guru inviting her to experience the ecstasy of tantra – normally only granted to those who have spent years in preparation. After the experience, which transported Valery miles above the Master's shag rug and into the stars, he told her that he must now sleep alone and travel to the astral plane where he would converse with his masters. He laid his index finger on her third eye and made a motion with his hands over her heart. Valery pulled her panties and sports bra back on, grabbed her lululemon yoga outfit, and backed out of the room full of The Aleph's seed.

When she arrived back home an hour later, the lights were on. Strange, she thought. Dawson was usually asleep and snoring by this time. Then as she entered the hallway she heard an unusual low sound coming from the kitchen. It sounded like the ancient Indian mantra 'Om,' but it couldn't be. She went into the kitchen and saw Dawson sitting on the floor in a Half Lotus with her yoga book on his knees. Valery stared as if in shock, simultaneously and instinctively feeling the Master's seed take root in her womb. She blurted out, "What's going on?"

Dawson looked up at her with a strange new glimmer in his eye. "I found this book under your pillow. Yoga. Wonderful, this is for me. I heard there is a marvellous teacher around here, The Aleph or something. What do you think?"

# WHAT MUSIC?

What is music anyway? A thing that tugs the heart, brings a tear to the eye, returns you to childhood, fills you with sentiment – your first go at masturbation … Or … is it the cry, the scream, the urge to revolution, war, the urge to obliterate, rip down the existing order? Do the makers of such music need musical talent? What is that anyway? Who the fuck defines that? Who are the guardians of the gate, the illuminati of musical taste? Fuck them and their rigid control, really, fuck them. Music is a weapon … This is 1978 …

Steve leaned back. Yeah, better leave out masturbation, but just 'fuck them,' or 'really fuck them?' He deleted the word 'really' and then took another drag on his ciggy. 'Fuck them' was a strong ender he thought and vaguely wondered if his editor would leave it in. Probably didn't matter – Steve's reputation as a difficult and controversial writer was now entrenched in the British musical press.

In his own fantasy life Steve imagined he was changing the course of music in the UK if not the world. The editor wouldn't dare fuck with him at this point. His editor was a middle-aged Beatles fan – bloody pathetic. The hooting wind of punk derision was now blowing in his face and if he wanted to sell this pathetic rag of a music paper he had better listen to guys like Steve.

Steve read through his piece, which ostensibly was about a new band called The Grubs. Their stance was vehemently anti-music, anti-government, anti-record business, basically, anti-life. Three young boys who raged at everything and somehow got it onto their guitars and drums in a chaotic howl. Steve saw and felt it as great writing material and felt not only kinship with it but also that it was the sonic equivalent of his own angst.

The essay gave faint description to the music itself, not much more than a cursory nod, but went into full overdrive as Marxist polemic about revolution, revenge and the new world order, as if The Grubs with their banshee howl were going to bring this all about. Three eighteen-year-old kids from the outlying and miserable London boroughs who, with a vague grasp of existing political structures and a pissed-off attitude, decided that they would decimate the old guard with their violent sonic scream. Amazing, the perfect band for Steve.

He smiled to himself and continued writing but this time without mentioning the band but ranting on about social anarchy, the failure of British society, diminished opportunity, the aesthetic of the ugly, Marx, Engels, Lenin and the Bolsheviks. Out with the old and into the icy gale-force wind of the punk revolution. Anything before that was dead, even Hendrix. The Stones were a toothless bunch of middle-aged losers – Genesis, Yes, it was all dead, dead, dead, the graveyard of rock.

Steve felt good and pleased with himself as he got all his rage onto the page.

The door opened and his girlfriend Polly walked in. "Watcha doin'?" chirped Polly.

"Oh, just writing," said Steve. "Nothing much."

"I hope it's not about that punk crap," said Polly. "I have great news for you. Yes are on next week at the Rainbow, I've got tickets, they are going to do the whole of *Close To The Edge*, the whole bleedin' album – heavenly."

Steve gulped. The horrible and deadly secret truth was that underneath his sneering punk-writer façade he was obsessed with prog rock. A huge fan, he worshipped Steve Howe, Rick Wakeman and Jon Anderson.

"Can I see what you've got there?" said Polly.

"Uh, no – it's not finished yet, Pol," said Steve, feeling a Jekyll and Hyde kind of emotion and quickly closing up his typewriter. "I'm done for the night, the music industry will have to wait. How about a shag?"

"Well!" said Polly, "I only shag Yes fans."

"Well, then, I'd be the man," smirked Steve, at once desperate to keep Polly away from his punk ravings and also filled with lust for the creamy skin of his Jamaican-Chinese girlfriend.

Fast forward one week: the London Rainbow Yes show is over and an after-concert party is happening backstage. There is a huge buzz at the party about how marvellous the concert had been, the virtuosity of the Yes music, Jon Anderson's vocals, Steve Howe's guitar, Rick Wakeman's mighty keyboards … glorious. Steve and Polly are there mingling with the crowd, holding glasses of shitty white wine and acting groovy, which is difficult for Steve, who has a beanie pulled down to his eyes.

Despite his infatuation with prog and being thrilled at the concert, Steve feels extremely uncomfortable as he is desperate not to be exposed as the writer of yesterday's ruthless and gutting piece about anything pre-punk.

No one at the party is aware that the enemy is among them. He smiles beneath the thick black scarf his Mum gave him last year for Christmas. There's a sort of twisted thrill to this. Steve in his double identity rather likes himself – feels cool, no one else could pull this off. He should probably be working for MI6.

But thrilled by the brilliant prog rock he has just heard, Steve is in a dazed state, half of his mind wrapped in the vicious polemic he has just spewed, and the other half besotted with the music of Yes. He's confused by his self-image as a vitriolic confrontational journalist – while also being a kind, serene fan who adores all the yearning sentiment of prog rock and its upward spiral to the land of Hobbits.

For a moment his mind plays with a few ideas. There must be a way to unite the two worlds. Prog–punk, punk-prog, pronk maybe. Pronk's good. Hmmm, he sees possibilities. Is it possible to bring it together? He suddenly sees himself as the bearer of a new standard, one in which somehow pronk would bring together the disparate factions of society – maybe getting old would no longer be a crime, as long as you had perfect pronk credentials.

Steve muses for a few minutes lost in reverie and then decides to go for a piss. He nudges Polly and whispers, "Pol, is there anywhere to go for a piss around here?"

"I dunno," replies Polly in a tipsy slur. "Shall I ask the heavy over there?" A brutish-looking thug was leaning on a door with stars on it – clearly the dressing room for the performers.

"Want me to chat him up for you?" says Polly.

"Yeah," mumbles Steve. Polly sashays over to the man and Steve sees her whispering into his ear and the bloke grinning. With a hand behind her back Polly wags a finger at Steve to give him the okay. Steve shuffles over to where Polly is standing. The heavy looks at Steve suspiciously and then grunts, "Alright, mate, in you go, be quick," and he pushes the door open. Steve walks through what looks like a dressing room – or maybe a wizard's lair, filled as it is with several fancy-looking costumes, books on spirituality, crystals and various esoteric objects, as well as a handmade bong.

He wants to stop and drink all this in as the symbols of prog rock but is dying for a piss, so he pushes open another door depicting an erect phallus or a mushroom and arrives in a small room where there are three urinals in a row. With a sigh of relief, he unzips and begins splashing the porcelain and then from out of nowhere there's a man standing next to him and he speaks.

"So ... Meathead let you back here, did he? You are a lucky man, he's big on beating most people senseless. I congratulate you on getting past him. Are you a fan or what?"

"Well, yeah," mutters Steve as he realizes that it's Jon Anderson talking to him and causing him to freeze midstream. Bloody hell.

"What do you think of all that crap tonight?" says Jon. "Can you believe they buy all this rubbish about wizards and rainbows, unicorns? It's fucking ridiculous ... It's hard for me not to go into hysterics while I'm bawling that lot out."

Steve, still trying to piss, can only come up with "Er ... ah ... um ..."

"What do you do, mate?" asks Jon Anderson, continuing to piss like Niagara Falls.

"Well, I'm a ... I'm a roadie," says Steve, feeling desperate and pissing on his Doc Martens.

"Oh, great," says Jon. "Actually we're looking for a replacement. One of our guys choked on his vomit the other night. Anyway, I want to start a new band. I'm into Albert Ayler, Coltrane, Archie Shepp – that kind of atonal shit, anything that doesn't have a

fucking unicorn in it. Have you heard the band The Grubs? That's
what I really want to do. What do you think?"

Steve pisses on his boots.

# HOTEL

By the time he got to his room he was exhausted. He was done in anyway, totally shagged out. Too many shows, this should have been a day off. "What the fuck", he snarled to himself, "are we doing here in this godforsaken town in the middle of nowhere?"

He needed to lie down, get still in the darkness for half an hour, let it all come back together before the bloody sound check. The show wasn't until midnight, too bloody late. But that was the way it was in this country – not much happened before 10pm, and that was early. He tried to throw his big black suitcase onto the case stand and felt something go in his back. Fuck, he shouldn't have done that. Too much baggage, as usual, but there was no easy way to tour. Maybe he was getting past it. The music was one thing, the life another. He pulled his toilet bag out from his suitcase, went into the bathroom and pulled out his contact lens case – at least that was where it was supposed to be – and then studied the bed and felt the pillows. The usual shit – big bouncy foam fuckers that were useless to sleep on. Who designs this shit? he thought, they should take a course in anatomy. He flung the pillows across the room, cursing them. He then took two big bath towels, folded them, put them where the pillows had been, and ripped one of the cases off a pillow and placed it over the towels. He went over to the pathetic thin light-revealing curtain praying for blackout blinds, but there were none. "Shit hotel," he cursed under his breath. He undressed and got into bed in his underwear and was just sinking back but felt filthy and decided he really needed a hot shower. He got up and went into the tiny bathroom and turned the lever of the shower. He pushed it to the red, presuming that meant hot, but after a few agonizing minutes, as he stood there naked with icy water spluttering onto him, he turned the shower lever to the blue mark that presumably meant cold as it quickly turned to a scalding hot. "Thank fucking God," he said and got under the shower that sprayed unevenly, much of it landing on the bathroom floor. "Soap – where's the fucking soap?" he asked no one. There was nothing in the shower itself. He stepped back out of the cubicle and saw a tiny packet of soap by the washbasin. He grabbed it and got back under the shower and tried to open the soap packet, but it was so tiny and economical that he couldn't get a grip on it and his hands were too wet to tear off the wrapping and it shot out of his hand, back into the bathroom, landing in the toilet. Okay, what-fucking-ever. He shook his head and tried to come up with some sort of philosophical line. "Whatever doesn't kill you makes you stronger" – yes, good old Nietzsche, he had one for every moment in life and fuck the soap. That should have been one of the lines as well. Consoling himself with that, he towelled himself with the small rag that the hotel had kindly provided and, sighing and naked, went back into the bed-room and got into the bed. With some difficulty he found the switch for the bedside lamp. It was on the wall where there appeared to be three switches. He pressed the one in the middle and the ceiling light came on. Cursing, he pressed the other two. The lamp on the other side of the bed came on, as did the light in the entry. "Fuck you, fuck you," he yelled. "Which idiot wired this bullshit?" Right, he thought. O-bloody-K. He found the wire of the bedside lamp and yanked the plug out of the wall. Everything went dark – momentarily – but within a few seconds he saw that the room was now lit up by a sparkling blue light on the air conditioner high up on the ceiling, making the room look like a bright Martian landscape. "It's like fucking daytime in here, what are they thinking?" he cried out loud. "Jesus," he moaned and buried his head underneath a pillow. A few minutes later and just as he began to drift off, the bedside phone rang. He groaned and picked it up. "Hi, Sull," said Martin, the band's tour manager. "We're all downstairs in the lobby ready to go to the sound check. Are you coming?"

# THE CLEVELAND INCIDENT

Slipped on wet tarmac with amp outside backstage door, door locked. Back in van, drove to McDonald's for dinner before gig. Felt nauseated after Big Mac, also knee hurting like hell after tarmac incident + rip in jeans but looks cool. Think have tarmac embedded in patella. Having knee-jerk response, ha ha.

Back to gig. Stage door now open. Lug gear in. Promoter arrives, comes from behind bar like Godzilla, beer in mitt, definitely a biker – or killer. Only stares – probably had his tongue cut out by other biker. Notice American flags hanging behind bar. Will have to cut certain songs. Brief sound check – seems pointless, totally knackered and fucked up anyway, better to save energy. Change guitar strings? No – fuck it, place not worth it. Dressing room like Chernobyl. Pass out on diseased couch. Pictures of hair bands on wall, sneering.

Show time. Quick look through curtains. About fifteen punters, locals, no women – looks scary. Think about doing a runner, low on gas, just enough to make nearest station – probably pointless and would get done over anyway. Start show trying to rock hard, hoots of derision, shower of spit and some spewed beer. They don't like our hair. Carry on anyway. Try a ballad – big mistake, drowned in fuck offs and maybe a couple of limey faggot lines. Oh well. Think about Nietzsche and various other European philosophers, actually get to Pythagoras during sixteen-bar break on 'Dead End Job'. There's a lot of hate in the room, keep turning up the amp, maybe volume will silence these fuckers, but the higher the volume the more the beer.

Come to end of short set.

Mood ugly.

# GIRLS WITH GUITARS

Peter Postlethwaite, the son of a GP on the outskirts of Dallas, had no interest in the medical arts, despite relentless encouragement from his parents and the vast majority of his relatives who were in the game themselves. No, he was obsessed with the guitar and at age thirteen he bought his first model. It was a Guild D-50, an acoustic steel string with a Dreadnought shape. A big guitar with a huge cowboy sound. Pete was small, a beginner, with red hair, and only knew three chords. He struggled manfully with this untamed beast, knowing nothing about the action, the string gauges, set-up or any kind of guitar stuff. After a couple of weeks and just about managing E major on the thing, he decided to sell it or swap it for an easier guitar, something that a human could play. He decided to go electric and saw a red Fender Bullet solid body in a local guitar store. To get the money for the Fender he sold the D-50 to his cousin Saul, who was in a folk group. Saul got tired of the recalcitrant D-50 in a few days and sold it to a woman who was also into folk. At first, she offered sex as payment to Saul as a way to get the guitar for nothing and enjoy herself, but Saul already had a girlfriend and was afraid of the woman who appeared to him like a witch. She gave him two hundred dollars and squeezed his scrotum on the way out of the house. Saul went back to his folk group, The Dangling Modifiers, who right then decided to go electric following Dylan's rebel example. Both Saul and Henry, the other guitarist, now had to get electrics. Henry decided he would play electric twelve-string, despite the lifetime he would have to dedicate to wrestling the beast into tune and, sadly parting with his Framus six-string, he picked up a Rickenbacker twelve-string and started chiming like an English cathedral.

Alice, the lead singer in the group, now wanted to play guitar as well. She felt vulnerable just standing there in front of the microphone. She was a curvy girl and she needed something to cover her blossoming female attributes. She asked around and found a college student, an Italian named Roberto D'Angelo, whose father played mandolin and cooked pasta fagioli. Roberto was selling the Guild D-50 that he had picked up from some kid in a folk group but had decided to switch to mandolin and learn how to make homemade pasta with his father. Alice felt deeply attracted to Roberto but, passing up the shot at getting pregnant at seventeen, jumped at the chance to get his guitar. He sold her the guitar for a very fair price and said let's suck noodles together sometime. She put a strap on the D-50 and wore it high on her torso. It did the job nicely in terms of coverage, but it was too hard to play, she needed a smaller, more feminine instrument, a Martin 000 or something. But right then her girlfriend pointed out to her that her band was now electric, and it was the twentieth century. She pushed the big acoustic under her bed, wheedled some cash out of her Dad, and picked up a battered Stratocaster from the local pawnshop. She posed in front of her bedroom mirror with it and snarled a few times at the glass. She suddenly saw herself in a shocking new light. She made the strap longer and dropped the guitar to somewhere around her pelvis and thrust a few times against the solid body. It felt good. She decided that she would let go of the pure yearning image of folk and get down – she would be the bad girl of folk. She let out a hysterical laugh and called her girlfriend Naomi who was also getting into guitar and just getting out of the bath.

"Ali … what's up?" screamed Naomi rhetorically, in her deep Persian-accented voice.

"Hi, Om," said Alice. "This guitar thing … it's such a turn-on."

"Yeah, it's a lot of vibration for sure. I'm into it. Have you got to C7th yet?"

"Is that the one like a triangle?" asked Ali.

"Yeah, a triangle with a bit on top – you can move it up and down if you want."

"Ooh, I like the sound of that," said Alice. "I think I'm going more folk rock now rather than just straight folk. I'm a bit bored with all that stuff about rivers and valleys. Hey! Can I come over tonight? We can do some guitar stuff together, you know, like ... jam."

"Sure," said Naomi. "But my guitar's not here. My cousin has it, he was desperate ... don't ask."

"Well, no problem," said Alice. "I'll bring my Guild D-50."

"Sounds high-class," said Naomi. "Okay, later, gator."

Alice was dropped off by her Dad in the early evening with both guitars in the trunk. Her father told her not to take drugs, drink alcohol or have unprotected sex with strangers, gave her a kiss on the cheek and drove off to a secret rendezvous.

The two girls greeted each other like undying soulmates and went to Naomi's room, a place that sparkled like Aladdin's cave with posters, shaggy-haired boy photos, current pop stars and signs of the zodiac. They sat on the floor chattering like parrots and finally opened the guitar cases.

"Ooh, that's cool!" said Naomi, eyeing Alice's Stratocaster.

"Easy, girl," said Alice, "it's just a guitar."

"What's this other one?" said Naomi, hauling out the Guild D-50. "Whoa ...! Bit of a monster this, but let's have a go!"

She placed the acoustic across her lap, carefully positioned her fingers in the shape of a D chord and gave it a twang.

"Yeah, nice sound, but sure is stiff," said Naomi, smiling.
"We don't want anything stiff," said Alice. They broke into hysterics and rolled about the floor for five minutes, and eventually, gasping and giggling, recovered and sat up again.

"Here, let me try that Stratocaster," said Naomi. She moved her hand around a few chord shapes on the electric guitar and said, "That's more like it, not so stiff. I can do stuff with it." They both went into spasms of laughter again.

"Oh my God!" said Alice. "You are a crack-up, Om. What shall we play?"

"Let's jam on one chord," said Naomi. "You know, just bang it out."

"Yeah," said Alice, "I've got that."

"Okay," said Naomi, "add the little finger here." She helped Alice place her little finger on the third string at the third fret.

"Okay, that C7 shape is very useful. It's what's called a moveable shape. You can move it anywhere on the guitar."

"Sounds like my bum," said Alice, at which remark they both fell over sideways, howling.

"Okay, c'mon," said Naomi, finally recovering. "We gotta' jam, let's go. C7 alright." And she started a fierce rhythm on the C7 chord. Alice got the hang of it after a couple of minutes and they bashed along happily, and then Alice started singing out a few notes above their jangling chords.

"Yeah!" called out Naomi. "Go for it!" Alice's voice rose higher as if some new force had been unleashed, now unfettered by false sincerity and feelings about old homesteads. And then Naomi did something that amazed Alice, as her friend started playing a bass line on the bottom two strings of the D-50. Alice sang out even more, really feeling like she was in a rock band. After about ten minutes of pure excitement and fun they came to a stop.

"Jesus!" said Alice. "Om, you are like a musician. That was incredible, what you were doing? Where d'ya learn that?"

Naomi smiled and said, "First of all, Ali, your voice, man – world class! You friggin' got it! God, I wish I could sing like that, but my stuff, well, I do practise a lot and I play along with all sorts of records, hours sometimes."

"But those low notes? Where do they come from?" said Alice.

"Yeah," said Naomi, "I don't know why I go there, but I do like warm round bottom."

"Let's not start talking about my bum again," said Alice. Once more they rolled around on the floor in convulsions. Finally, Naomi sat up and said, "I think I'm a bass player, I should get a bass."

"Yeah," said Alice. "Then we could be, like, a band."

"Ain't got no money for a bass," said Naomi.

"I know where there's a bass," said Alice. "Down at the pawnshop where I got this Fender, we could trade up the D-50."

"Great idea," said Naomi. "Are you sure, Ali?"

"Sure," said Alice, "that thing is more like a boat than a guitar. Glad to get rid of it."

"I think you have to be sitting on a horse to get anything out it," said Naomi.

The night ended in cackling laughter as the girls, full of excitement, hugged each other goodnight.

The next morning, they turned up at the Use It or Lose It Pawnshop. The sun was out in a peerless Texas sky. They pushed open the door with a jangle and stared into the cave-like gloom. Their eyes adjusted and they made out the shapes of a vast array of objects, from car parts to furniture to paintings, toys and musical instruments, including brass horns like tubas and sousaphones, and one stuffed parrot.

"Christ! Where does this shit come from?" gasped Naomi.

"It's like hell," whispered Alice.

"Yeah?" a croaky voice came from the back of the store. Alice edged forward in the gloom.

"Um… um… we want to ask about that Fender bass guitar hanging in the window," she said. A man with wild frizzy hair, a thick beard and bifocals emerged through the crepuscular light from behind the counter.

"That's a Fender Jazz Bass," he said.

"We were wondering if we could trade this beautiful Guild D-50 for it?" said Alice. "It's in good condition, I hate to part with it, but my friend really needs a bass. Can you help? I think this is a rare instrument, might be worth a few thousand dollars."

"You are a sweet girl," said the man. "But it's not worth much, they're out of style now. There's another one back there gathering dust…"

"It's so important to us two young girls, sir," said Alice with a beseeching look on her face. "Can you find it in your heart to help us and, well… how much is the bass?"

"Fifty," said the man with a deep sigh and an inward wish that he was the same age as these beautiful young girls, with their lives stretching ahead of them.

"Any chance we could do an even swap?" said Alice.

"Hmm …" he said. "Give me five dollars and I'll do it. It will be my good deed for the day. Let me get it out of the window. By the way, it doesn't have a case, which is why I'm practically giving it away."

"Okay," said Alice. "Thank you very much, sir."

Meanwhile, Naomi was holding her breath and saying a silent prayer. The man returned from the window with the bass in his hands. "Who's the bass player?" he asked, staring at the girls.

"Me," said Naomi meekly.

He handed it to her and asked, "Wanna' plug it in and make sure it works?"

"Sure," said Naomi. "Good idea." The man hauled out a dusty looking Fender Tweed amp and plugged it in. He fished a guitar lead out of a drawer and plugged the other end into the Fender Tweed, then switched on the amp and said, "There you go, check it out."

Naomi, feeling scared, tried out a few tentative notes and then, growing in confidence, moved her hand up and down the neck, the notes booming resonantly from the amp. "Oh, this is so me," she whispered.

"You gotta feel for that thing," grunted the man. "You'll do well with that."

Naomi was almost on the verge of crying, so huge was her joy. "Heaven," she murmured, "Heaven…"

Alice stood there beaming. "This is great, Om, we're going to be famous!"

# "ARE YOU FUCKING HER, RICHARD?"

"**A**re you fucking her, Richard?"

Colette leans back against the kitchen counter, a glass of Sauvignon Blanc in her hand.

"Of course I'm not fucking her," Richard flings back.

"Yes, you are, you're fucking... fucking her. I know it."

"I'm not fucking ... fucking her," yells Richard in exasperation, almost chopping his hand off with a kitchen knife.

"How would you know, anyway? Got yer little spies out?"

Richard waves the blade in the air as if this indicates little spies.

"You may be a big man at the weekends, Richard, down the pub with your squidgy little Les Paul, but I know what goes on. Think I'm daft?"

"Not daft. Insane, maybe," growls Richard. "I go there to play music, my music. I have to, otherwise I'd go insane. Life's not all about a mortgage and a semi-detached, you know."

"Really, sweetheart? Thanks for filling me in – maybe there's a song in there somewhere. Anyway, what about Davina and her big twenty-two-year-old tits? Does she like your Les Paul? I thought she would be more into Stratocasters. And as for your music ... you're a car salesman, love. Did you forget?"

"What's that supposed to mean?" spits Richard, stabbing at a carrot. "A man can't have soul or express himself outside of this shit, or rise up against... against...? I don't fucking know. You know, rise up with the voice of his guitar, spread his wings – rip it up a little?"

"Not if it means fucking around on his wife."

Colette swishes her white wine a little and takes another sip. "Who knows what nastiness you might come home with? And also, you haven't even paid for that guitar yet. It's not actually yours. I'm the one making the payments. I'm thinking of taking it back or giving it to a friend of mine, another guitarist. How's that salad coming? Anyway, Dick, how come it's taken you so long to realize that you are a bluesman? Why didn't you go for it when you left school? Not good enough? Didn't have the balls? The chips didn't fall right? You could have been the Eric Clapton for millennials. I don't see how a burning player like you got missed. A bit more avocado in there, if you don't mind."

Richard hacks with ferocity at an under-ripe avocado.

"I can see it." Colette gargles some more Sauvignon Blanc. "There you are, down at the office shuffling papers. You act a bit mysterious, a loner, an artist, despite the mediocre trappings you are passing through, the crappy menswear suit you have on. But, my God, it works. The little office sluts are interested, and you can't wait to get your mitts on Davina's juicy little knockers."

"You're drunk, you bitch!" Richard points a leaf of romaine at Colette.

"You going to stab me to death with that? Ooh," cackles Colette, spluttering into her wine glass, "death by lettuce. Love it. Don't you see, Richard? This is what it's all about, the blues and all that, and a lousy cheating husband. Lyin', cheatin' bastard. I gotta right to sing the blues, don' I?"

"You don't know anything about the blues," snarls Richard.

"How come I feel like shit all the time then? That's the blues, innit? Not to mention the Devil growing inside me … B-A-B-Y asshole, and a lousy cheating husband to boot."

"Yeah, you got the devil inside ya, alright," snarls Richard with his head inside the refrigerator. "Yeah, the spawn of Satan, you were born with it. My lucky day."

Colette leans at a perilous angle to the left and begins singing in a low voice: 'I gotta kid right here inside me and a man who ain't in sight / Yeah, I gotta kid here deep inside me and that cheater gone at night / I'm gonna chop his balls off / I just gotta make it right / Whoah oh-oh-oh.' Colette's voice, soulful and blues-drenched, echoes around the kitchen walls.

She slides down the cabinetry and slumps into the position of a broken marionette. Richard stares at her in amazement with a cucumber in his hand.

"My God, Colette, I didn't know you could sing like that."

"You never asked, asshole," slurs Colette.

Richard leans over her to help her up, accidentally sticking the cucumber in her left ear while doing so.

"Shit, Richard … geddafuckawayfrome – tryin' to kill me with a cucumber …"

"But darling! We could be a band."

"I'm joining another band, want the guitar back. Where's the goddam salad?"

"Really … I mean …" Richard lets out in a falsetto voice.

"What? The Blues Motherfuckers? Is that what you're thinkin'? Make the bloody salad, will ya?"

"My wife the blues singer." Richard does a little pirouette around the kitchen, three unpeeled radishes falling from his hand, one hitting Colette on the head.

"Motherfucker," moans Colette.

Richard leans over Colette and says, "But darling, we don't have a baby."

"Open your eyes, bluesman, I'm three months gone," slurs Colette.

"What?" moans Richard. "What do you mean? A baby? I thought we were being so careful … Really? We're having a baby?"

"That's right, old buddy, baby is a comin'. But it ain't yours, it's Eric Clapton's."

"Whaaat? You …" Richard slashes savagely at a radish and lets out a huge scream as his left index finger rolls neatly off the cutting table and onto the kitchen floor.

Colette gives a huge laugh and falls over sideways.

# READING IVAN ILYICH

He bent forward, legs akimbo, black Les Paul swinging between the dark triangle of his jeans which snaked down into the thick slabs of his bovver boots as they hovered over the gleaming silver buttons of his pedal board, onto which his sweat fell like thick gobs of rain. His face and hands obscured by a thick plume of black hair, he bent the B string at the fifteenth fret of his guitar up from D to E and then, with a fast sideways motion of his left-hand ring finger, produced a singing vibrato.

The crowd roared. He moved the D to E a few times, accenting the pain and the joy that it elicited. It was a bent string imitating the human voice, it was the sad whine, the anguish and moan of distress. Some called it the sobbing woman. It came from the blues by way of Africa. B.B. King, Albert King, Freddie King, they all did it and they were the masters of the blues form. It was the need, the urge to sum it all up with one singing note and even here, with this mostly white audience, it hit home, penetrated.

Sullivan bent even lower over his guitar, swaying with the drummer's pulse and holding the vibrating E with his left hand while he tapped a G# on the string at the nineteenth fret, which made the notes trill like a bird. The audience broke into spontaneous applause as he finally straightened up, raked the strings of a mighty E sus chord, stared down at the neck of his Les Paul with a considered rock star arrogance and then, with a forceful swing of his right arm, hit the ultimate chord in perfect time with his drummer. And as that final triad rang out he did a tricky move on his pedal board, making the chord balloon in volume and then swallow itself as if disappearing into an underground cave.

The lights went down. He looked to his right at where a crew member in a black T-shirt was signalling to him with a flashlight.

Getting on and off stage had become a serious issue. Two years ago he had fallen in the dark at the back of the stage and broken his right leg, all because some bozo wasn't paying attention and guiding him through the backstage darkness as per instructions. What a pain in the ass that was. Also, it was the time when he had broken up with his long-time girlfriend, so he was alone, apart from his assistant who came in every day.

What misery.

Crutches at the beginning and then the big boot on his right leg so he couldn't drive or go to the local store. Getting in and out of the shower was a deadly trial every morning and sleeping with the thing – what a drag, it was a monster. But on the upside he did get in a lot of practice, wrote a new album and went back into the studio while still on crutches. And, thanks to the new miracle of social interaction on the internet, was able to keep up his profile with his fan base. In fact it had worked well for him. He got sympathy from well-wishers all over the world, Japan in particular, so apart from the physical wound it seemed to have been a good career move. But he still had a few months to get through before he was really up and about and he couldn't handle living in this big house alone now, it actually seemed dangerous. It would be dead easy to fall down the stairs with these bloody crutches. He needed a live-in housekeeper.

He called up his manager, Barclay Williams, who, thinking of his own financial future, agreed instantly. He called back next day and said, "You won't believe it, we have hundreds of applicants. Some you will really like. I'll bring over their résumés."

Around midday his manager swerved into the driveway and got out of his silver Porsche with a thick folder in his hands. Sullivan, after a slow, tortuous descent down the stairs, was sitting in the kitchen watching CNN.

"Look at this lot," said Barclay Williams, waving a sheaf of papers as he strode in. "I don't know if you want to start a harem or have a live-in cook."

"Both probably," replied Sullivan, staring at another outrage in the Middle East.

"Check it out," said Barclay. Sullivan pulled the stack of papers over and began leafing through and then gave a low whistle.

"Jesus, they all seem to have PhDs in housekeeping and some of them are like … shit … beautiful."

"Let's break it down to five," said his manager. "Otherwise this is going to get out of hand."

"Right," said Sullivan. "It's a tough job but someone's got to do it." He shuffled through the resumés for a while and finally made a small pile of five papers.

"Let's meet these," he said. Barclay Williams took a look. "OK, hmm … two Japanese, one Swede, one German, one French. Nice."

"How about all five," said Sullivan with a raised eyebrow.

"Okay, let's not get crazy," said Barclay. "How about I have them come by at different times tomorrow, discreetly timed so there is no embarrassment."

"Good management," said Sullivan. "Set it up, should've thought of this in the first place."

"Get some rest," said Barclay. "I'll call you in the morning. And comb your bloody hair."

Sullivan spent the rest of the day idly watching some old Bogart movies, playing some guitar and writing a few lyrics, before finally hauling himself up the stairs in anticipation of tomorrow's meetings. The phone rang at 10am.

"You up?" came the voice of Barclay on a crackling cell phone.

"Up, yeah," yawned Sullivan, moving his hands up and down the neck of his Triple-o 1925 Martin.

"Okay, we have Sasha at 11, be prepared."

"That's my motto," said Sullivan. He sat there on a low chair in the kitchen drinking Nespresso Livanto, crutches on the floor beside him, guitar cradled in his arms. I look good, he thought. Pathetic – no – vulnerable, they like that. He realized that, instead of housekeeping, his mind was roving over the sexual possibilities. A live-in housekeeper-cum-sex partner when needed – a happy practical arrangement at least from the un-PC male point of view. Food, sex, clean house, shopping – the happy life of a spoiled invalid. Fuck it, he thought, I make so much money for other people they should look after me.

The doorbell rang. It was Barclay with the first applicant. "In there, please," he heard Barclay say. A slim, petite and beautifully dressed Japanese girl walked into the kitchen and bowed to him. "My name Sasha is," she said and gave him a smile that broke his heart. "I am cordon bleu chef and sushi master."

She came over to Sullivan and shook his hand. "I love your music. Here is my CV." She handed him a paper with a smiling photo of herself at the top of the page, followed by a list of her accomplishments. She had studied in France, spoke French, was from Kyoto and had worked in restaurants in that city where her father owned the number one sushi restaurant in Gion precinct.

"Well, it's lovely to meet you," said Sullivan. "Would you like to live here? As you can see I am having a little problem at the moment."

"Yes, I would," she said, "I make you better. Good food, lots of attention," and then, as an afterthought, she added, "and healing vibes." Sullivan chuckled. "You are wonderful, Sasha. We will be in touch very soon."

He raised an eyebrow at Barclay, who was watching attentively from the corner with a smirk on his face.

"Thank you, Sasha, thanks for coming. Let me show you the way out and we will call you this afternoon."

He disappeared with Sasha and then reappeared a moment later, grinning. "Well, how do you like it so far, lord and master?"

"She's got the job as far as I'm concerned, ain't going to get better than that."

"You might want to check the others," said Barclay. "They're all pretty high-class."

"Probably a bit out of my league," said Sullivan. "Can you knock me out another Livanto?"

"You don't have to fall in love and marry them," said Barclay, pulling the lever down on the Nespresso machine. "Just check 'em out. Something to do today, isn't it?"

"Yeah, 'spose you're right," said Sullivan, sipping on his fifth Livanto of the morning.

The other girls turned up at hourly intervals. All highly qualified and each one seeming to be more beautiful than the last. The Swede, like a double of Agnetha of ABBA, the German in a short leather skirt and legs to the eyeballs, the French girl with emerald green eyes and an accent to die for, another Japanese, tall and slim with white make-up and the movements of a gazelle.

Finally, after they had all left, Barclay lit a cigarette, stared out of the window at the swimming pool and said, "Well?"

"I'm completely fucked up now," said Sullivan. "They are all fantastic."

"That's what managers are for," said Barclay, blowing a stream of Marlboro Light out of the open kitchen door. "It's going to be a couple of months, so be sure."

"Okay, I'll go with Sasha," said Sullivan.

"You and Japanese girls..." laughed Barclay.

"Yeah, I know, I know," said Sullivan. "Why is that? Can she start today?"

"Sure, I'll give her a call and try and get her here tonight. I'm taking off now. I'll call you later. I think she's got a car. Okay if I give her your cell phone number?"

"Yep, hook it up," said Sullivan picking up his Triple-o and starting into a slow blues.

A few months after moving in, Sasha had proved indispensable. She tended to his every need, was sweet and intelligent, and knew what he would need before he had even voiced it. As his broken bone mended she helped him practise walking again, her arms around his waist as he struggled across the floor of his TV lounge. He fought an overpowering urge to fall in love with her, be with her and of course be in bed with her. The feeling between them was strong but she remained resolutely professional. She went to her own bedroom every night and he would lie in his bed imagining her in hers, hopefully imagining him in his. He finally started to walk again, to come back to himself. He began looking forward to being back on tour after this prolonged break, and he would take Sasha with him.

He came downstairs one morning to find a note on the kitchen table. It was from her, briefly saying that she should leave now, he was healed, he no longer needed her. She wished him luck and love. Sullivan almost broke into a sob, he was so bonded with her. He stared into a void. He was just working up to proposing to her. She left no forwarding number or email – she was just *gone*. It was devastating. He couldn't understand it and he cursed himself for not making a move while he'd had the chance.

Sasha – come back, come back … It flashed through his brain as he stood there on the edge of the stage, gazing over a sea of up-raised arms and smiling faces.

He took a few bows and then got the rest of the band to come out to the front of the stage, where they all bowed together and finally, with cheery waves and thumbs-up to the audience, exited stage right, leaving the crowd rammed up against the stage edge, arms raised, mouths wide open yelling for more.

He walked into the semi-darkness at stage right, where his man-ager was waiting beside the monitor guy. Everyone was smiling. "Great show, Sul," said his manager. "You're back!"

"I never left," said Sullivan, grinning but happy to have pulled off a good one. It was what he did best. And now he walked slowly, fol-lowing the flashlight through the darkness, down the steps where he held onto the handrail and finally into the narrow backstage cor-ridor that lead to his dressing room.

He got in and closed the door behind him, he was drenched. All his clothes were wet and sticking to him like a second skin. He pulled off his silver bomber jacket, peeled out of his red T-shirt with the snarling dog, unlaced his paramilitary boots and finally – the most difficult of all – got out of his black jeans, which was like an exercise using paint stripper. He pulled a fluffy white hotel towel out of his gig bag and stepped into the shower, praying for hot water. It came and he started soaping himself, luxuriating in the steam and heat, and then realized he still had his socks on. "Oh what the fuck …" they needed washing anyway, crazy asshole. He still felt good from the show. Really, there was no other life experience that matched it, he knew it and he felt lucky, so very lucky, and then Sasha came into his mind and he felt something like a jolt in his heart. She should be here sharing all of this with him. He felt pain at her absence, how could this be? He finally stepped out of the shower, dried himself off and put on a complete set of clean clothes, the nightly process, checked himself in the mirror and opened the dressing room door.

Barclay Williams was standing outside guarding the dressing room. This was a well-rehearsed routine. They had a strict protocol over the way things would go after the concert, a controlled system, or else Sullivan would disappear immediately without seeing anyone, which in these times was not welcome. "You ready, mate?" said Barclay. "They're all waiting. C'mon, let's slay the beast, down here on the right – see this little room with the green door, surprise, surprise!"

A look passed across Sullivan's face. She was in there, he knew it. Sasha, she had come back. Barclay pushed the door open and Sullivan was confronted by an almost rabid mob with outstretched arms and a sea of hungry cell phones.

No Sasha.

He let her go with a brief thought that he would dream of her later and then waded into the green room, which was packed with fans, well-wishers and anyone who had somehow managed to finagle an all-area access pass.

Sullivan hated this, but it had to be done, it was part of the gig these days. There were sponsors mixed in with children mixed in with relatives mixed in with spouses, CEOs, sales associates, representatives, corporate accountants. If you did a tour in the US these days you were part of the Walmart family, or the Target family or the Best Buy family, etc., etc. But it was the new normal, there was no other way unless you wanted to play to tiny audiences in tiny clubs, and they were disappearing, too. You could be a rebel as long as you had sponsors. It was mind-numbing. All you could do was smile your way through the whole thing, be gracious and laugh through gritted teeth, even if it took more energy than the actual performance, and you couldn't get through it every night by drowning in alcohol because there was another show tomorrow. Moan – moan – moan. Poor little me, thought Sullivan. Man up, mofo, this is the job. He walked into a storm of iPhones flying in his face, the old records, the EPs, the cassette tapes, the vinyl LPs, CDs, bootlegs, paper napkins, programmes, the glossy photos. His past like a mighty ocean come again to drown him. But no time to think about it, just here we go, selfie, thank you, selfie, thank you, selfie, thank you – everybody's famous. I'm a lucky guy, he thought resolutely.

Where's Sasha? Am I a rock god or is that an old concept? Oh, your Mom likes me, that's lovely, and your grandmother, too, even better. Celebrity, youth, money – these are the things that rule.

C'mon, touch me and get some of this shit, you can be famous, too.

Sullivan worked his way through the crowd smiling, beaming and signing, his manager close behind him. Finally he climbed up onto a table and addressed the packed room. "I want to thank you all so much for coming tonight and thanks for your wonderful support. Here's to you!" He swallowed a glass of champagne. "Now I must go and get some beauty sleep and a few more drinks." The crowd cheered him as he jumped down from the table and got out into the corridor, Barclay Williams close on his heels.

"Christ, there were some lookers in there," he said to Barclay.

"Careful, amigo," said his manager. "Those days are over. Serious jailbait, no, no, my friend."

"Yeah, I know," said Sullivan. "Well, back to Hotel De Shit then."

"De Shit it is," said Barclay. They grabbed his stuff from the dressing room and piled into the limo that was waiting for them backstage. They arrived back at the hotel where he signed a few more records for fans who were waiting at the lobby door and made straight for the elevator. "Bar?" shouted Barclay behind him.

"Maybe," said Sullivan. "I'll be there in fifteen or not at all."

"Whatever," said Barclay. "I need a drink."

"Finally," breathed Sullivan, as he slumped against the door of the elevator and pressed his floor number. He got out at the eighteenth and struggled for a few minutes trying to find his room in the endless maze of corridors. After circling around for about five minutes he finally arrived at his room, waved the plastic card over a panel that opened the door and walked into the pastel silence. "Thank God!" he said. He slung his bag on the bed and then crashed down beside it, his head sinking into the soft pillow. It felt good. I'm done, he thought, what a night. I wonder if there are some women in the bar.

Sasha floated into his mind and the bar idea went out of his head. Can't do that any more, might as well paint a target on my back – no, thanks. Well, I guess it will be me and Ivan Ilyich. He took off his clothes, slid between the sheets, snapped open his Kindle and began reading.

# THE JAZZ WIFE

Reggie was in a panic. He stared up at the white-painted ceiling. Something was wrong down there. He knew it. It had been a long time since anything like this had happened to him, goddammit. He was a jazz star. A bona fide jazz star playing down here in South America to adoring fans. Too adoring, maybe.

Why the hell hadn't he used a condom? She – Inez – had come on real strong, he couldn't resist her pouty lips, firm body, short skirt, stilettos and soft Brazilian purr. He had fallen for the whole thing. After the show and a few drinks later they were back in his hotel room and swallowing more Grey Goose. She had asked him to play. So he'd pulled out his Gibson ES-175 and played a couple of ballads for her, 'Stella by Starlight' and 'All the Things You Are'. Clearly she loved music and was practically swooning by the time he got through the Cole Porter ballad.

He laid his guitar down and moved toward her. The drunken sex match took place with the word "Baby!" being called out several times in the next hour and then it was blackout time. He woke up in the morning with the Rio sun gently breaking through the flimsy curtains. Inez was gone. But despite the pounding in his head, he woke up smiling. He felt like a true jazz musician, like Bird or Lester or something – just another night of music, alcohol, a couple of toots and sex. Sure, what's the problem? It's the jazz life, it is what it is.

She, his wife Roberta – or big Rob as some of his associates called her – would never know. When he returned home she would ask him if he had been a good boy and then drag him into the bedroom and take repossession of the man she had put on the map. She was his manager. She made all decisions about his career. She was good at it. He provided the raw material, his nimble fingers and juicy guitar chords. She had built the career that he was now enjoying and now she was encouraging him to explore his singing.

He had two nights left at the new Bossa club in Ipanema, then back to NYC for a week and some dates in Canada. But now, right now, something was up and it sure as hell wasn't preoccupations with his career or a guitar chord. It was the appendage between his legs. He pulled himself up from the sheets and made for the bathroom. Anxious and paranoid, he started to piss. Damn! It hurt! He knew the signs, man – Inez had left him with a love letter.

He took a shower. But he could only think of one thing. His confrontation with Roberta. She would kill him if he returned and did not have the usual demanding sex with her, or said how about they use a condom? If he said that, it was a dead giveaway. He was a good-looking guy with a guitar and she remained a hundred per cent suspicious at all times. She would start in on him and that would be it. She controlled everything. She could pull his gigs, cancel his tours. She was now managing several other young cats and maybe didn't need him. All the bank accounts were in her name. The only thing she didn't do was the music.

Reggie felt sick. What was he gonna do? He was on a flight tomorrow. Could he extend the tour in South America, pretend the flight was cancelled? No, she could check up on all of it. He was fucked and he knew it. He would have to call Ignacio, see a doctor. He emerged from the bathroom and struggled into his clothes. He picked up the telephone and dialled. The phone rang a few times and finally was answered by a gruff voice.

"Hey, Iggy, it's me, Reggie. I – um – got a little problem."

"Yeah, Reggie, what's up? Good morning, by the way."

"Yeah, man," said Reggie, "I gotta see a doctor."

"What's going on, man?" said Ignacio. "You got dengue fever or something?"

"No, man, it – it's something else."

"What?" asked Ignacio.

"You know," said Reggie. "Something down there ain't right."

"Your dick?" asked Ignacio.

"Yeah, that's right," whimpered Reggie, "I think I got an STD."

"What does that stand for?" said Ignacio. "Small tiny dick?"

Reggie couldn't even laugh and just said, "Do you know a doctor? It's gotta be private."

"Man, Roberta's gonna kill your ass," said Ignacio. "I told you not to go with Inez, she goes with everybody. Well, yeah, I gotta doc. I'll pick you up in half an hour, meet me in the lobby." Ignacio hung up and Reggie, awash in shame and paranoia, stared at the wall, which featured a sun setting behind the Cristo.

Half an hour later Reggie climbed into Ignacio's Toyota and they drove through morning traffic to the doctor's office in Copacabana.

"He's a cool guy, this doctor," said Ignacio, as they walked to the elevator. "He's used to fixing things like this. He has probably had a few Inez victims before," and cackled loudly as he pressed the elevator button. Then he said, "Don't worry, man, everything's going to be fine – you're just paranoid."

They entered the office of Dr Blauensteiner and were directed into the waiting room, where they plonked themselves down on a plush couch. Reggie sat there with visions of hell in his head as Ignacio talked about more girls he was inviting for tonight – the last show.

Fifteen minutes later the secretary came in and motioned for Reggie to follow her. She directed him into a small room that had a bed, a few shelves with medical paraphernalia and a picture of the male urogenital system. More time passed, with Reggie having Hieronymus Bosch-like hallucinations. Finally, the door swung open and a man with a hawk-like nose, steel-rimmed spectacles, a white coat and thermometer walked in.

"*Bom dia*, Reggie," he said with a thick German-Brazilian accent. "What iss ze medizinisches problem today?"

"Mmm ... I seem to have little problem down there," said Reggie, pointing south.

"Ah, I see. Haf you been a bad boy, Reggie? Okay, I need you to pee-pee in this little bottle and I will be back in a few minutes." He handed Reggie a small plastic bottle and goose-stepped out of the room. Reggie unzipped and carefully aimed into the bottle, trying not to piss on the carpet. He peed and it caused a stinging sensation.

Fuck, he thought, I'm done, this is it. It's over. His mind was spinning with thoughts of Roberta's rage, his career ending, no one remembering him, ending up homeless and forgotten on the streets of New York. Yeah, that's where it would all go just for the sake of one stupid night. Would he ever learn? He cursed himself.

Dr Blauensteiner walked back into the room. "Oh good, you did well there, a full bottle. Let's haf a party! I am just going to run some tests and we'll see what's going on. Now, lay down there and please pull your Yamamotos down." Reggie lay down in the medical bed and gingerly eased his pants and underwear down as Blauensteiner snapped on a pair of rubber surgical gloves and then, standing over him, briefly felt Reggie's testicles and then squeezed his penis, only emitting a light "Hmm …" as medical evaluation.

"Okay, mein Herr, you can put your clothes back on. I will be back in twenty minutes with the test results." He left the room and Reggie sat there again, his mind extrapolating on his future. Maybe he could work at McDonald's or at garbage disposal, become a waiter or maybe do janitorial work. He saw those scenes: Reggie swabbing down tables, Reggie carrying out the trash, handing a menu over to a fat cat white guy, arguing about rent with a rat of a landlord … He probably would have to go back to Cleveland. No doubt it would be instant divorce from Roberta and she would take everything, including his guitars. He held his head in his hands and stared at the Persian rug, which seemed to be laughing in his face. He felt sick.

Blauensteiner walked back into the room. He stared at Reggie with a look that was a mix of pity and cruelty and said, "I don't know what you have been up to, young man, but mein Gott …"

And just as his lips parted in a thin smile, Ignacio burst into the room with a shocked look on his face.

"Reggie," he blurted, "Roberta – she's … there's been an …"

# THE STALKER

Zebediah had long ago decided that he only wanted to be known, metaphorically speaking, as a man fading in and out of mist. He was there or he wasn't there – elusive butterfly. Inspired by avid reading of books about pop music – including various shadowy fringe figures – he found this image attractive. He would be known for his faint Mona Lisa smile that said nothing yet implied a deeper mystery. They would come to him. Women would swoon.

Well, at least that was the way Zebediah's fantasy went, but he hadn't reached that elevated stage yet. He was the lead singer and guitarist of his own completely not famous band, although that ownership, that unknownness, was hotly disputed by the other band members. The band was called Only Child. God knows why, but the four of them had somehow picked that out of the hat in a pitiful democratic process where each guy put in twenty names of his choice and then a neutral party wearing a blindfold had the unenviable task of pulling out the name. Zebediah had put Z on twenty slips of paper, thinking that he'd probably ace it, and then he would shrug with an ironic smile as he took on being the dude, sort of implying that the gods had chosen, or that fate had taken a hand. But that fantasy didn't play out and they were Only Child – actually the name of a woman who had once hired them for an underpaid gig in a bierkeller in the Schwabing district of Munich.

And although he was pissed off about what he thought was a shit name, he would only let himself be known as Z, and anyway, whatever the band was called, he was still the singer, the front man.

So, like any other young band, they started doing gigs, travelling all over the UK and eventually to countries like Belgium and Holland, where they began to get a following. Young girls picked up on their youth and Z's good looks. The music of Only Child was middle-of-the-road pop, not bad but not particularly original either. The great hit, the one that would really put them on the map, eluded them.

And then they were offered a song by a kid on the internet – not something they would have normally looked at, as they all imagined themselves to be great songwriters. But the song was called 'What Me a Narcissist' and the internet kid had cleverly rhymed narcissist with one off the wrist, think I'm pissed, boo she hissed, it's the drugs I missed, put your face in my fist, etc., etc. It was a song for morons, the band knew it, but Z sang it in a broad cockney accent and lo and behold they had a huge hit. It was a pub song, and for a couple of weeks it rocked the UK. The band were happy to have a hit but wished it hadn't been this beer-soaked anthem. They thought they were a lot cooler than that. But suddenly the tabloids were taking an interest, at least while they were in the charts, but fame, that dodgy little tart, slipped away and they were back to the shitholes of Belgium.

Z was desperate, he had to become really famous before he turned twenty-two. He started thinking. Maybe he should leave the band and go solo. Everyone knew him now because of their one crap hit. But maybe that was going too far and he should stay with the guys – maybe? He thought about it, dreamed about it. I *am* the fucking band, he thought, it's me, I am the whole thing, I don't need them, it's obvious where the talent is. And then, paranoid and in-secure, he would retreat from that position. What if it didn't work and then he was just another wanker without a band, plus they could fucking replace him. He did a mental revision and tried to work up some kind of warped loyalty to his band mates and then padded that out with some imaginary public response like: "Good old Z, he's stuck with his original band all these years but we all know that he is the real star," and that was followed by a sicken-ing vision of them playing at the end of a pier when they were forty in Scunthorpe or somewhere, just as desperate, when they should have been selling out stadiums in America. He went through a list of famous career-making moves: suicide, drug overdose, car accident, both his parents dead in a plane crash in Majorca, gas explosion in his house, electrocuted by his own guitar due to faulty wiring by a Glaswegian roadie, sex change.

And then with a shock he got it. STALKER. He needed a STALKER. Right! He would get on the front pages with a stalker and be the embattled pop star, a tragic but heroic figure who through the power of his charisma and music had attracted a nutter. He could probably get on the cover of *The Sun* or the *Daily Mirror* for weeks if he played it right. *The Sun*, the *Mirror*, that's where he should be, his heart gave a little spasmodic jerk at the thought. It would have to be managed and plotted to get the maximum effect. And that would be topped off by another massive hit. But who could play the part of the stalker? A professional actor or …? Again Z hurt his brain thinking about it. Maybe there would be someone in their fan club who could do a convincing job. It would have to be a girl, preferably attractive and someone who could handle it – late nights, dodgy weather, lots of hanging around and making sure she got photographed by the paparazzi. He couldn't tell the band about it – it should be a secret shared only by him and the stalker, and perhaps a publicist.

She appeared in his mind like a dream – he knew her! Mandy! That was her name, Mandy. She was in the fan club and came to all their gigs around London. She had arrived in their dressing room one night after a gig to get her records signed, and Z had given her more than a second glance but then declined the possibilities – don't mix with the fans – and she had a look in her eye. Perfect material – not bad looking, always dressed up for the gigs, kinda sexy, perfect. If he was going to be stalked, it had to be by a sexy-looking chick – otherwise what was the point? This was simple. They had the names and emails of all their fans. It should be dead easy to contact her and arrange a meeting. Karen, their fan club secretary, had all of that information. He would get the list from her and give Mandy a call.

The next morning he phoned Karen and casually asked if he could get the fan club list from her. Karen slightly quizzed him on it, which made him uncomfortable, but he waffled through the moment and said he was thinking of a song where he would use some if not all of their names. Karen thought that was a terrific idea and said she would pop over the list via WeTransfer in a couple of hours.

Z stared at his computer screen for a while, thought about sex, went over to the bedroom mirror and practised the Mona Lisa smile, played Rock Band for ten minutes and then picked up his real guitar and worked on a few Hendrix licks against his iPhone metronome.

Halfway though 'Purple Haze' the list popped up on the screen. He opened the file and ran down it. There she was, the only Mandy in the fan club. She lived in Croydon – didn't they all? – and there was her phone number. Z stood up and walked around his bedroom for a couple of minutes. Should I do this, he thought, should I? Should I? Right then a red admiral butterfly fluttered in through his open bedroom window and alighted on his bedpost as if sending him a sign from the universe. After a brief moment it rose back into the air and left through the open window.

Z stood there stunned. I am that butterfly, he thought, and he almost wept at the beneficence of nature and the underlying causation of all things. He knew. He rehearsed a little speech to Mandy in his head and then dialled the number. A South London voice responded, "'Ullo … Mandy …"

"Uh, hello, Mandy," he said, surprised at his own nervousness.

"Ooze this?" asked Mandy.

"It's Z from Only Child," he said.

"Christ," said Mandy, "can't believe it – what? Really? It's you?"

"Yeah," said Z. "Bit of a surprise, I s'pose, but I have something I want to talk to you about. A job offer, actually."

"But I got a job," said Mandy breathlessly.

"Yeah, I know," said Z, "but this would be outside of normal office hours."

"Sounds sexy," said Mandy.

"No, nothing like that," said Z, his fingers still on the E7#9 on his guitar neck. "I think you might think it's fun. Could we meet somewhere and talk about it?"

"Yeah, sure," said Mandy, "would be an honour."

"Do you know somewhere we could meet for a chat?" he asked.

"Well, I could meet you after work tonight if you like. There's a McDonald's right by our office."

"Okay," said Z, "give me the address."

Mandy breathed it into her cell phone, Z jotted it down and then said, "Well, thanks, Mandy, I'll see you at 6:30 at Mickey D's." All he heard from Mandy's end was "Fuckin' 'ell!"

At the end of the afternoon, Z travelled on the Northern Line down to Tottenham Court Road, wearing black sunglasses for the whole journey, occasionally raising them slightly to make sure he didn't miss the stop.

He got out and walked over to the McDonald's on the corner that Mandy had breathily mentioned. He entered the bright light still wearing his dark sunglasses and looked around. She was sitting in a corner. She saw him and gave a shy little wave. He nodded, smiled and walked over to her.

"'Ullo Z, can't believe it's you 'ere come to see me like..."

She looks good, thought Z, better than I remember. Hmmm, hope this doesn't complicate things. I have to remain neutral – no involvement whatsoever.

"Uh yeah, good to see you, Mandy. Let me tell you a bit about what I have in mind."

"Yeah, awright," gushed Mandy, "ready when you are."

"Um, well, like it's like this," said Z. "I know you are a fan of our band and our music and you would probably like to see us do well. Get more hits, maybe?"

"Yeah," said Mandy.

"Well, it's difficult these days, you know, and we could always use a little help."

"And what would that be?" said Mandy, raising an eyebrow over her Styrofoam cup.

"Well, I've thought about this a lot," said Z, "with the guys, of course, and what we have come up with is that I should be stalked. You know, have a stalker and get it into the papers. Create a bit of drama like, you know, *The Sun* – front page of it, millions of people reading..."

"How d'ya know I'm not doing that already," smiled Mandy. "You are stalkable, you know."

Z laughed. This was going well. "I think it will be fun. No harm to anyone, just a bit of a lark, and you'll get paid."

"How much?" asked Mandy.

"Two hundred quid for a week."

"Make it three and I'll do it," said Mandy.

"Sure, okay," said Z. "You could be a manager, you've got the right stuff."

"Yeah, maybe," said Mandy. "So what do we do?"

"Okay, here's a rough plan," said Z and outlined the plan he had dreamed up with his devious publicist Keith Wrenchman. Mandy took it all in with a few 'ooh's and 'ahh's, and nodded in agreement. She was up for it.

He left Mandy with a wink and a light kiss on her hand as she sank her teeth into a Big Mac and extra-large fries.

A couple of nights later, as planned, Mandy hid herself in the bushes outside Z's house. Z took photos of her for evidence when he went to the press. This was repeated for the following two nights and then finally on the fourth night, Z leaned out of his bedroom window and yelled at her to fuck off. A paparazzi photographer was there as arranged by Wrenchman and took a flash photograph from behind Mandy, and up at the window where the pop star appeared with a raised middle finger.

This picture appeared in the *Daily Mirror* the next day, but only as a small item toward the back of the paper. It was disappointing. Z and Wrenchman knew that they had to kick it up a bit if they wanted to get full and ongoing tabloid coverage. They decided to go for a video that they could try to get on the BBC, Sky, or any six o'clock news if possible. They called Mandy and let her know what the plan was. She was to be outside Z's at midnight, only this time Z would open the window and sing to her with his guitar in his arms and then would yell out, "Would you now please fuck off?" Romeo and Juliet in reverse. That should do it. Mandy was excited. She was loving all this; she would become famous in her own right and she was completely besotted by Z – loved him as no woman had ever loved a man before. She turned up at midnight and started yelling out "Z, Z, Z" and chucking a few pebbles, but this time broke a window, having miscalculated the strength of her throw. Z appeared at the window with a guitar around his neck.

"What the fuck are you doing?" he yelled. "How do we end this?"

"Sing me a song," yelled back Mandy.

Right, yeah, thought Z, and sang and played an Only Child song. Then he yelled again, "Good fucking night, go away and don't come back!" and slammed the window shut. This was all captured on video by a lone paparazzi hired by Wrenchman who, after the incident, filmed Mandy giving a heartfelt sobbing interview saying that her life was dedicated to Z and that she was prepared to end it all unless he accepted her. Mandy felt pleased with her performance and thrilled to be in this deception with Z. But in fact she truly did love him and her thoughts about what she was doing became confused because in her heart of hearts she really was that person. She didn't need to fake it.

Wrenchman circulated the video the next day when it not only got shown by Sky and the BBC that night but also went viral on social media. There was a lot of reaction. Some condemned Z for his cold heart and some put the blame on the hapless girl with her unwanted attention. But all this produced the desired effect – there was a big buzz around Only Child. The tabloids were now taking a big interest and the story of Mandy and Z was selling papers. The people wanted more of this *Fatal Attraction* tale and the tabloids kept it going. For Z it was now over, and he was ready to move on, although he still hadn't made the front page of *The Sun* and that nagged at him. But still, he was a lot more famous than a few weeks back and the bookings for the band were going through the roof and the tabloids kept it going. They put a big picture of Mandy on the front page showing a generous amount of cleavage, tears on her cheek and the headline, 'Where is she now? Bring her back Z', for the general public had taken to Mandy. Mandy herself knew that Z had now lost interest in her and she started to connect with a new feeling of rage. As Z went on to fame and fortune, didn't call her any more and was seen with a young Victoria's Secret model, she felt dumped and alone. She started to feel a different emotion. It was hate; love turned to seething hate. She still kept her mouth shut about the set-up it had all been, but now she would show that bastard. If she couldn't have him then no one would. She knew that she could reveal the truth to the tabloids, but that understanding was lost in the huge wave of anti-Z rage she was drowning in. She called the paparazzi guys and let them know about a photo opportunity.

She turned up at Z's house on a Thursday night, after a couple of drinks at Callwells, a nearby pub. There were a large number of paparazzi hiding in the bushes and trees. "Hello, boys," she greeted them like a star and then, powered by three vodka tonics, yelled up at the window, "Z, you bastard, come out here or you're gonna get it."

Z appeared at the window and yelled back, "Really, Mandy, please fuck off. It's over now. Don't you get it? It's over!" and slammed the window shut. Mandy started crying, sobbing loudly enough to wake the whole neighborhood, and to complete the ghastly scenario it started raining. It was a hard, unrelenting English rain and it beat down on Mandy like so many iron nails. Mandy stood there wet and sobbing while the cowardly paps, thinking that's fucking it, quickly disappeared into the wet London night. The darkness and deluge beat down like a hard fist on Mandy, who was now a crumpled heap on the lawn. The front door of Z's house opened and Z stood, looking around to make sure that there were no photographers lurking, before running across the lawn to Mandy with a raincoat. He came to her in the dark and said, "Look, sorry, Mandy, this is getting out of hand. Here, put this on and come inside." Mandy's hate immediately dissolved and she followed Z into his house, where there was a nice fire in the hearth, a guitar on the couch and a couple of brandy glasses on the table.

He turned to her and said, "Look, Mandy, why don't you have a nice warm bath after all that? You'll feel better. I'll run it for you, it's upstairs." Mandy, almost in a state of shock at this intimacy, followed Z up the stairs into the bathroom, which smelled like an English meadow. Z turned on the taps and the bath quickly filled up. "There you go, sweetheart, I'll leave you to it, there's a bathrobe on the hook." He exited the bathroom and Mandy slipped into the bath and luxuriated in the warm, scented water. She felt as if she was in a dream and thought like maybe he's not an asshole. The water eventually cooled down and she climbed out of the bath and snuggled into the terry cloth robe. Her clothes were not there, as Z had put them in a dryer, so she went down to the lounge where he was playing the guitar in front of the fire.

"Oh, you look a lot better," said Z, smiling at her as she came in. "Here, sit down, have a glass of brandy."

"Oh, thanks," said Mandy, suddenly aware that she was here in only a bathrobe with the man of her dreams, who only a half hour back she'd wished dead. She took the glass and popped out "Brandy Mandy".

"Oh, that's good," laughed Z. "You are a good sport, Mandy." Mandy raised her glass and thought, I don't want to be a good sport, I want to be your woman, then downed the glass in one gulp.

"Whoa, easy on there, Mand," said Z. "You're supposed to sip it slowly."

"It's doin' me good," said Mandy. "'Nother one please."

"Certainly, Madam," said Z, pouring her another snifter and noticing that a luscious right breast had slipped out of the gown.

"I think I'll have another one, too. Try and keep up with ya."

They both had a couple more. Mandy was feeling more than tipsy after three brandies. With the heat of the fire and Z's bluesy licks on the guitar all combining to push her into feeling that she was standing on a slope, she practically shouted at Z, "I'm completely pissed." Z waved his glass drunkenly at her.

"Yeah, we're partners in crime, Mand, what a laugh. C'mon over here." Mandy slid out of the overstuffed armchair and onto the rug beside Z. They clinked glasses and then both fell over sideways on the rug, where the natural thing was to kiss and kiss and eventually ride through the gates of heaven together. Instead, they both fell asleep right there.

Several hours later, just as the dawn was beginning to crack the sky, they both awoke shivering and with the distinct feeling that somebody was running a hot iron through their skulls.

"Fuck," said Z. "How did that happen?"

"You plied me with alcohol," croaked Mandy, her face down in the rug.

"You gotta go," said Z.

"Yeah, I know. You done what you wanted, now it's sling-out time."

"No, it's not like that. I got an interview in less than an hour, wass the time?" Z looked up at the clock on the wall. It was 7:45am. "Fuck, my interview's at nine."

"You'll never make it," said Mandy. "All that hair and make-up – ain't gonna happen."

"You gotta go," said Z.

"Yeah, I know," said Mandy, pulling herself up. "'Ope I ain't pregnant."

"For fuck's sake, don't say shit like that," said Z. "I got enough trouble already."

"Yeah, rich little pop star … Christ, I need a fag … Awright, I'm going, gettin' out while the goin's good." She stood up and went to find her clothes. Z laid back on the rug and thought, fuck, what was I thinking? Fuck fuck fuck ... The door slammed and he reckoned that was bloody that, but there really was an interview with British *Vogue* and a particularly notorious journalist who was known to have a nose like a bloodhound when it came to scandal.

There was an imperious rap on the door using the brass knocker.

Fuck, thought Z, this is bloody it.

He opened the door to Penelope Stone, one of the UK's scariest journalists.

"Who was that poor girl just leaving?" she asked. "She looked terrible and the tears were streaming down her face like Niagra ..."

"No, no Viagra," said Z, confused and forgetting that he was an arrogant pop star.

"No, not Viagra. I should hope not at your age ... oh, forget it. I'm here to talk about other things." Penelope Stone grimaced at him, feeling that this was a complete waste of her time. Z asked her to sit down and stumbled into the kitchen to make them both some tea.

Stone interviewed him for about an hour on style, popular culture and how the internet had destroyed the record business, before finally she asked, "Success. What is that these days?"

Z did his best to sound like someone with a brain but it was hard if not impossible in the state he was in. He mumbled a lot and went for more of an elliptical take on things rather than coherence.

Finally, Stone turned her tape recorder off and said that will do for now. She patted him on the head, adding, "Next time, sonny boy, do some preparation." She stood up and left as rapidly as if she were on horseback.

Back in her office Mandy, bedraggled and hung over, found her hatred of Z returning like a tsunami. I am a used woman, she thought. That fucker has taken advantage of me in every possible way. Well, that's it, he's gonna get it. She picked up the phone and made a call to her paparazzi friend. "That's it," she said to Johnny Ragman. "He's done it now. You wanna get the real story? I'm ready."

"Great, Mand," said Johnny, "but you do know that you're on the front page of *The Sun* today."

"Fuckin what?" cried Mandy. "I don't believe it. Fuckin 'ell, 'ang on, I'll call you back." One of the girls in the office had the rag and she showed it to Mandy with a smirk on her face. There she was, a crumpled heap on the lawn outside Z's house. The headline said, MANDY – THE END. At the side of the lurid shot was a vindictive column about Z and pop stars in general.

That was it for Mandy, she dialled Johnny in a frenzy. "Are you ready, Johnny? Here's the real truth, no effing varnish." And she laid out the whole story about Z and the fake set-up, how he had planned the whole thing with Wrenchman and had taken complete advantage of her, and Mandy added, "When I say complete, I mean complete." Johnny breathlessly held his Sony micro recorder next to his cell phone, which he had on speaker, and kept murmuring, "Yeah, go on, go on," until he had the whole filthy story and could hear Mandy sniffling at the other end of the line.

"Brilliant, Mand," he said. "Z will be on the cover of *The Sun* tomorrow and it won't be good for him. The bastard," he added for effect.

"Okay, I have to get this all written up. It has to be on the editor's desk by 2pm sharp. That's an hour and a half from now to make tomorrow's deadline."

"Yeah, the rat deserves what he gets," said Mandy. "Thanks Johnny, thanks a million, mate."

"Okay, my love, you'll get a cheque for this," said Johnny. "And let's have a drink sometime."

She put the office telephone down and, with her brain on fire, tried to return to her office duties. Around ten past two her cell phone rang. It was Z.

"Hi, Mandy," he said, sounding nervous. I just wanted to apologize for this morning and kicking you out and all that. I'm really, *really* sorry, I can be an idiot sometimes."

"Yeah," muttered Mandy.

"But there's something else, Mandy," he said. "I realize that I am in love with you. I want us to be together, like forever. What do you think?"

Mandy fainted and fell onto her desk, on top of Tuesday's issue of *The Sun*.

# GLOWING RED MOUTHS

You walk out. Hot dazzle, darkness, a rising sound coming at you, a shell to the ear, waves crash on sand. What is it? You know it. Hands pressing together, you acknowledge their presence and your arrival, but this is the scaffold. You are up here, and they are there in the pit. You can feel them, they have paid the price to see you, you are part of a transaction, part of their lives. This is how you got here and they are invested – now what? You are it, the thing, the next two hours, all eyes on you – what are you going to do? Standing in the glare, as fragile as a paper cup, under lights that hit you like the Arizona sun. Black space, vague outlines of faces, the penumbra of the balcony stretching away to the left and the right like a corridor. The barren stage, the smooth floor sloping up behind you like a sucking tide, the metallic taste that fills your mouth – it dissolves only when you finally part your dry lips and say something. Fracture the silence with a funny comment, a joke, a self-deprecating remark … Well, who are you or who am I, like there's a garish question mark hanging over the hungry audience, which is red and green and winking and blinking with harsh flashes like a weird owl's eyes, but that's just your mind playing tricks. There's a guitar hanging off you, the strap biting into your shoulder – is it a noose or an anchor? It's heavy tonight, leaden, but it will be your protector, your way through to the other side, somewhere in the middle of the fifty nights that you signed up for. You see roads, freeways, hotels, motels, women with glowing red mouths, parking lots from Mars – it's all there again, the endless loop. There's stuff under your feet – small rectangular pedals with silver switches and coils of wire, like little black snakes hissing as they speak to each other and make the connections that are supposed to make your guitar sound bigger, better, to make it shimmer and echo as if you were playing in a canyon or from the surface of the moon. That blue one makes it roar as if inciting a mob to action, the crazy little white one makes the guitar sound backwards as if it is speaking in a lost and forgotten dialect. You stare at them quickly to see if in fact you are connected – if the shimmer pedal is turned on, if the little red light is off. You will play the first song and it will sound slightly dull, as if some kind of magic is missing. In the first moment of being out here, it's a shock sensation as you sometimes miss what someone else had missed. It has to be there ready to go, you can't think straight enough to see things like that, switching it off is misplaced efficiency. You are orienting, mapping, getting the shape, the feeling of this place, your position in this strange but always familiar territory; tight scared. Then you will drop a couple of lines into the darkness, laughter will come back and you ease back into it as if falling into your mother's arms.

Okay this is it.

You step up to the mic…

"Hi, I'm glad to be here. I'm glad to be anywhere…"

# SURFIN' USA

*Surfin' Fretboard – interview with Duck Davis*

**SF:** "So Duck, tell us – I mean our readers, I mean our hot doggin' surf guitar freaks – how you got started. Where the inspiration came from. How did surfin' and guitar playin' come together?"

**Duck:** "Well, which fuckin' question is it?"

**SF:** "Sorry, Duck, too much fuckin' sun, man. How you got started, man, is what I, like, mean."

**Duck:** (taking a long drag) "Well, I started out in my old man's garage in Pasadena. Y'know, the usual, just dickin' around out back amongst the grease and the tools, bored outta my teenage skull. One day I see this plank lying upside the shed. So I slung it in the pool and jumped on the fucker. As it happens, I landed on my feet like standing upright. I thinks whoah baby, hot dog! I'm ridin' the chlorine, fuckin' A. That's how I got started."

**SF:** "Wow, Duck, that's heavy, dude, but how did the electric guitar surf style …?"

**Duck:** "Well, yeah, of course I was a guitar player. Mostly polkas and waltzes, coming from a Polish family. If I didn't play a fuckin' polka every day my ol' man'd whup me upside the head. That's how I got the surf thing. He smacked me one day and it was like a wave going through my head. It had a rhythm – y' know, salt water poundin' on the sand. I even heard drums with it. And a weird melody

– 'Misery Guts' – kind of an A'rab thing, must have been the fuckin' sand or the whup on the head. My ears are still ringin'."

**SF:** "So … did you start a band?"

**Duck:** "No, I went to the fuckin' beach. Venice Beach to be exact, and I started surfin' on my plank. I just had this vision – Southern California, sexy chicks, me bangin 'em all, drivin' a hot rod and whackin' away at my Slamocaster."

**SF:** "Fuck, Duck, that sound went right round the world. You must be a rich man."

**Duck**: "I ain't fuckin' rich, but I got a few T-shirts."

**SF:** "So how did it go from there?"

**Duck:** "Well I looked for some guys with good tans and good hair and got them all instruments from the pawnshop – taught the fuckers the basic stuff and we were off and ridin' the waves."

**SF:** "Just like that?"

**Duck:** "Yeah, there weren't much to it. One rhythm, pretty much one chord and we were off and running, I mean surfin'. I tried adding more chords but it got too complicated – no one needed more than three and that'd be pushin' it."

**SF:** "But you have such a distinctive guitar sound. Where did that come from?"

**Duck:** "Well, promise not to tell anyone. But one day we were practisin' back outside my pop's garage and the sun melted the controls on my amp. Could never move 'em again, couldn't afford a repair or a new amp, so I got stuck on that screaming treble and it sort of caught on. So my philosophy was well, fuck it, if they like it they can have it."

**SF:** "Deep, man. And what about technique?"

**Duck:** "What about it?"

**SF:** "Well, those incredible runs you do all the way down the neck, for instance."

**Duck:** "I just figure it's a hell of a long way from one end to the other, I better get there as fast as I can."

**SF:** "Some people say your guitar sounds like the sea."

**Duck:** "That's because my guitar is a cheap piece of shit."

**SF:** "No, really, man, when I hear your guitar I think of the ocean."

**Duck:** "You need your fuckin' head examined."

**SF:** "Well tell us how you came to compose 'Inside the Big One', or 'Cresting in the Curly', or 'Hang Fifteen', or 'Head Up Surfs Down' – any of those godhead pieces."

**Duck:** "Well, I ain't really a religious man. Surf, maybe that's my religion, some of those waves are awesome. But when I am out there hangin' in a roller, I do hear a voice and it sings to me, even shows me pictures of the guitar neck and where to put my hands. That's how I get it, sort of a mixture of salt water and guitar frets. Hey, that could be the title of my next record. Fuck…!"

**SF:** "Cool, man – like rad."

# RACHEL

She stood right in front of him for the whole gig. Singing every song word for word. Her dark hair was pulled back from her face. She wore red lipstick and gold earrings. As he sweated and played his way through the set his eyes kept coming back to her. He found himself playing for her alone, occasionally throwing a pose for the large crowd and the mob of photographers pressed up against the security rails but always returning his attention to the girl in front of him. It was a good situation. A beautiful young woman – an angel – in front of you, paying rapt attention to every note you played. Wasn't this the name of the game? What it really was all about? The oldest cliché in the book … Why do you play the guitar? To get girls, you fool!

But it was difficult for him to catch her eye. She knows I am looking at her, he thought, but she's shy, too shy to return the gaze, because we are close, only a few feet apart – it's intimidating for her. But I feel her, and she feels me, I'm up here, she is down there. I bet she would like to meet me. Is that her boyfriend standing next to her? He doesn't look up too much. She's probably going to dump him after tonight – sorry, amigo, she's a little bit out of your league. I'll be taking over soon. I wonder what her name is? Could it be Rachel? I bet it's Rachel. There's a vibe between us. She knows it, I know it, we have a thing, and we haven't even met each other yet.

It came to his next guitar solo. He bent forward over his guitar and positioned himself in front of her. He played with his eyes closed but halfway through opened them and looked down at her. She was staring at him and her face broke into a wide smile as he caught her eye … Ha! They had connected! He finished the solo with a flourish and straightened up. She was still smiling. They finished the show with all the flash and bang that was expected, and after bowing and waving to the ecstatic audience he came forward to the edge of the stage and bent down on one knee in front of Rachel.

He took her hand and placed his signature guitar pick in her palm.

She burst into tears as he left the stage.

# VINTAGE

Gilbert parked his car behind Bob's Rare Guitars store in the parking lot. That way he could save three dollars on the parking meter out in the street. He could relax and have a couple of hours of guilty pleasure staring at premium vintage guitars that were out of his financial reach. But what the hell, he liked to come down here to Bob's Rare Guitars once in a while, dream a little.

The store was filled with beautiful old vintage electrics that in Gilbert's mind were so undervalued at the time of their making but had now become sought after, like priceless antiques. The world had caught up. The old ones were best, no matter what any detractor said. They had an undeniable mystique that just wasn't there with the new guitars. He had studied up on it, read a few books and had some knowledge. The most desirable would be all original, and that meant tuning pegs, nuts, control knobs, potentiometers and pickups – and no re-fret jobs, no broken headstocks, perfect as the day they first came off the bench.

It was all a bit crazy. In the rough and tumble world of guitar players back in the day, they were just guitars and probably saw a lot of rough handling in the typical guitarist's life. Thrown into the back of car trunks or Chevy pickups, bashed into mic stands, hurled off stages, wielded in fights, who knows. Nobody told a cowboy guitar player to go easy with that Les Paul Gold Top or that '54 Strat. That's the way it was, they were just havin' fun. To Gilbert's mind they were made in what seemed like the golden age of guitar-making and American ingenuity. These days the prices were breathtaking, some of them going from fifty to two hundred thousand dollars depending on date, serial number, condition, who had played it, etc. Long gone were the days of a guitar for fifty or a hundred bucks.

He entered the store. There they were, hanging like jewels, like precious fruit slightly out of reach. Bob, red-faced and overweight, was behind the counter, deep in an intense conversation with an Asian guy who was staring at a Fender Jaguar on the countertop. Gilbert caught little bits of their conversation.

"How do I know? You say early sixties – I don't see the stamp. Is that the right neck?" The Asian man was pushing Bob on a lot of questions as to the authenticity of the guitar. Typical, thought Gilbert. He's probably a serious collector, or he will sell them on the Japanese market for five times the price. Well, it's probably astronomically priced already, and the guy wants to know if it's the real thing. It's such an industry now. He wandered through the store looking at various old electrics, some vintage acoustic Martins and a Gibson J-200 from 1937 that made his heart beat faster. In his dream world he really would be a guitarist –living it, being it, being in a band, playing every night. But it hadn't worked out.

He had been in a few groups as a teenager but even he felt something was missing from his playing. He could not quite get the rhythm thing – the beat, the pulse, whatever it was you were supposed to feel naturally. He was stiff. So, he let go of that ambition and pursued a career in retail. He was currently a store manager at Big Buy. But his son Frankie, now sixteen and a keen guitarist, really seemed to have it – the inborn talent. Maybe Gilbert's dreams would be realized through his son. He would be proud if that came to be. A guitar suddenly caught his eye. It was a Les Paul. It looked very old, probably mid-fifties. He picked it up and started playing a few chords. It felt good in his hands. All the finish was worn off the neck, which seemed to add to its authenticity – a real player's guitar. It was wonderful, better than any guitar he had attempted to play before this moment. He felt weak, as if he had fallen into the arms of a beautiful woman. He had to have it – this old guitar with its history, its warmth, its soul. He knew he couldn't do it – the money – his wife would kill him, but he felt the seduction and something like the call of Satan. He carried it over to where Bob was standing behind the counter.

"Hey, Gilbert," said Bob, greeting him with a shit-eating grin. "What you got there?"

Gilbert, in his dazed mind was going over his bank account, thinking if I work extra hours for three months, I can do it.

"How much, er, this one," he stammered. Bob looked up at the ceiling for a second and then said "sixty-five" and stared at Gilbert.

Bob's eyes were like bullets entering Gilbert's brain. "Sixty-five," thought Gilbert, shrinking in Bob's glare. "He can't mean sixty-five dollars, he must mean sixty-five hundred." His brain whirled like a pool of vodka and then, shrinking under Bob's animal lust for a sale moaned, "I'll take it."

"Good man," smiled Bob, "great guitar. How would you like to pay?"

"Er, Visa," said Gilbert and fished in his pocket for his cards. He hauled out his wallet and handed over the Visa card, actually the company's business credit card which had an extended credit line. In his dazed condition Gilbert thought he could swing that. He was the one who turned in the accounts and he would have it covered before anyone looked at it. Bob ran the card which took a couple of minutes, and then went through.

"Okay," said Bob, "she's all yours. Let me get you the case." He went into a room at the back and returned with a battered brown case saying, "This is the original case. You're lucky, don't see many of these any more."

"Thanks, Bob," said Gilbert and carefully placed the worn old Les Paul into the pink crushed velvet of the case.

"See you next time," said Bob.

Gilbert left the store, placed the guitar on the back seat of his car and started the drive home. He felt good, flushed with something like passion – he had done something bold, gone for it. He was proud of his acquisition. Maybe if he practised, he could ...? He laughed out loud at his own enthusiasm, but – yeah, man, he had finally got one of these old beauties and there was no question about it, they were the real deal. The modern ones just didn't sound as good. No magic, not even close.

This was a starting point. Maybe he would write a book about vintage guitars and their inherent value, something like *The Truth of Vintage*, with a '52 Les Paul on the cover or an early Telecaster ... No, wait a minute. *The Veracity of Vintage*, that was it! Brilliant – killer title! He could do it. It felt like his whole relationship with the guitar was coming together, like if you weren't a player per se, you could be an expert. Yes, that was it. The man who knew. Maybe he could have his own vintage guitar shop. Really be that guy, the old dude who had the encyclopedic knowledge, the go-to guy. Maybe he could get Big Buy to invest, help get this thing up and running. There was money to be made. He dreamed and drove and then, glancing down at his fuel gauge, realized that he was almost out of gas and only halfway home. He pulled over into a Chevy station to refill. While the tank was filling he pulled out his credit card wallet to take a look at the receipt. He let out a huge choking sob as he stared at the numbers. He felt faint and sick. It was sixty-five thousand, not sixty-five hundred. How could he have been so stupid? He hadn't asked Bob to define the number exactly, because he was trying to be cool, like he was a rock star, like he did this every day – like – like … like he was an idiot. And as for Bob, well, he was just an outrageous thief. Sixty-five thousand for this beat-up piece of junk? What a thief. Not a dealer but a stealer. He had no choice. Almost in tears, he pulled out of the gas station and headed back to Bob's Rare Guitars.

There followed a tense scene with several people witnessing a fierce argument between Bob and Gilbert, with Gilbert threatening to call the police. Eventually Bob relented and tore up the credit card slip in front of him. Gilbert left the store and drove home feeling chastened but victorious. He had stood up to a challenge, if not a beast. He had won the day, he could breathe again, that nightmare over. He pulled into his garage, happy to be home. He heard a guitar playing in the house. It sounded soulful, bluesy, authentic. Wow, what a sound, he thought, and despite the disappointment of the last few hours, this playing and tone thrilled him in the way that the vintage sound always did. It was coming from Frankie's room. He knocked on his door and walked in. Frankie was sitting on his bed absorbed in playing what looked like a Les Paul.

"Great sound," said Gilbert. "What is that you're playing?"

"It's a Taiwanese copy," said Frankie. "Eric leant it to me. They're only two hundred dollars, can you get one for me, Dad?"

# VIBRATO

T ry as he might he could not get that sound. What was it, this thing that he heard, that they did – a sort of trilling, wobbling sound in a high register? It sounded like a woman sobbing. There would be a string of nice notes and then the crying thing. It seemed to hang in the air for a few seconds and then slide away again, like a woman burying her head under the sheets, not that he had any knowledge of stuff like that. But it must be on the guitar somewhere. Maybe it's this, he thought, sounds like one of these. He stabbed around the upper register of the guitar above the twelfth fret, but it didn't come out right, all he got was a flat choked sound. Where was that singing note? He decided to chuck it for the night. Maybe he would be a drummer instead. He went downstairs to watch *Top of the Pops*, trying to focus on the paradiddles of the various drummers, instead of the chugging chords of the guitarist out front.

Sitting on the worn-out floral sofa with his parents, Thomas watched with mixed emotions as various guitar players swung their guitar around, barked out poppy choruses and generally had a great time. I wish I was American, he thought. But I'm not; I'm just a fifteen-year-old English nerd living in the middle of nowhere, a schoolboy with pimples and no technique.

He thought of his guitar upstairs in his bedroom lying there, taunting him. He knew there was magic there, buried somewhere in those pickups, those strings, but how did you bring the corpse to life? He knew it was possible. It was there right now in front of him on the telly. The lead guitarist of The Vanities smirked and stepped into the spotlight to rip a solo. "They look like a load of monkeys," said his dad before swallowing another mouthful of PG tips.

After school the next day he decided to go to Strikes, the local music shop. He had broken a string last night in his frustration and, although of two minds about whether to chuck the whole guitar thing, he decided he might as well do it and ignore the Jekyll and Hyde contest whirling in his brain. They had a lot of guitars and it was always fun to go in and stare at some unattainable American solid-body electrics. The Stratocasters, the Tele's, the Les Pauls – they were the ones with serious cachet, the holy grail of guitar playing, normally only ever seen in the hands of someone on TV. But even so, it was inspiring to stand close to them and gaze up at their beautifully lacquered surfaces, gleaming frets and artfully curved whammy bars: American legends incarnate. He had been learning for about a year now and his teacher said his playing was fair, that he had some feeling for the guitar – but it would take practise, practise, *practise* …

As he was gazing up in rapture at the jewel-like instruments on the wall, he heard a soft sequence of rapidly played guitar notes behind him. He turned around. It seemed to be coming from behind the counter, but all he could see was a mass of blonde hair. A girl's head bent over a guitar, her fingers moving with speed up and down the rosewood fingerboard. And then she did it, the crying thing, actually did it, but what string did she do it on? It was fast and he couldn't quite tell and then she was off again – now striking a loud E chord as if to re-establish the foundation of the thrilling virtuoso lines that seemed to shower like rain from the palm of her hand.

He stood there frozen, speechless. A girl? A young girl? Wasn't possible, no way, couldn't be, what? And then she looked up, smiled and said, "Can I help you?" His tongue felt thick in his throat, his power of speech paralyzed, a general numbness pervaded his being. Not only was she a goddess of the guitar, she was a goddess, period. He tried to answer but all that came out was a mumbled "strint" – he couldn't even say "string".

"Sure," she said. "Strings! What gauges are you playing on these days?" as if one virtuoso was in conversation with another. "Gauges?" he whispered in his own head. What's that – a railroad track? "Nine through forty-two, eleven through forty-six, twelve through fifty-two – are you replacing the wound third with a B string?"

Dazzled by this brilliant technical guitar talk he stood there dazed and confused, everything seemed hyperreal…

She put down her guitar and stood up to reveal a lissome figure in tight blue jeans and a cowboy shirt, long blonde hair cascading over her shoulders. She came around the counter and up to where he stood rooted to the spot.

"I'm Lizzie," she purred with a soft Californian accent.

"Thomas," he mumbled back.

"What's your axe?" she smiled.

Axe? He desperately imagined his head on the chopping block, a silvery blade inches from his neck held in the hairy arms of a beast in a black mask. Henry the Eighth, Anne Boleyn, Thomas Cromwell…

"Guitar?" asked Lizzie.

"Oh, right," said Thomas. "Um, uh – a Burns Marquee."

"Oh," Lizzie smiled, "a Marquee. I've heard of those. Sort of an English Strat copy, right?"

"Yeah, that sort of thing," nodded Thomas.

"Does it have strings?" said Lizzie, smiling.

"NO! no strings," Thomas cackled maniacally and Lizzie burst into laughter along with him and something flooded into his soul, a warm fuzziness, the body of a small bird, ketchup… Indeed he felt as weak as a kitten, soft, pliable, obedient, enslaved. Her presence washed through him like melting honey.

"Shall we look at some strings? C'mon – over here."

She guided him to a set of drawers against the wall. "Let's have a look at the Marquee." Thomas set the long, heavy guitar case on the floor. Lizzie crouched down beside it and snapped open the locks to reveal the Burns.

"Well, not bad," she said. "At least they tried to do something. Wonder what these pickups are? Hmmm, you're missing an E string." A flush of shame drained through Thomas's body, he felt like a little kid, an amateur, a Martian. He should have stuck to making balsa wood model airplanes.

"That's an easy fix," she smiled up at Thomas. "Do you want just the single string or a whole set?"

"A whole set, please," gulped Thomas.

"Okay," said Lizzy. "Custom or standard?"

"Um, custom, I suppose," said Thomas.

"Same again?" she smiled up at him.

"Think so," he agreed, full of self-loathing.

"Okay, I'll get my micrometer to check the gauges."

"Christ," thought Thomas, "micrometer. What the bloody hell is that?"

"Hmmm," said Lizzie as she crouched over the guitar with a small silver device in her hand, applying it to the strings.

"Well," she turned her face toward him, "this is a heavy set. Starting with the second, you've got fourteen, seventeen, twenty-four, thirty and, wow, a fifty! Are you into jazz? That's more like those jazz guys use, Kessel, Farlow, etc. I'm strictly blues – Buddy Guy, B.B., Johnson. I like to get a good bend going."

Thomas felt his brain drowning in a sea of unfamiliar terms. How could she possibly know all this? BB, what was that?

"Yeah, blues for me," said Lizzie, bent over the Burns. "Do you want more of a blues set on here? I think you'll find it a lot easier. How long you been playing?"

"About a year," said Thomas.

"I'd like to hear you," said Lizzie. "Let me change your strings and then I'll plug you into that Fender Champ, okay?" Thomas felt himself drowning as an Arctic wave of panic swept through his every fibre. A silent voice screaming, Noooo, can't possibly play in front of her – no, PLEASE.

NOOOO…

Lizzie had the guitar up flat on the countertop and was expertly and rapidly changing the strings. She tightened up the top E string and then casually tapped a silver tuning fork on the counter and wound the A string to pitch, and from there tuned the other strings by ear to the standard guitar tuning.

"Better," she said and pulled a couple of quicksilver runs up and down the neck, casually throwing a high vibrato E into the pot.

"Fantastic," breathed Thomas, "how do you do it? Are you American? You're amazing… my God!" Thomas felt the blood suffusing his face as he stared at his shoes hopelessly.

"Yeah," said Lizzie. "I'm from California, LA to be exact."

"But what are you doing here in Ridgehampton? It's awful."

"Yes," said Lizzie, "funny how things turn out. I'm here with relatives, this is my uncle's shop. I had nowhere else to go."

"What happened?" said Thomas. "I mean…"

"My Dad was in Vietnam. He never made it back. Never made it… My Mom… Well… I got sort of farmed out… No choice, I was under age. She disappeared, my uncle invited me and agreed to look after me until I'm eighteen, then I'll probably go back, unless I'm in a blues band in London. I would like to be."

"Yes," said Thomas, "I can see that. You'd be great – great. You play so well."

"My Dad taught me," said Lizzie. "He was a great player. I've been playing since I was five, I won't ever quit."

Thomas felt himself almost on the verge of tears. He was so in love with this girl, everything about her – the angel face, the figure, the amazing guitar playing. A star, a true goddess.

"I love America," he blurted.

"You're sweet," said Lizzie, smiling. "I'm glad to know you, partner."

What was left of Thomas almost crumbled at the word "partner". His head felt like a hive of bees, the words "I love you" buzzing in his throat like an angry hornet.

"Let me plug you in," she said. "We'll play a slow blues together…"

# MAXIMUM BASS

"Jamaica!" Ger shouted and jumped for joy as his feet touched the ground of the Caribbean island. "What do you think, Caroline? Isn't it great?"

"Don't know, Ger," said Caroline, "me feet ain't touched the tarmac yet."

Gerald's girlfriend Caroline was still on the steps of the plane as she adjusted her Yves Saint Laurent knock-off shades and the fake Hermès bag around her shoulder before popping down the last two steps to join the line into the airport lounge. Already they could hear the voice of Bob Marley.

"Great!" said Ger, "Marley never gets old."

"It's old for me," said Caroline, "I like punk these days."

"Really, Caroline?" said Gerald, spinning to look at her and walking backwards. "You are a bit mad, girl – punk, ha ha!"

"Well, punks like reggae," came back Caroline. "They don't accept much outside of punk, but they got a soft spot for Marley and Tosh. Not for me, though. I like a bit more energy. I like the hardcore shit. Punk is real."

"What? You don't think that reggae is real, then?" said Ger. "These people have hard times, too. Just because they live on a beautiful Caribbean island doesn't make them imperial to hard times."

"*Impervious*, you twit!" said Caroline. "Ooh, look, there's my stuff." She pointed at the number two carousel where sat an over-sized pink suitcase with a Mickey Mouse sticker on the side and a travel sticker that said '*BOURNEMOUTH. GIVE IT A SHOT*', with a picture of a golfer, but someone – probably a lowly baggage handler – had crossed out the 'O' in shot and substituted the letter 'I'.

"Where's my case and my guitar?" said Ger. "Fuckin' 'ell."

"Welcome to Jah-maica!" piped Caroline.

"Hard luck, Ger. Welcome to paradise."

"No, really," said Ger. "This is no joke. That was a Les Paul Black Beauty, bloody expensive, took me years to get it. Still paying it off. I could have been the next Robert Fripp with that thing."

"King Crimson is not reggae, sweetheart," said Caroline, fiddling with the zip on her pink suitcase.

"Well, I know that but, you know, just saying," said Ger.

"So, what?" said Caroline. "Sort of prog, sort of reggae? Like, proggae, maybe?"

"Yeah, something like that," said Ger. "But, whatever, talent will out."

"That's what I'm afraid of," said Caroline, "but you do have a talent and it's nice when it's out."

"Ooh, you're a smasher!" came back Ger. "Wait till we get to the hotel, I'll show you talent. Where the Tooting Bec is my Black Beauty?"

"Why didn't ya bring your Taiwanese copy?" said Caroline. "You can't tell the difference anyway."

"I can!" said Ger. "I bloody well can!"

"But you only know three chords," said Caroline. "Anyway, looks like your lucky day. Look."

Gerald turned around to see a skinny Jamaican porter coming toward him carrying his backpack and his guitar.

"Thank God!" said Ger.

"Thanks be to Jah, more likely," laughed Caroline. The porter stood in front of them, still gripping the guitar case and the backpack.

"He ain't giving you those until you tip 'im," said Caroline.

"I've only got a twenty quid note ..." said Ger.

"Give it to 'im and then we can be off to the local flea pit. What say you?"

"Fuck," moaned Ger, and handed the porter a twenty pound note.

"I hope they have an ATM at the hotel," said Ger, "or we're done for."

"I reckin' we are anyway," said Caroline. "We could have gone to Bournemouth, good punk scene down there these days."

"Yeah? I heard it was a bit rough now," said Ger, staring at the exit.

"Yeah, sex capital of the south," said Caroline grinning.

"How would you know?" said Ger.

"There are some things you will never know, my man," said Caroline. "Now come on, let's get out of this excuse for an airport."

They got outside and, after a difficult misunderstanding with the taxi driver, finally made their way into Kingston. They were happy in each other's company – this was an adventure if only for a mad three days. Ger could only get three days off from the bank where he worked, and that with his manager threatening that if he wasn't in the bank at nine sharp on Monday morning then he should seek employment elsewhere. He was determined to have a great time, realize his reggae dream and have a sweet little holiday with 'Carolily', as he called her. He was lost in these thoughts when the taxi came to a jerking halt and dropped them in front of a small grubby-looking building.

"Looks great," said Caroline as the taxi sputtered off, leaving them bathed in a garish red and green neon glow that fuzzily said Paradise Hotel. They went into the lobby, where a well-fed and tired-looking Jamaican lady leaned across the reception counter.

"Yah," she yawned as they entered.

"We have reservations," cooed Caroline.

"Yeah, right," said Ger, looking depressed.

"Who are you then?" she said, staring at Ger. "You look like Sherlock 'Olmes."

It was true. Ger was about six foot tall, skinny, had a hawk-like nose and was dressed entirely in black. He bore a faint resemblance to Basil Rathbone.

"And I'm Dr Watson," piped up Caroline.

"No, you look like Elizabeth Taylor," said the receptionist.

"Well, thanks," said Caroline. "Other people have said that. I don't get it." Caroline was a pretty, dark-haired girl of about five foot six with a unique dressing style. Tonight she wore a rainbow striped beanie, some kind of sari thing and tight-fitting gold-coloured jeans.

"Would it be the honeymoon suite?" said the receptionist.

"Naturally," said Caroline. "Can't wait!"

"It's our most popular," said the lady. "People, dem 'ave a good time in dere."

"Sounds kinda stinky," muttered Caroline.

"Very kinky!" said the woman, thinking she was echoing Caroline. "Okay, tell me your names?"

"Gerald Hawes and Caroline Cookson," said Ger.

"Okay, Horse and Cook." The receptionist yawned again, scribbled in her entry book and then said something like "Two lefts and a right."

"Let's go," said Ger. They picked up their bags and trudged off down the seedy corridors that had a few pictures of Jesus on the walls, and finally arrived at a door with green flaking paint.

"How very, very romantic," said Caroline to the flaking green paint.

"Lovely green though," said Ger as he pushed the door open. "Sort of Sherwood Forest."

"Honeymoon suite or honeymoon bitter?" said Caroline.

"Let's go!" shouted Ger, and hopped across the room to land with full weight on the bed, which immediately collapsed under him. Caroline laughed and screamed.

"You're bonkers. Alright, you asked for it!" She jumped onto the broken bed beside Ger and started kissing him. Within seconds they were ripping their clothes off and taking great pleasure in each other.

The night passed. Sunlight woke them at 7am along with the sounds of children's voices singing 'All Things Bright and Beautiful'. Caroline extricated herself from the broken bed, went over to the window and said, "Christ, we're right on top of a school. Look at all these school kids, so sweet…"

"I wonder if we get a discount for that?" moaned Ger from across the room.

"The Lord God made them all," said Caroline. "Brekky?"

"Let's get some sleep," muttered Ger, his voice sounding muffled between the sheets.

"Come on, you duffer," his girlfriend said. "This is Jamaica. We've got three whole days and I'm jumping in the shower and hitting the beach." She disappeared into the tiny bathroom. There was a loud scream. "Ger"!" she yelled. "There's a bloody spider in here and the shower's bloody broken!" Ger scrambled up out of the twisted sheets, grabbed his guitar and rushed the full three feet into the bathroom.

"There! In the corner!" Caroline squealed. "Get it!" A big black spider lay motionless in a badly tiled corner of the bathroom. "Right, you bastard!" yelled Ger, as he lunged at it with his Black Beauty but missed and instead chipped a large oval-shaped piece of paint out of the lower bout of the instrument. "Damn!" he cursed as the insect shot up the wall and out of the open window.

"Told you – you should have brought the Taiwanese," laughed Caroline. "Sorry, you are my hero. Thanks, Ger, but what about this abomination of a bloody shower?"

"Right," said Ger. "I will now go and speak to the authorities. Back in a sec." He disappeared out of the room and returned five minutes later. "The receptionist said she would send the engineer to fix it and breakfast is at half price for the inconvenience."

"Shit!" said Caroline. "I feel so grungy."

"Maybe we can swim in the hotel pool?" volunteered Ger.

"Brilliant!" said Caroline. "Let's go!"

They found their swimsuits and got into them.

"Right," said Ger. "A swim. That should do the trick."

They left the room and marched down the gloomy corridor and out to the patio at the back of the hotel. There was a swimming pool, but it was empty and mostly filled with dead leaves.

"Well, that fucks that!" moaned Ger.

"All things bright and beautiful," said Caroline, as a tear rolled down her cheek. "I wanna go home."

"Oh, come on, Carolily, we will have fun, I guarantee it. I know people, Jamaicans, Rastas. They're great! I'll tell you what, let's get the shower fixed, take a nice hot one, grab our swimsuits and get a Piña Colada at the nearest beach. What say you?"

"I love you, Ger – Rasta man," said Carolily, wiping another tear from her cheek.

They trudged back to the honeymoon suite and saw that the door was open and noise coming from the bathroom. They peered around the edge of the bathroom door to see a man working away with various tools on the pipes and singing under his breath.

"Hey there!" said Ger, taking the lead.

"Oh, mornin'," said the plumber. "Sorry about de problem 'ere, I fix him. I know this one. Goes wrong every two weeks, dis an old 'otel." As he said this, a violent sputtering spray came down on his head and he burst out laughing. "I win da war!" He looked at them grinning. "Trench Town rock, oh yeah, you be okay now. Hey, zat your guitar on the bed, mister? You a musician?"

"Well, sort of," said Ger. "I love Jamaican music."

"I am a guitarist, too," said the plumber. "Everybody knows me. Fat Willy!"

"Fat Willy," said Caroline. "Sounds a bit like you, Ger."

"Stop it, you bad girl," said Ger. "Hey, you wanna play my Black Beauty?"

"Okay," said Fat Willy. "I've had a few Black Beauties me'self long time ago."

"Yeah, I bet," said Caroline, poking Ger in the ribs.

Fat Willy went over to the bed, sat on the edge and picked up Ger's guitar.

"Nice action," he said, playing a first few chords. "Nice guitar." He went into a suave reggae rhythm, humming along, and from there into some perfectly executed bluesy licks.

"Yah s'good," he smiled at them. "Very good guitar, man!"

"Wow, you play great, man," said Ger.

"Yeah!" echoed Caroline.

"Yah, been doin' it all me life. Praise be to Jah," said Fat Willy. "Just fillin' in wit a bit o' plumbin' here and there. Gotta lot of kids to feed, you know how it is? Hey, what you people doin' tomorrow? Would you like to come to Big Bang?"

"Big Bang?" said Ger. "You mean the church of reggae … all those hits – Lee, Bob, Tosh … wow!"

"Dat's de place," said Fat Willy. "I work as a guard there some nights – I can get visitors in sometimes. I'm der' tomorrow – it's pretty relaxed, you can bring your guitar, maybe play with the band."

"My God!" said Ger, "that would be a dream for me."

"Okay," said Fat Willy. "Your dream will come true Saturday night. Be at Big Bang at ten. You know what? I can pick you up if you like? Make it easy."

"Bit late, isn't it?" said Caroline.

"It's the chance of a lifetime," said Ger. "We gotta do it."

Fat Willy packed up his tools, gave them a smile and said, "Okay,

I see you young people Saturday night. I pick you up at 9:30. 'Ave a nice day."

"I'm taking a shower," said Caroline and disappeared back into the tiny bathroom. This time Ger heard the sound of a shower and Caroline singing 'All Things Bright and Beautiful'. She emerged from the bathroom, "Shall we now go to the beach and get our full money's worth? … What's wrong? You look upset."

"Sorry," said Ger, "I'm a bit anxious about having to play on Saturday night with real reggae players."

"Don't worry about it," said Caroline. "Just smoke some ganja with them and melt into the groove. C'mon, man, let's have a day at the beach."

"Okay," said Ger, brightening, "let's find out where it is. We'll ask the expert at the front desk."

They pulled their few things together – paperbacks, suntan lotion, sunglasses, towels – and headed out the door. The same woman was in reception, looking even more tired.

"Hello," said Ger. "Good morning again. We want to go to the closest beach."

"You can go to Hell!" said the woman.

"That's a bit rude," said Ger and Caroline almost in unison.

"Hellshire Beach, it's the nearest one. We call it Hell around here."

"Oh," said Ger. "How do we get there?"

"You need to take the number 1a and go to Hell – I mean, get out, yeah?"

"Where's the bus stop?" asked Ger anxiously.

"It's at Halfway Tree."

"Where's that?"

"You need to take a taxi there."

"Christ!" said Ger. "Bit complicated."

"Why don't we just take a taxi straight to the beach?" said Caroline.

"Yeah, how much is the taxi?" Ger asked.

"Twenty-six US," came the reply with a raised eyebrow.

"C'mon Ger," said Caroline. "We can do that, can't we?"

"Yeah, s'pose so," said Ger. "Can you call us a taxi, please, um … Yolanda," now noticing for the first time the nametag on her blouse.

"Okay, I get you a taxi, take a seat now."

They sat down on a tatty couch in the reception. As soon as they settled Yolanda looked over and said, "Cab's here."

They groaned together, got up and went outside, where a worn-looking taxi was sitting in the sun.

They slid into the back of the cab and its searing inferno heat, the fake leather seats like burning metal on the skin of their legs. "Christ!" they screamed in unison.

The driver looked in the rear-view mirror and spoke in a low phlegm-ridden voice. "You going to Hell?"

"Yes, we are going to Hell, unless we're there already," said Ger.

"Okay," coughed the driver, "you asked for it." He slipped the car into first gear and pulled out of the driveway.

Fifty-one minutes of non-stop coughing from the driver later, they pulled up at Hellshire Beach.

"Welcome to Hell," said the driver. "Twenty-six US."

"Here you go," said Ger, putting thirty US dollars in the driver's hand, who just said thank you, and didn't proffer any change. Ger thought about it for a second and then, getting it, didn't ask for anything back but just said to Caroline, "Okay, let's do it!"

They got out of the taxi and walked into the beach area, which turned out to be a row of shacks that ran almost to the water's edge.

"Finally, paradise," said Caroline, as they edged their way through crowds of Jamaican families. Earsplitting Jamaican dancehall music blared out across the sand. "What happened to Bob?" said Ger.

"That's old-fashioned now," said Caroline, "they're into gangsta rap these days. You gotta keep up with the times. Here's a spot." She pointed to a tiny gap between some sprawling Jamaican families.

"Yeah, nice and private," said Ger. "This is the life."

"Well, let's make the best of it," said Caroline. "At least we can get into the water." They dumped their bags and towels down on the sand, smiling at the families around them, who stared back with looks of disbelief on their faces.

"Do you think we stand out?" said Caroline.

"No, I think we are blending in nicely," said Ger. "Let's hit the water." Without much thought, they stripped down to their swimsuits and made for the water.

They got in the water up to their waists, where a few gentle waves lapped against them along with various ice cream wrappers, old potato chip bags, condoms, plastic bags, a beach umbrella and what looked like part of a deck chair.

"I'm not feeling too good in here, Ger," said Caroline.

"Yeah," said Ger, "time to get out of Hell and back to the hotel?"

"Yep," said Caroline. "Great swimming pool there."

They got back to their spot. Their stuff was gone. "Oh fuck! Not that as well!" cried Ger. He looked over at the nearest family.

"Excuse me," he said. "Did you see anyone take our stuff that was … that was lying here."

"Yeah, Mister, dat guy over dere, he got it, him keepin' it safe for you."

"Oh, thanks," said Ger, staring across the sand at an aggressive-looking young man.

"Hang on, Carolily," said Ger to his girlfriend. "I'll deal with this." He crossed the sand to the man and said, "Hi, that lady down there told me you were keeping our stuff safe for us, right?"

"What stuff is that?" said the man.

"It was lying right there on the beach – a red towel, a blue towel, a couple of bags. Where is it, please?"

"Maybe I seen it, maybe I don't seen it, you never know around here. You want to buy some ganja?"

"NO … I don't want ganja!" said Ger, now starting to get upset as he raised his voice and people on the beach started staring. "I want our stuff back. Give it to me or I will call the police."

The man laughed. "I *am* the police," he said, flashing a small silver badge at Ger.

Ger was stumped for a minute.

"Buy some ganja, you can go home, have a nice smoke, look at your stuff… Easy…"

"Okay," said Ger, "I understand you, officer… what is your name?"

"Bob Marley," said the man. "You can call me Bob."

Ger realized that he would be lucky to get out of this with anything. Affecting a more respectful attitude, he said to the man, "Please, Mr Marley, give me my bag. It has my money and my credit cards and I will be pleased to buy some… um, um, some er… herbal remedy from you."

"Okay, now you getting it. It will be two hundred dollars US. I have a square here on my iPhone so I will just run your card – ah, here it is." The 'cop' fished in Ger's bag, pulled out his wallet and extracted a card.

"Hmm. Barclay Bank, British card – okay I'll give you a break and just call it one hundred and fifty pounds sterling."

"Jesus!" said Ger. "You're killing me. I haven't got that kind of money for dope. That's my life savings. How about five dollars? Please, er, Mr Bob?"

"You want to get out of here alive?" rasped Bob as he sliced Ger's credit card through his square. "Is that your nice little girlfriend sitting down there? She looks like Elizabeth Taylor … cutie pie …"

"Yeah," said Ger in a panic.

"Be careful with her, my friend. You never know what might 'appen in a place like this. Okay, here we go – all clean and square."

"Where's the ganja?" asked Ger.

"Okay, you have another problem, my friend," said Bob. "If you take the ganja out of my hand I am going to arrest you. It's not legal in our country. You need to show more respec' …"

Ger realized he was fucked, no way out. The Rasta proffered his tote bag with a big grin. Ger grabbed it and ran back to Caroline who was lying on the sand with a towel over her face.

"C'mon, quick, we gotta get outta here now. NOW! For fuck's sake …!"

Caroline, who had been dozing nicely in the Jamaican sun, woke with a snort. Ger grabbed her by the arm, yelling incomprehensibly as the Jamaican families around them dissolved into laughter, slapping the sand. Caroline started grabbing her things but she didn't seem to be latching on to Ger's fast rambling monologue as they ran back toward the taxi rank. They threw themselves into the first cab in line, with Ger yelling "Paradise Hotel, Kingston."

'Bob Marley' watched from his little hut, smirking and chuckling as he blew large blue clouds of smoke from an oversized spliff.

Inside the cab, Ger desperately explained the dodgy situation to Caroline, who listened grim-faced and whose only rejoinder was, "Told ya we shoulda' gone to Bournemouth."

About ten minutes later she pushed up close to Ger, who was

morbidly staring out of the window and said, "Sorry, Ger, that wasn't fun. You saved the *day*." Ger turned to kiss her, but right then an insect flew in through the window and stung him on the lip…

"A fuckin' bee, a wasp, I don't believe it. For fuck's sake… let's get the hell out of this hell hole." Just as Ger was screaming all this, they screeched to a halt at the Paradise Hotel.

"Christ, I need something. My lip, my lip," moaned Ger. They staggered into the hotel foyer. Yolanda was sitting there in her usual place.

"Yolanda!" yelled Ger, "I've been stung. Stung on the lip. Do you have anything for it?"

"Depends," said Yolanda. "What kind of insect was it? There are some really deadly ones on the island, for instance…"

"Forget the 'for instance'," moaned Ger. "Do you have any Dettol?"

"Yah, right here, mister." As if performing a magic trick she pulled a bottle of Dettol up from under the counter, with a box of cotton wool.

"Don't worry," she said. "We get this every day. Just a dab 'o Dettol, ya be right as rain."

"Oh my God, thank you," mumbled Ger through his swollen lip.

"And let me get you some ice, too," said Yolanda, disappearing into a room behind the counter. They heard some clunking noises and she reappeared with a small bucket of ice cubes.

"There you go, mi darlin'," she said. "Go to your room, ice your lip and rest. You'll be good as gold in a few days."

"A few days," moaned Ger. "But we're on holiday."

"Wha 'appen, 'appen," said Yolanda sagely. "Ya be aright soon."

Ger and Caroline hobbled off to their room, embracing each other like survivors. Once in the room, Ger collapsed on the bed and said, "Christ, what a day. Now I could really use a big fat joint."

"Well, you're in luck there," said Caroline. "Look what I got." And from behind her back she pulled out a perfectly rolled joint.

"Jesus!" said Ger, "where was that?"

"Brought it from London," said Caroline.

"How?" asked Ger.

"Up my arse," she said and doubled over cackling.

"No," said Ger.

"It was in a packet of Marlboro Lights, Rasta man," wheezed Caroline, blowing out a heady stream of smoke. "Dead easy ... want a hit?"

"Thank God!" said Ger. "Hand it over."

Ger took a long drag on the joint and said "'Appy days."

"All we gotta do here," said Caroline, "is survive."

"Yah mon, be survivin'," said Ger. He took a long hit and spluttered, "'Ow does mi lip look?"

Caroline went into a laughing-smoking-coughing fit for a few minutes and pointed her finger at Ger. She finally stopped hacking and said in a sweet little falsetto, "Mmm ... think it's going down, Rasta man. Are we still invading Big Bang tonight? Show 'em a bit of proggae?"

"Fuck yeah!" said Ger. "I need to practise."

"Well, nothin' 'appenin' before ten," said Carolily. "Wanna try something else to get that lip down? Shall I give it a kiss?"

"Carolinnius," said Ger.

Caroline crawled over to the wreckage and they proceeded as usual with youth and passion.

Some time later they woke up, Caroline found her little wristwatch and said, "Jesus – it's eight thirty! Fat Willy's comin' here at nine, we better get our shit together."

"I need to practise," said Ger. He got up from the busted bed, opened his guitar case, and immediately started hitting the strings in an approximation of a reggae rhythm. Caroline started swaying around the room in time with Ger. And then Ger broke a string. "Fuck! The top string just broke," cried Ger. "I don't have any spares."

"Ooh, that's not good," said Caroline, "What to do? Nix Big Bang?"

"But we gotta go, whatever," said Ger, and he banged away at the remaining five strings. There was another twang and another loud "Fuuuck!" from Ger. "Now it's the bloody B string," he said. "What's going on? *Voodoo?*"

As they were contemplating the string disaster there was a knock at the door. Caroline opened it. Yolanda was standing there. "Im waiting for you ... Mr Fat Willy."

"C'mon, let's go," said Ger, throwing his guitar into its case.

"Cast our fate to the winds."

They rushed out of the room and found Fat Willy at the front of the hotel, his car engine revving noisily. "Ah, I and I my friends, sorry about mi car, I gotta keep the engine going or she dies but we'll get there."

"Okay, thank you, Willie," they both mumbled and sank into the back seat, Ger holding onto his guitar for dear life. They drove for about twenty-five minutes, the car jerking spasmodically the whole way. Neither Caroline nor Ger said anything on the journey. They both felt somewhat apprehensive, a little bit freaked out. They were entering unknown territory. Ger idolized Bob Marley and all the great reggae artists but now wasn't sure if he wanted to get this close after all. It was a bit real and he only had four strings left on his guitar and he had his girlfriend with him. He had to protect her. He was doing well at the bank where he worked. He didn't want to blow that, which was why he couldn't dare take more than three days away, sacrifice it on the altar of reggae. No, they would get through this, get home and he would buckle down to some good hard work. Advance his prospects.

Caroline was thinking, this is nuts, we don't know these people, they might kill us, torture us, anything, disappear us. We ain't in Hounslow anymore. She saw headlines in the *Daily Mail*: 'British tourists die in Jamaica,' reports on the BBC's six o'clock news, pictures of her at eleven years old, and her mum in tears and in an interview saying that she – Caroline – was always a bit of an adventurer. Then she thought of the animal shelter service that she supervised in Ealing. God, what would they do without her? And her mind ran over the names of all the corgis, Alsatians, Labradors and collies she was looking after.

As they were both lost in these thoughts, Willy called out, "'Ere we are then. Big Bang, safe and sound." They pulled up in front of a big barbed wire gate and two men with guns on their shoulders.

"Christ!" said Ger. "Bit scary."

"Yeah," said Caroline, "you sure about this?"

"Don't worry," said Willy, "they ain't gonna shoot you. It's just security. I don't think they got any bullets anyway. Let's go in."

They climbed out of the car and followed Willy through the big gate and into the studio entrance. "This way," said Willy. They nervously followed him down a couple of corridors and then Willy pushed a door open and they walked into Studio A.

The unmistakable stink of leaf. Through the haze Ger and Caroline could see various shadowy dreadlocked men. "C'mon in," said Fat Willy. "Let me introduce you. Yah mon'," he said to the various figures. "This is Ger and this is Caroline. They visiting from London, they are my special friends. I want you to treat them right. Gerald has brought his guitar, he would like to play with you when you are ready." There was obviously a lot of respect for Willy and there were general nods of heads in their direction. Willy turned to Ger and said, "Okay, I gotta go and do some guard duty, I leave you 'ere, 'ave a good one." Ger and Caroline stood there, sightless and almost paralyzed in the blue fog.

"This is another planet," whispered Caroline.

Ger just gripped his guitar with white knuckles. A figure appeared out of the haze. "Hey man! I'm Michael," he intoned like it was a song. "I am the guitarist with the band. You wanna play with us, I help you plug into an amp and all that. You ready to jam?" Michael gave Ger a big smile and offered him the joint he was holding. "Oh yes, please," said Ger, and took a drag on the oversized joint and passed it to Caroline, who took a small, nervous puff.

"C'mon into the studio," said Michael, "let's get you set up." Ger followed Michael into the studio with Caroline trailing behind him.

"Okay, let see your guitar," said Michael. Ger put his guitar case on a chair and hauled out his Black Beauty and showed it to the guitarist. "Nice one," said Michael, "high-class."

"Hey man, you're missing a couple of strings!" he laughed. "Wha' 'appen?"

"Yeah, they broke tonight," said Ger. "I haven't got any more."

"Okay, I fix it now," said Michael. He went over to his own case and pulled out a packet of strings. "Here you go, E and B, let's get 'em on there." With fast and expert precision, he got the strings onto Ger's guitar, tuned them up and handed the guitar back to him, commenting again on what a nice guitar it was.

"Okay," he said. "Let's do some playin'. Let me introduce you to the other guys. This is Zee, our drummer, and this is our bass man,

Rob the Robber."

Ger gasped as he recognized the policeman from the beach, who just grinned at him and took a hit on a joint. "And this young man over here," Michael went on, "is Julian Marley. He's going to sing with us tonight, ain't you, Julian?" The boy nodded and grinned up at Ger, who smiled back nervously.

Caroline was sitting on the floor with her back against the wall, anxiously watching out for Ger and hoping and praying this situation would end soon. The band started playing a soft slinky reggae rhythm. A gentle groove so cool that Ger forgot he was supposed to be playing also.

Michael the guitarist called out to him "G". Luckily Ger knew that chord and struck it hard. It rang out over the band. "Yeah," called Michael, "just hit the one with that chord – we be alright." Ger didn't know what Michael was talking about or where the *one* was. He hit the chord again and saw Michael grimace, obviously not in the right place. "Okay, I count," he called. "One two three four and one." Ger managed to half hit the chord on the *one* and tried desperately to count the other two three four and do it again. He had never been so on the spot and he felt as if a huge white searchlight was on him with about a million people watching. He saw his life passing away like a small dribble down a drain. The band – the rhythm felt like a steel trap. He saw no way out; this was humiliation reggae style. Yet here he was, Black Beauty in his hands in a Jamaican studio – the apotheosis of his dreaming.

The band was great, really the real thing, he must acquit himself well, where was that *one*? That downbeat? He listened carefully to Michael, who was still counting, got ready and this time around hit the one. Michael smiled. Ger did it again and then again and somehow he had it. The one. He stayed there hitting the chord where he was supposed to. It made a sort of sense to him. He hit the chord on the one and the bass drum followed on the two – this was Jamaican reggae rhythm. He relaxed and stayed with his chord on the one part. The eleven-year-old started singing in a wordless falsetto voice over the band and it was the perfect highlight to the seductive and authentic groove below. Finally, they ended and Ger breathed a sigh of relief. He had got through it. Michael came over to him and said, "Well done, mon', that's not easy, most people can't get it. We been playin' together for years, it's natural for us." Ger, ready to faint, thanked Michael and said, "Yeah, that was really cool, thanks for letting me sit in and thanks for the strings."

"Yah mon, you be cool," said Michael and disappeared back into the vaporous distance of the control room. Ger went over to Caroline, who looked in a state of shock.

"Do you believe that?" asked Ger.

"I was fucking terrified," said Caroline. "You did well, I can't believe it."

Michael reappeared in front of them. "C'mon you two," he said, "you can sit in the control room. We are going to record some new songs." He let them back into the studio control room and motioned them toward a big velvet sofa against the wall. "Enjoy," he said, smiled and went back into the studio. Out of the darkness a hand appeared in front of them with a giant joint and a voice said, "'Ave a good time." Not knowing what else to do and not wanting to appear rude, Ger took the proffered joint and smoked it with Caroline until it was not much more than a stub. From there, as they leaned in a daze back on the sofa the music seemed to get deeper and deeper as various elements came at them from the oversized speakers. The bass line luminous and loping like a giant rabbit, the drums making a steady pumping hallucinatory heartbeat, the guitar interjecting its precise, biting rhythm hits before it ballooned out into an operatic wah-wah solo that sounded like a trombone player in a hall of mirrors.

Was it the ganja or was it the music? Neither of them knew any more as they passed into a deep trancelike sleep of the ages.

Then a hand was shaking them on the shoulder. It was Fat Willy.

"Hey, you know it's time to go. It's 4am. My shift is over, y'wanna go home?"

They opened their eyes and stared up at Willy.

"Yeah, okay," they mumbled from some deep hungover space. They struggled to their feet and Willy said, "Hey don't forget your guitar. Okay, I got it." He picked up Ger's guitar and they waved through the haze at those left in the control room and staggered out.

As they were driving back to the hotel Caroline said, "Christ, we have to leave at 7am. We gotta be there two hours before the flight."

"Right," said Ger, not really comprehending what his girlfriend was saying. They got back into their room and the shipwreck of a bed. Caroline set her alarm. "It never fails," she said. "Let's get two hours of kip at least, we can sleep on the plane. I hope you enjoyed all that?" she said, looking at Ger.

"Yeah it was great!" said Ger, "what a night. God, I'm fucked."

They crashed for two hours and were jolted back to life rudely by Caroline's very loud and shrill alarm. "Okay, Ger, let's go," she said. "We gotta hit it, you can't miss tomorrow morning or you'll be in for it. Deep shit!"

"Yeah, right" said Ger, and pulled himself up. They left the hotel a few minutes later with the Paradise cab that was always there and arrived at Kingston airport half an hour later.

"I feel like shite," said Ger in a Belfast accent.

"Ditto that," said Caroline in a posh BBC voice, handing her pink suitcase over to the check-in lady. They showed their passports, got their tickets and went to immigration. On the way across the airport Ger suddenly said, "Wait a minute, let me just check my guitar."

He placed it on an open seat and opened the case. Inside sat a cheap yellow guitar that looked not remotely like a Les Paul Black Beauty. "NO! NO!" said Ger. "It's the bloody cop again. I don't believe it."

"Shit!" said Caroline. "Well, we can't stop now. We gotta get on the plane, we'll be lucky to make it."

"I'm coming back with a posse, I'm gonna kill that … kill that … aagh!" Ger's face was screwed up in a mix of pain and rage.

"Serious drag," said Caroline as she went up to Passport Control and handed in her passport. Ger followed quickly behind her. He didn't want any more trouble. As they passed to the other side they heard a voice shouting, "Ger! Caroline!" They looked back. On the other side of Passport Control they could see Fat Willy. He had Ger's Black Beauty and stood there frantically waving it at them. *"Last call for Hawes and Cookson,"* came a voice over the PA.

# ROADIE

...that was a rough fuckin' ride up here today, I'm fuckin' knackered. I bet those cunts will be late, they're getting a real fuckin' attitude now. Snotty about fuckin' everything, "Ma heels broke, the dressing room's too small, where's ma make-up? Tune ma guitar ..." Blah blah blah – plus I ... yes fuckin' me – have to fuckin' knock on their dressing room door to get in and get a beer.

Where the fuck is this goin'? It's all goin' to shit just 'cos they got a pissy little tune in the charts. They shoulda listened to my idea. They woulda had a number fuckin' one instead of a bollocks number nine and goin' down, as we speak. I got ma finger on the pulse. I know what the people want 'cos I'm one a them. These cunts are outta touch now – fuckin' stars who are above ridin' in the van these days, need new hairspray at every gig, where the fuck am I supposed to get that from? Ah don't have time to trot down to the fuckin' chemist when ah'm testing the amps, testing the fuck-ing fuse box so they don't get fuckin' fried like my mate Alex – yeah, that wuz rock 'n' roll! Out in a blaze of light, one hand on the strings, one hand on the mic stand. Deadly but glorious.

Did they learn a fuckin' lesson? Fuck no – they wander on late every night now full of piss and vinegar, plus the fuckin' nightly powder and just expect that I – me, meself, alone have got it all sorted. No fuckin' danger to their little asses. Well, take note, lads, that you don't go up in a blaze of extreme wattage one night if you keep givin' me shit. Yeah, really – ah'm not kidding. Remember, ah'm from the back streets of Glasgow where life is cheap – very cheap.

Ah, fuck it – think this is ma last gig with these tossers. Don't even like the outfits they're wearing now. Fuckin' glam rock. They used to look like real geezers, black leather, studs, chains and the like, could 'ave bin the nephews of Gene fuckin' Vincent but now they look like a bunch of girls with eye shadow and fuckin' pink blouses. Ah'm not dressin' up like that. If I went up to Glasgow lookin' like a daffodil ah'd get done over before the first beer.

I thought there was loyalty, some stickin' together through thick and thin, but now I think ah'm just a fuckin' embarrassment. Long hair, black leather jacket, boots, that's always been the gear but ah guess ah'm not in vogue anymore. Well, suck ma dick, school boys, ah'm rock 'n' roll and you … you're just a bunch of daisies. Who showed you the chords to 'Purple Haze'? Ah got more music in ma underpants than the lot of ye'.

Wass'up with this Les Paul? Well, fuckin' Taiwanese copy of a Les Paul, the fuckin' neck is goin' – cheap wood, no doubt. The strings are about an inch off the neck – that's the overnight in the van that did it. Too many temperature changes. He's going to sound like shit tonight when he tries to play the opening chord of 'Twisted Little Fingers'… good fuckin' luck, guitar man. You should have opened a pet shop like ah said.

What about this Strat? Christ, what do they do to these instruments? This was in perfect nick when we got it. Looks like it went to Vietnam and back – they got no fuckin' pride. Look at that, fuckin' fag burns on the headstock, chewing gum on the pickup and fuckin' beer stains all over the body. These instruments are just a decoration now – they're more into their fuckin' hair. Now it's like havin' five fuckin' women on stage, apart from the fuckin' towels they shove down their jeans every night.

Ziggy Stardust's got nuthin' on this lot.

# TRANSITION

The hair … it was going. He stared in the mirror. He didn't like it. He was a rock star. He needed his hair. Should he shave his head? Go for it? That was a look these days. Did it increase his sexual power or take it down a couple of notches? He could have one of those implant things done at huge expense. But the effect was one of thin, weak hair that looked like a worn-out lawn in suburbia. He was vain and he knew it, but he felt that it was his job to be vain, keep up the looks, exude sexual power. But fuck, it was getting harder as the hair receded like the Red Sea. The reality was that his was a life lived through photographs, and tiny pictures on hand-held devices where he visibly aged in public. Every time he released a new album, he had less hair. He started retreating into the shadows for his publicity pictures, which caused a huge row with his publicist. Why the fuck was rock music associated with masses of hair anyway? It was so sixties. It was time for a new paradigm – a lean, stripped-down look with a hard, toned body, a stubble beard and a tough shaved head. That would make a deliberate fearless statement. Maybe 'rock' was over anyway, loud guitars and all that, stacked Marshall amps – the stone age. This was the age of Cyberia, not bloody Aquarius. The digerati were here, armed to their digital fangs. A concert could be reduced to 0's and 1's. Instead of drums and guitars it was iPad, iPhones, 'I' bloody anything. Tiny digital devices, small intelligent machines – projections, holograms, digital illusions and the ability to reach millions instantly. This was the miracle of the internet.

This was now.

You wouldn't have to bother with musicians and their moody demands any more, the show-off guitarist and thundering drummers. It was going to get very sleek and sophisticated.

It was time.

He saw a new vision of his future.

He stared at the mirror and lifted a razor to his scalp.

# A CORPSE IN TINSELTOWN

May 1933. I got out at Union Station and fell in love. Maybe it was the sun, maybe youth, but I was crazy for LA. I was flying high like I was walking into a silver fantasy. I knew this was the place where you made it. I didn't know it could break a guy like a straw. I was a guitar player. I was good. I was young. I was fresh meat. A lotta big shots back east told me to get out to California. I might even make it in the pictures. I had a couple of numbers from a drummer back home and a bucketful of confidence. But to work I needed a fixer. It was a system. You had to have a fixer to get a gig and to a man they all had to swing their dirty little power to make you bow before 'em. You had to be real nice to them if you wanted to work and that was a problem. Bein' nice didn't come easy. I'd come up with a bunch of hoodlums, the only difference bein' that I played the guitar, and I had my own ideas about that, too. Those guys made sure I was employed – I had to sing their song. But I only wanted to play jazz, Eddie Lang, Joe Venuti, Duke Ellington style, no dance band schmaltz for me, and that's what I told 'em. I thought they'd be impressed. But bein' high and mighty with fixers cost me plenty. I was living in a low-rent joint in Silver Lake with a couple of bums and I was about two bits from skid row. So I greased up my phone style, took the edge out, softened my pitch up like I was trying to woo a dame. But it seemed like the word was out. My edge had cost me. I was a corpse in Tinsel Town and the train back home was already in the station. I'll fix 'em, I thought. Yeah, I'll fix 'em good.

I made a call to Chicago and then, like an angel, one of the fixers called and said there might be a gig downtown with a Hawaiian outfit. I could go for a try-out and then he added, "But if you want it, you have to play lap steel Hawaiian style."

"No problem, Mr Barfus, it's my favourite style," I said. I heard a grunt on the other end. So much for sticking to your guns.

He gave me the details of the joint for the try-out and then the phone slammed down. I hung up and figured my next problem was where to get one of these new tin guitars used for the Hawaiian style and get good on it real fast.

I had heard about the Dopyera Brothers and their new all-metal guitar called a Dobro that was made especially for Hawaiian music. They had a place over on Normandy, so I hitched a ride over there to take a look. There they were, all lined up like a row of tin soldiers, steel guitars with big resonators like built-in speakers and some fancy decoration on the back. I picked one up and ran my fingers over the strings. One of the sales guys came over and asked, "Whadd'ya think?"

"Sure is heavy," I replied. "You could stop a bullet with this thing, but it's loud, I'll give ya' that."

"That's what they want now," said the guy.

"How do you play it?" I said, hitting the low E. "The strings are three inches off the neck!"

"Let me show you," he said. He took the guitar, placed it across his knee, pulled out a small steel bar and with his left hand moved it up and down the neck. "See, it's real simple."

"I bet," I said. "Okay, I'll take it." I'd seen some of this stuff with blues players back east so I reckoned I could get it. This Hawaiian stuff had caught on with a bunch of players like King Bennie Nawahi, David Kane and Sol Hoopii. It was all the rage, and a lot of these guys were playing Dobros. I handed over my last few greenbacks and took possession of a Dobro called a Triolian with the bitter thought that I'd have to hock my Gibson Lloyd Loar F5. I had no choice. It was either this or back to the meat yards.

The surprise for me was I took to it pretty fast. The tuning was simple, a C6 chord and I seemed to have a natural vibrato with the left hand which held the steel bar. I thought I could make it, be good enough for the audition. I learned some Hawaiian tunes playing along with the radio 'til I got the style. It was simple, sentimental stuff, although hearing someone like the virtuoso Sol Hoopii with his flash was another matter. "I'll get to that," I thought, "Lemme get the job first." I would be trying out for an outfit that had a permanent set-up downtown, but the guitar player had keeled and was bye-byes. The day came. I borrowed a Hawaiian shirt, played some more tunes and got a ride down to Main Street and a place called The Flaming Palms. The club was empty, the chairs stacked on tables as cleaners moved around the joint. But there was a bandstand with a bunch of musicians sitting there looking like zombies. I saw a greasy guy leaving with a guitar case. He wasn't smiling. The bandleader, an old Hawaiian-looking, guy beckoned to me. We introduced ourselves. He was Fred Kapaapa, the orchestra, The Island Serenaders.

I gave him a line about touring around the country and made up a Hawaiian-sounding band name and added that I was now settling into LA due to so much work being available out here. He was gentle and it made me feel a bit more relaxed. Then he said, "So, my friend, what would you like to play with the orchestra?" I named a couple of standard South Sea numbers and off we went. He conducted the introduction by the orchestra and I took the melody. I played along with the violins and saxes, smiling, being genial and playing the sappy melody effortlessly. I wanted this gig, a guy's gotta' work. In those times you never knew what was coming. The world was crazy. I wanted a good ride and music was my way. I looked good and I knew it. I seemed to have a natural knack for playing with a steel bar in my right hand. From where I came from it could easily have been a .38 Special. The guitar across my lap was making all the right sounds and the musicians around me seemed to be nodding like I was alright. And then Fred said, "Now I would like you to accompany our singer, Miss Rose Balanchine." As he said this a young and beautiful female walked out onto the stage. She was a real looker and my heart started beating faster. We looked at each other for a beat, and then at the music to choose a couple of songs to try out, and came up with 'On the Beach of Waikiki' and 'The Moon of Manakoora.' Her voice was sweet but also strong, with a natural vibrato and perfectly in tune. She had it for sure. I played along with her, admiring her curves and her voice, thinking, sure, I'll play with you, anytime, anyplace, anywhere. We finished the two songs. She walked over to me, smiled sweetly, put out her hand and said "Rose," adding, "that was nice, mister."

That was the signal. I was in. Old Fred nodded and I started that night. It went swell. This was an easy gig for me. The Palms was busy most nights and packed at the weekends. Each show would begin with old Fred stepping up to the mic with a smile and saying a few words in Hawaiian that I couldn't understand. Then he would say "Welcome, ladies and gentlemen, to the sounds of happiness", and off we would go.

I settled into the band, got to know the other musicians and worked on my duets with Rose. Every night we wowed the crowd with our act, and I knew I was on to a good thing – a guy gets lucky sometimes. She was a draw. People came to see her, hear her or maybe just to drink in her good looks. I guess she was a star in the making. I haven't got that much time, I thought. She's gonna get into the pictures, the big time, Hollywood. I gotta make a move or it's curtains for you, Buster. She had this effect on men. I could see it. They would send her flowers after the show with little cards, sometimes with a telephone number. I wasn't much different. I was obsessed with her, in love with her. I would talk to her backstage, being careful not to rush my romantic intentions, and she was friendly but guarded – maybe some heel had broken her heart already. We were working together, so we had to keep a certain type of professional reserve, but it was difficult. I didn't want to put the make on her too fast, she must have had it up to the eyeballs.

One night after the show, thinking we were getting closer, I suggested that maybe she could come over to my place in Silver Lake and we could practise away from the club, be in a different atmosphere. I nearly said explore our chemistry but stopped just short of such a loaded remark. She looked at me with a raised eyebrow and said, "Okay, let me think about that."

"Here's my number," I said, handing her a small slip of paper with my number scrawled on it in pencil. She didn't call. I kept practising anyway and my lap steel playing got real slick. I practised alone in my apartment in Silver Lake in the afternoons, my right hand getting faster, the left-hand vibrato really singing. I knew this was the chance. It had come from a sideways direction, but I had a shot.

I wanted the guys back east to be proud. I stayed with it and Fred started giving me solo spots, where I would do fast knock-offs like Sol Hoopii's 'Hula Girl'. I was good, Rose was good, and between us we pretty much had the whole thing sewn up. And then out of the blue, she called. The phone rang around two in the afternoon just as I was getting outta bed.

"How about I come over later?" she said. "Around four maybe? We can run a couple of numbers."

"Sure thing," I replied. "I'm in. Here's the address, just ring." I rushed out to the diner on the corner to get some breakfast, eggs over easy, orange juice and black coffee. After that I went to the flower shop on the corner and bought a big bunch of roses. I wanted my crummy place to look good. Now that I had a regular paycheck I had kicked the other bums out. I had meant to move but just hadn't gotten around to it. I wanted to impress her. I cleaned the place up, made the bed, wiped the windows, put away the dirty plates and dishes, emptied the ashtrays, cleaned a few glasses and put out a bottle of Scotch just in case. Just as I finished this frenzy, the bell rang. I opened the door and there she was, lovely as always.

"Gee," I said, "I never seen you in daylight."

She laughed and said, "That sounds kinda dirty," and walked past me into my little lounge, where I had a couple of guitars on the couch including my F5 which I had gotten back out of hock, seeing as I had a little dough now thanks to the South Sea malarkey.

"That's not Hawaiian," she said, pointing to the Lloyd. "You play that as well?"

"Sure do," I said. I picked it up and ran a couple of Lonnie Johnson lines. "Beautiful," she said. "I love the blues."

"That's where I come from," I said. "Blues... jazz... this Hawaiian thing is new to me, but I gotta work just like anyone and it's harder with the jazz thing."

"Well you sure play nice," she said. "You've made the band better."

"Well, I sure like playing behind you," I said. She laughed again and said, "I bet you do."

We both laughed. I was desperate to kiss her but that would be too fast, but I thought we're alone and this is going well, she's looser than I would have expected – is there a chance, *any* chance, for a sap like me? She must feel it. What's stopping two people like us, we could go the whole distance. My brain was doing double time but in an effort to be relaxed I offered her a drink. I needed a drink, too. But she just wagged her finger and softly said, "It's too early. Maybe tonight. Let's play some songs." She stretched out on the couch like a cat and looked up at me and said, "Ready?"

"Sure," I said, taking a quick slug. "We can work up a coupla new ones, surprise old Fred."

"Dear old Fred," she said, "he's so sweet. Been like a father to me, but I'm afraid he may not be long for this world."

"Really?" I said. "What's wrong?"

"I dunno," she said. "But he's got something … something that's gonna get him."

"I'm real sorry to hear that," I said, "I like him, too. I'm having fun with this band and a lot of it's because of him and, well, you."

She put a hand on mine for a second – was it a warning off or a maybe someday? – but as usual around her it felt like a bass drum bangin' in my chest. I thought I was a tough guy, able to resist any dame, but around her I was mush. I picked up my Dobro, placed it across my knees and whipped out three lush chords.

"What will you sing, Miss Balanchine?" I asked.

"Okay, how about this?" she said, pulling out a couple of pages of sheet music of a brand new Hawaiian-style hit, something about a grass shack. We worked on the song for a while until we had it sounding sweet. I sat on the couch next to her and never felt so good. She was classy, cool, elegant – so different from the hot and ready chicks I had known on the streets of South Side Chicago. The city I had grown up in with its gangs, mobsters and guys with their kill-or-die style. I still felt affection for it. They let me alone because I was a kid with a guitar. They liked that, Italians were always soft for music. I learned to play a lot of old-style Italian songs for them. It was my protection. I had to talk tough and act tough, but I knew one day I was going to get out, head west. I never even left my ma and pa a note; I just jumped a train one day figuring I'd get back to them later. This little movie was flashing through my head as I played along with Rose, and somehow it just made me put more feeling into what I was playing. She finally turned to me and said,

"You sure are playing nice today, Jake Benedetto." I lit a cigarette, blew out some smoke and said, "It's you, it's you."

"Maybe it's us," she replied, and she stared out of the window as if something was catching her attention. "We're good together."

"That's nice," I said. "That's what I feel, too." I was fighting an overpowering feeling to take her into my arms, but then she said, "Good musically ... we're good musically."

I was about to splutter some foolishness, but I covered it by asking her where she was from. She looked me in the eye, smiled and said, "I'm from Pittsburgh."

"Well," I said, "I thought maybe you were from Switzerland or something. So ... Balanchine, is that your real name?"

She smiled again and said, "Sure sounds good, don'it? My name is Jones, Rose Jones. My family is Welsh. My grandfather was the original immigrant. Our family are all coalminers but we all sing. I've been singing since I was two. What about you?"

I wanted to ask her more, know everything about her, but instead I briefly told her about my background, making it sound better than it was. I told her my father had been a musician in Chicago, although the truth was that he worked in the meat yards and was still there. I left the mob out.

After my little speech she just said, "Well, it's amazing to be out here, isn't it? Los Angeles is like paradise."

"Yeah, I love it," I said. "It's a whole new world. No one to bother you out here ..."

A look passed across her face and she looked as if she was going to say something, spill the beans, but instead she stood up and said, "Well, I need to go back to my place and get ready for tonight. See you later, Benedetto." I sensed something was up, like I'd touched a nerve, but I followed her outside into the street and stopped a cab, put a twenty in the driver's hand and gave him her address in West Hollywood. She waved through the window as they drove away. Did I see a tear? I went back to my room and played a fierce blues.

That same night old Fred died on the stage. It was a dramatic and tragic moment. Rose and I had just done the new song about the 'Little Grass Shack in Waikiki' and Fred was saying something about it when his face suddenly went purple, he clutched at his throat and fell to the floor. That was it, stone dead from a heart attack. We all packed up that night without speaking and in a state of shock, wondering what would happen next. I was just about to leave when the maître d' came up to me and said, "Bill wants to see you in his office. Can you come now?"

I went to Bill's office. We talked about Fred for a few minutes with mutual respect and then he asked me if I would take over the band, be the bandleader. I protested lightly, saying that maybe there were others in the band that had been around a lot longer who were more deserving of the job. Bill said he could see that but that I was the one with charisma, with the out-front personality to run the show, and then finally he said, "You are the new bandleader, we'll change the sign out front." And that was it. I figured I could do it and the best thing was that it would keep me close to Rose.

Next night I took the stand, made a little speech about Fred and did Fred's Hawaiian spiel to keep things comfortable. The band knew I was the new leader as approved by the manager. All I could do was smile at them, shrug my shoulders in a "wasn't my idea" kind of way. "It's a lousy job, but somebody's gotta do it." They seemed okay with it. The truth was I probably was the best choice. I was younger, the crowds liked me, and Rose and I were knockin' 'em dead every night. But no one gets a free ride in this world and naturally, now that my star was finally rising, I got some trouble to go with it.

I noticed a shady-looking guy coming in a few nights a week. I knew he was a thug. I could spot 'em like a piece of tar on a white sheet. It made me nervous. There was always an angle, what was this punk after? He sat there at the back of the room in a dark corner. Sometimes another hood would arrive and say something to him. He would nod but never take his eyes off Rose. I wondered if she could see him. Maybe to her he would look just like another guy with a drink and a Lucky Strike. One night I had an idea. I would go over to him between sets and offer to buy him a drink, get him a little more juiced up and then lean back as he spilled his guts. If he was trouble, I could make a call.

I walked over to his table, nodding at various patrons as I moved through the tables. He was sitting alone with a half-empty glass.

"Good evening," I said. "Thought I'd come over and say hello. I've seen you in here a lot, you're one of our regulars now and I want to thank you for that. Mind if I sit down? Can I get you a drink?" I waved Carlos, our waiter, over and told him to bring a bottle of our best champagne.

"Jake Benedetto," I said offering my hand. "What's your name?" The hood just looked at me and then swallowed a full glass of champagne. Okay, I thought, not the talking type. I moved on, "Where are you from, if you don't mind my asking?"

He just stared off into the distance like I was a fly on his wrist. This was harder than I thought. I glanced at the bulge over his left breast – he was packin' for sure. At this rate it would be the slab mañana. I stubbed out my Chesterfield and tried a final inquiry.

"What line of work you in, mister?" He gave a sozzled snort and slurred out, "Exports, wadd'ya think?" Then he slammed his fist on the table and barked, "She's my wife. She's my wife." I was confused. Who was his wife?

"Who, mister?" I asked. "Who's your wife?"

"Her. Rose, the goddam singer," he spluttered.

"What?" I replied, gripping hard on a metal ashtray. "Rose? She's your wife? I never ..."

I got up from the table and stomped to the back of the stage. I felt cheated, stupid, another sap, another sucker. How could I have not seen it? This was what was holding her back. We went on stage. Rose and I were beginning the set with 'The Moon of Manakoora' as a duet. We started into the song. I was full of bitterness but I kept my eyes on the back of the room staring at the hood. I knew something was coming. Just as we hit the word 'moon' he stood up, staggered, pulled out his pistol, drew a bead on Rose and fired, I mirrored his every move, whipping my metal guitar up in front of the woman I loved.

# WHAT STRINGS DO YOU USE?

*The Incredible Guitar Nerd Interview: Mikey Van Stoker*

**IGN:** "Thank you for agreeing to the interview today, we are incredibly honoured. We would like to do an in-depth piece about your music, your life, the trail that you have blazed, the millions that you have thrilled with your amazing and inspiring guitar playing. The readers of *Incredible Guitar Nerd* are really thrilled. May we begin?"

**MVS:** "Well …"

**IGN:** "What strings do you use?"

**MVS:** "Yes, it's true that there is an African influence in my playing, mostly from the Yoruba but with a trace of the Gabon and maybe the Côte d'Ivoire, but some say it runs parallel to West African high-life music, but I believe it comes from my collection of fetish dolls and an in-depth study of the Mau Mau."

**IGN:** "Thanks. What strings do you use?"

**MVS:** "Was I influenced by Hendrix? Well, that's a matter of conjecture. Actually, I think it was the other way round. While he was wasting time in New York, I was already tripping on acid, experiencing the white light and walking through the door marked X. In other words, while Jimi was merely sucking on an occasional reefer I was living the full psychedelic life. Word crossed the Atlantic and as you know, the rest is history."

IGN: "What strings do you use?"

MVS: "I see chords as shapes of sound, blocks of sonic fabric, cosmic vibrations, if you like, melodies as strings of light. They come to me as if in dreams. I am a catcher of dreams, if you will..."

IGN: "What strings do you use?"

MVS: "Of course this just proves that I am someone who has synaesthesia. Shape, sound, colour – it's all a big crazy mix to me. For instance, when I see a cauliflower, I hear an E7 sharp 9 and should I, by coincidence, see a carrot right after that, I hear a bright high A major chord and a pulsating yellow. There have been others like me, of course, for instance the Russian composer Scriabin. I think in fact we are related, but that's another story, probably more for *National Geographic*."

IGN: "What strings do you use?"

MVS: "I think my music is reaching for a vision, some sort of utopian future no doubt, one where music, peace and harmony reign supreme. That's what I try to express with my guitar, but I suppose that's obvious enough. Obvious enough that I am an avatar."

IGN: "What strings do you use?"

MVS: "You could say I am like Nabokov in search of blue butterflies – the elusive, the rare – that's what I am after."

IGN: "What strings do you use?"

MVS: "It's true that my music in many ways runs parallel to quantum physics. I go deep. For instance, I'm down there in some sub-harmonic zone like a deep sea diver. I listen for a note and then when I hear it, it stops playing, and then when it thinks I'm not listening it begins again, and thus we go on, it's like a game of hide-and-seek. This is not available to most people, of course..."

**IGN:** "What strings do you use?"

**MVS:** "Okay, I own up, mushrooms are a big part of who I am. In fact, I am mostly mushroom now. They have influenced me and obviously through me many millions of young people. Amanita muscaria, Psilocybe cubensis, Claviceps purpurea – these are my friends, these guides are my brothers. The music I play is theirs."

**IGN:** "What strings do you use?"

**MVS:** "Will I ever retire? Ha ha, how can you retire when you are immortal? Are you on drugs?"

**IGN:** "What strings do you use?"

**MVS:** "Thank you, this has been a great interview. Oh – one last thing…"

# HALCION DAZE

Sullivan boarded American Airlines Flight 1207, Nonstop Los Angeles–Sao Paulo, Brazil. It was going to be a long flight, twelve and a half to thirteen hours, a big one. He felt pleased to be going back to Brazil, good about going on tour but clouded by a tinge of anxiety that stemmed from the immediate circumstances as soon as he got there. Not to mention the fact that this week he had broken up with his girlfriend, Julie. They had been together for three years but both felt there was too much conflict between them. It didn't suit her to be with a constantly touring musician. She wanted something more stable and, typically, here he went again and would be onstage within hours of arriving in Sao Paulo, playing fast and tricky jazz-fusion on acoustic guitar. It was demanding – you had to be really on top of your playing on the steel string to pull it off. It was just him and a high-speed Russian/Brazilian virtuoso, with no drums or bass to fall back on. He laid back in his business class seat, going over the set list in his mind. It was all there – he had practised enough, he could see all the notes, the lines, where his hands would be. It would be okay, they had done it a few times before. Challenging, yes, but it would be good.

An old Japanese lady arrived at his row struggling with a carry-on bag that she was trying to stuff into the overhead compartment. He got out of his seat to help her. They struggled together and actually laughed as they shoved the recalcitrant case into the black maw of the overhead, but in it went and they both gratefully got into their seats and sank back in comfort. She turned to him, said "*Arigato*," and started preparing herself for sleep. He picked up the flight dinner menu and noticed that it was also in Japanese. That's right – Sao Paulo had the biggest Japanese population after Japan itself.

Sullivan's mind flicked back to the Kurosawa film *I Live in Fear*, where the grandfather of a family in Tokyo has recurring nightmares about the dropping of another atomic bomb. Set in 1952, the grandfather is determined to get out of Tokyo – out of Japan – and has extended arguments with his family about selling his factory and moving the whole family to Brazil. He dreams of a farm, sunny landscapes and a new life. But the family doesn't want to leave Tokyo, so they plot against the old man and eventually get him declared insane by the court. Naturally it all ends in tragic disaster full of Kurosawian irony. That was a good one, he thought, can't beat Kurosawa.

He studied the menu – fish, beef, hmm ... Eat light, make it easy on yourself. You need to sleep for at least twelve hours to be ready for tomorrow's onslaught. The plane took off and, after the usual safety routines and the dinner, which he kept light with only the fish course and two glasses of red wine, he decided that it was time to get to sleep. It was still afternoon for him but, what with the time change, the flight duration and the pressure when he landed, he needed to get down now. He kicked off his boots, took off his jacket, checked his jacket pocket to make sure his passport was there and, just before fully reclining the seat, searched in his carry-on bag for the new sleeping pills that his doctor had given him.

He found them. They were called 'Halcion'. He didn't know much about them, other than they were supposed to be pretty effective. Well, I'll just take one, he thought, emptying one pill into his hand and swallowing it with the last dregs of red wine. Then some nasty thoughts of high-speed acoustic jazz guitar fusion went through his mind along with the concert, which was just hours after landing and barely time to rehearse the difficult shit. No, better take two, gotta sleep he thought, and swallowed a second and then, to seal the deal gulped down a third. He glanced over at the old Japanese lady; she was fast asleep. *Sayonara, sweetheart, see you in the land of nod*, he messaged to her in a haze of red wine. He took one last look out of the window at the ocean as it disappeared beneath a veil of clouds, pushed the recline button and got horizontal.

Now followed a brief dream fragment of a large hypodermic needle being inserted into a vein on his left arm, foggy images and distant voices, a sensation of being laid on a bed and more vague, muffled voices. And now he opened his eyes to look across a few inches of pillow at the low afternoon light pushing through a window. Words floated through his mind like small white flags being waved from a long way off: Hotel-Brazil-Concert-Guitar-Play … He got up as if on automatic, unaware that he had got out of bed fully dressed or that there was anything strange about this. He left the room and walked down the corridor as if in a normal routine to find the tour manager, Luiz Paulo. Ignoring the fact that the corridor appeared tilted and looked like something out of *The Cabinet of Dr Caligari*, he went to the front desk, looked at the receptionist and just said, "Luiz Paulo." She smiled as if she knew him and with a brief, slightly astonished, purse to her lips said, "Luiz Paulo, room 46." He went back up the Caligari stairs and found room 46. He knocked on the door, it opened. Luiz Paulo stood there looking at him and then gently said, "Hello, buddy, you okay?"

"Yes," Sullivan answered, like a robot. "When is Hector coming? We have to practise."

Luiz Paulo gave him a puzzled smile and said, "He's coming soon. Shall we get a coffee?"

"Okay," he replied. So far this was all as expected, their usual routine. They went to a café, Luiz ordered two coffees and asked, "How are you feeling, man? Okay?"

"Yes, I'm fine – why?"

"A little bit strange coming in this morning," Luiz said with a Mona Lisa smile. "Maybe we'll talk about it tomorrow. Hector will be here soon. Are you okay to rehearse with him?"

"Yes," he said, "of course," vaguely wondering about the question. "Okay, I'll go and play for a while."

"Okay, my friend." Luiz slugged down the last drop of his espresso. "I'll bring Hector up to your room in about half an hour." Sullivan went back up to his room and got his Martin acoustic out of its case. He sat on the edge of his bed and started running a few scales and licks. He felt a lot of energy, well-rested, not tired, he must have slept well on the flight. Good to be back in Brazil.

There was a knock at the door. It was Luiz, with Hector right behind him, who came striding into the room shouting, "Hey, man! Welcome back, good to see you. How are you?" There were mutual hugs all round and then Luiz said, "Okay, I leave you two to play," and he quietly closed the door behind him.

"Well, okay," said Sullivan, "let's have a go. Here's our set list from last time." He pulled out a crumpled piece of paper from his guitar case which had a list of songs on it written in black magic marker. "Shall we start at the top and just do it like it's the concert?"

"Yeah, okay," said Hector, giving him a slightly bemused smile. They started working their way through the list of songs, Sullivan playing with unusual energy and vigour. Somewhere in the middle of the practice Hector said, "Wow, man, you are on fire tonight. Lot of energy!"

"Yeah, I feel pretty good," said Sullivan. "I slept the whole way here." Hector looked at him and said nothing. They played until about 12:30am and then decided to call it a night and get some rest – the first concert was tomorrow.

Sullivan finally climbed into bed and sank back into the pillows.

About one hour later he sat bolt upright as if a flash of lightning had just burned through his body. *What the fuck!* How the hell did he get here? His mind groped for what should have been an easy recent memory … seat on plane – seat on plane …? But it was as if that strip of film had been edited out – zero. And now he was here with no memory, just a black gap, a void where there should have been a picture of greetings at the airport: hugs, back to Brazil etc., etc. – *fuuuck!* And really, how the living Jesus did he get off the plane, get through immigration? Where were his carry-on bag, his boots, his suitcase, his passport? His brain fizzed as he grasped the giant fuck-up he had just gone through. He got out of bed, found the light switch, got the lights on and started looking. But there was his suitcase, there was his carry-on bag, there was his passport, there were his credit cards, there was his guitar. What the fuck …? Finally he crawled back into bed, feeling fucked up and blessed that he wasn't dead – big hypodermic needle? How the fuck do you ex- plain that?

He arrived at the little breakfast room at 9:30am. There was Luiz Paulo, who grinned when he walked in. "Okay, Luiz," he said, "give it to me." Luiz started laughing uncontrollably then spluttered, "You almost died, man. You're lucky, ha ha ha!"

Luiz thumped the table, almost choking, but finally calmed

down and said, "Sorry, man, but it was so crazy. You came off the plane like you were completely drunk. You were staggering all over the place from side to side in the corridor. Nobody at the immigration desk could understand you. I was outside waiting and waiting. Finally, one of the immigration officers brought you out and asked if anybody knew you. 'I am his friend,' I said, 'I'll take him.' Obviously you were really fucked up and needed a doctor, and lucky for us there was a medical office at the airport with a lady doctor. She took one look at you, felt your pulse and said that you had about one hour to live. She gave you a big injection and said you needed to stay in the airport for three hours. So we waited three whole hours and she kept watching you and feeling your pulse. When finally she said it was okay for you to leave I took you out of the airport in a wheelchair. You don't remember nothing?"

"Only the needle," said Sullivan, feeling shocked and incredulous. "Jesus fucking Christ! But the plane. How did I get off? My stuff… my shoes, passport?"

"I don't know," said Luiz. "Incredible, but there was an old Japanese lady. She came over when the immigration officer brought you out and asked if you were okay. She had sat by you the whole way and when you landed, she helped you with your bag and shoes. Then she left, she said her daughter was waiting for her. …Oh, she said her name was Tomoko. She gave me this card."

"Bloody hell!" said Sullivan. "Well, she saved me, God bless her. How the hell did I play last night like everything was normal? Did Hector know?"

"Yes," said Luiz. "He was sort of amazed by you and that you could play."

"Well, I guess I had about twenty hours of sleep," said Sullivan. "There's well-rested and then there's very well fucking rested. Are we still playing tonight?"

"Well," said Luiz, "we are playing a gig but, there's one thing. Eveni is our promoter. She was waiting at baggage claim the whole time, very, very nervous and smoking one cigarette after another. I came out with you in a wheelchair and she said "Where is Sullivan?" I pointed to you and said "Here he is!" She was very freaked out. Unfortunately, there were some press people, they took pictures, but I kept going. Good rock star press for the tour."

"Christ!" said Sullivan. "Can't believe it. Bloody incredible. Must have been the Halcion. I don't remember anything. But still, we are playing tonight, right?"

"We are," said Luiz, "you are a lucky man, but unfortunately we have another problem. You won't believe it. Look …" He pulled out a newspaper and showed Sullivan the front page. There he was in black and white, wearing dark sunglasses but in a wheelchair with a headline along the lines of 'ROCK STAR ARRIVES IN SAO PAULO', followed by what Luiz described to him as a somewhat scathing commentary about musicians and their irresponsible lifestyles. Sullivan groaned. "Christ!" he said. "It all comes at once. Another shitstorm."

"But wait a minute," said Luiz, "the promoter called me and said that because of this newspaper photo the ticket sales have tripled. She wants to move the show to a much bigger venue. We now play on Tuesday night instead of Sunday night, which is tonight … remember?"

"If you say so …"

"So … everything is okay."

"They probably all want to see me die on stage," said Sullivan. "What a start."

"Let's get sushi tonight," said Luiz. "Or do you prefer Figuera?"

"Sushi should do it," said Sullivan.

Sullivan sat in his room for the next two days feeling chastened and swearing to himself never to try *that* again – *bloody hell!* He practised for several hours, making sure his playing was up to speed, that the songs sounded good, that he could do it. He also felt more remorse as he had found a note from Julie slipped into his carry-on bag that said, *'I'm sorry about us but I think we both know it's not right. I wish you well wherever you are and wherever you go – love Julie x.'*

He had almost broken down after reading her note. He needed a drink – wanted to raid the minibar but couldn't start in on that after what he had just survived. The break-up had been coming for a while. This tour would provide the time and space to let it happen. It was mutual and although they tried to part without rancour, neither he nor Julie would miss the endless fights and arguments. But he was missing her badly. He pulled out his cell phone and dialled her. But it went to voicemail. He left a brief message that hinted that maybe they were making a mistake and then he regretted leaving it. So be it, he thought – it wasn't right, time to move on, but still, it was painful. He focused on the music as tears began to roll from his eyes and his hand sped up and down the guitar neck, securing the trickiest passages, the most difficult time.

Tuesday evening arrived and Sullivan came out onto the stage with Hector to thunderous applause. The audience stood up and cheered. This is incredible, thought Sullivan as he took a deep, theatrical bow as if acknowledging the bad-boy lifestyle, but here he was anyway. They are cheering me on because ... because ...? Because I'm a survivor. He raised his hands to the audience in a brief namaste gesture and picked up his guitar. They sat down and launched into 'Frevo' at lightning speed. They played a stellar show, and Sullivan felt very pleased with himself and the whole crazy mix of the last few days – maybe his luck was turning around. They came off stage to a huge audience response and three encores – they had, in the proverbial phrase, gone down a storm.

Sullivan stood in the middle of the dressing room as most of the audience – typical of Brazil – crowded into the room. He and Hector stood in the middle of all this having their picture taken over and over and over, until Luiz Paulo emerged from the dense throng and said, "I made a call and I have someone special for you to meet. Here she is!"

He stepped aside to reveal the Japanese lady from the plane. "This is Tomoko, your friend from the airplane." And there indeed she was. Tomoko stepped forward and gave him a big smile that somehow also contained the bond that they had already made. "Are you okay?" she asked in perfect English. Sullivan gave a foolish grin and threw up his arms as if to signify, "I'm a crazy man!" and they laughed together. He gave her a little hug and said thank you – "*Arigatou.*"

"Very good music," she said, and then, "this is my daughter. Her name is Moon." A beautiful girl stepped forward and, putting her hand in Sullivan's, said, "Wonderful music – beautiful guitar. I loved 'Stone Flower'."

Sully looked into Moon's eyes as his heart began a drum roll. She…

The phone in his pocket rang.

# SAGEBRUSH

Two cowboys are riding across the desert. One is called Gene the other is called Roy. Gene and Roy are heading down to Texas. Gene rides a chestnut mare, Roy rides a piebald. The days are long and pleasant. They are not in a hurry. The ride will take them a couple of months. But it's the cowboy life and they find a *certain comfort*; they are men of the saddle. The West is beautiful – God's country, some would say. The only dangers are Indians, rattlers and wolves, but they both carry shotguns and Colt 45s and they look out for each other. They are happy to be out in the wide open spaces where a man can bide his time, know his own self, fall back on himself if needs be. They are returning from a long cattle drive up north in Montana. Cattle are a huge industry now and that's where the work is. Men of their time out in the West have become used to the life and are glad of it. They have a code of ethics, their own cowboy talk and strong skills with a lasso. They don't have much use for city slickers.

As they ride one day looking over at the round brown hills to the west, Gene says, "Those hills sure are round and brown."

"Sure are, sure are," says Roy. They trot on for a few more minutes in silence and then Roy speaks. "We might be in for some weather, look at those high and mighty clouds – durn it."

"Yep," says Gene, "reckon you'd be right."

A wind starts blowing and tumbleweed starts rolling across the landscape like an army of ghosts. The horses get skittish so that Roy and Gene have to pull hard on the leather reins to stop the piebald and chestnut from breaking into a gallop.

"Roy, head for those round brown hills!" yells Gene. They both pull their horses' heads to the right and make for a wall of huge round brown boulders. The huge stones protect them from the wind, although some tumbleweed follows them in as if it, too, is looking for shelter ...

"Boy," says Gene, "we made it outta there. This is gonna take a while to blow over – might take a while – yep, might take a while, I reckon."

"S'okay," says Roy, yawning. "My chaps were making my legs sore anyway, helluva ride today."

But inside the shelter of these mighty old boulders they feel protected, safe from the devil of a storm out there in the great lonesome. Out there beyond their shelter, black clouds fill the sky, cactus bends in the wind, sand blows. In the spectral gloom between the big rocks they unpack some blankets from their horses and spread them out on the sandy ground. By dint of the good Lord they have found this little dome-shaped hollow, not much more than twelve feet across, but it is shelter, and even the horses sense it. They sleep.

"Goddam, Roy!" says Gene, waking up suddenly after a piece of tumbleweed blows in to tickle his stubbly chin. "We are snug as a bug in a rug."

"Yeah," says Roy, snuffling. "Time for some of the good black stuff and some music, I reckon."

"Yeah," says Gene. "The stars are out, let's git a fire goin'."

They search around and manage to come up with enough tumbleweed and twigs for a small blaze. Roy shreds the tumbleweed into tinder and uses his trusty flint to get it started, and it takes about fifteen minutes of striking along with a sprinkling of salty curse words. But spark becomes flame and flame becomes fire and the two of them huddle in front of it, thankful that the Lord has provided.

Roy unwraps his guitar from a thick blanket. It is a small instrument with an unusual headstock with the tuning keys all on one side.

"Ain't never seen a guitar like that before," remarks Gene.

"Yeah, I know it," says Roy. "But I know a bit about it. Got it from a fella in Tombstone. He was broke, had to sell everythin' includin' his soul, I reckon. It was made by a German man livin' in New York City by way of Vienna. Anyways that was what the Tombstone fella told me and this bit where the strings are tied on is called a Stauffer head – I think Stauffer was some old guy in Vienna who was tryin' to do somethin' different."

"Vienna, where's that?" asks Gene.

"Ain't sure," says Roy, twisting one of the tuners. "Europa or Russia mebbe." He strums an E minor chord.

"Sure sounds purty," says Gene. "Let's make up a song. You go first."

Roy hits the E minor again and softly sings, "The night is cold, the night is black…"

"Agin' the boulders my cowboy back," Gene rejoins in a high falsetto.

"I know a little girl down Texas way," Roy croons.

"The night is black, can't wait for day." Gene bull's-eyes a note in the middle of the E minor.

Roy stares into the fire for a few seconds and then comes out with, "Where is that girl with the eyes of a cat?"

"I need her now and … and …" Gene stops, spits in the sand searching for the right word. Roy pipes up with, "I need my hat." Gene comes back with, "She ain't no rat."

"That's not very romantic, pardner," says Roy. "We need something sweeter."

"Well," says Gene, "how about, 'If she was here, I'd doff my hat'?"

"Yeah, not bad," says Roy and he sings the line and bunches his fingers into various little knots on the neck of the guitar. They sound good to him.

"Dang, yer good on that thing, Mr Stauffer Head," laughs Gene.

"Yeah, I know it," says Roy, somewhat morosely. "I could have played in the saloons, I reckon, but I'd miss the life out here. All I really need is a prairie and a pony – that's the way it is with me."

"We're in the desert," says Gene. "The prairie is five hundred miles east."

"Well, I bin to the prairie one time," says Roy. "Hey! Notice something?"

"What?" asks Gene, looking puzzled.

"The storm! It's done," says Roy. "Let's take a looky."

The two men get to their feet and make their way out through the boulders into the open where they are greeted by a sky with a massive blanketing of stars. The luminous starlight pours down from the heavens in a spectral glow that envelops everything in radiant light, an announcement of love from the universe. Roy and Gene stand in silence. A tear rolls from Roy's eye. Gene sighs deeply and says, "I like being a cowboy."

Roy can only squeeze out, "Mmm ..."

After another few minutes of drinking in the starlight Roy says, "Well, better get us some shut-eye, I guess."

"Yep," says Gene. They turn around and head back to the boulders, their horses and thick blankets.

They sleep well, the night refulgent with dreams, stars and sagebrush. Around 5:30am the sunrise sends a stream of light into their little shelter in the rocks. They begin to stir, grunting into the rays that greet their sleep-filled eyes.

"Goddam, what a night," says Gene, his voice muffled by blanket.

"I dreamed I crossed a river with a snake up my ass," replies Roy. "Shall we get some beans a cookin'?"

They rise from their blankets and the sandy ground and start fussing with their utensils. As they are doing these small chores, they both hear a scratching sound like claws on rock.

"Goddam!" says Gene. "Sounds like a bear."

"Or mebbe a wolf," whispers Roy. They both listen intently. The sound continues but doesn't seem to be coming any closer.

"Mebbe we should take a look," says Roy.

"Or maybe get the heck out of Dodge," says Gene in a loud theatrical whisper.

"C'mon, let's take a look," says Roy. "Probably ain't nuthin'."

They emerge from the rocks with their Winchesters and look up. The sound seems to be coming from further up. "It's up there," says Roy cautiously, and he begins to climb upward. As they ascend the sound becomes louder and then suddenly stops, as if an animal is sensing danger. Roy and Gene, alert but wary and wearing their guns just in case, keep looking around. And then, "Over there!" exclaims Roy, spotting a flash of colour in the rocks.

"See that? What is it? Whatever it is, it ain't movin'."

They climb down the rocks, and to their amazement see a woman, a young woman, an Indian maiden.

"Goddam!" says Gene. "How'd she git here?" They both edge a bit closer and see that she is trapped in the rocks somehow.

"Her leg's between them rocks," says Roy. She was crying. "That's what we were hearin', reckon she's hurt some."

The girl looks at them terrified, thinking that they are going to cut her throat, as Roy has just whipped out a dangerous-looking knife. Roy sees that she can't move.

"She musta' been runnin' from somethin'," says Roy. "I mean how the heck, ya know, injun an' all – don' make sense. We gotta get her out, she's gonna die otherwise, get baked in the sun."

"But she's an injun," says Gene.

"And we are good men," says Roy. "D'ya forget? Help me."

The girl lies there trapped and mute. She is afraid of what these white men might do to her. Roy studies the situation, whistles and says, "Gene, this is going to be difficult. We gotta move that rock off her leg, but how?" He scratches his head for a minute and then says, "We need a lever, gotta get that monster off her."

"I gotta better idea," says Gene. "How about we grease her leg up and slide it out?"

"Durn!" says Roy. "Gene, sometimes I swear you amaze me. Go and get that can of bear grease."

"Sure thing," says Gene and heads off back down the rocks. Roy tries speaking to the girl, but she remains mute and staring into space. Gene returns with an excited look on his face. "Got it! Let's free the injun."

The girl is motionless. They study her leg for a minute, stuck as it is down in the cracks between the rocks.

"Okay," says Roy. "Here goes." And he pours some of the grease down the hole and onto her leg. "Wiggle your leg," he says to the girl, but she doesn't understand and remains still. "Okay," says Roy, "let me help." He leans forward and puts his hand on her thigh and moves it side to side. The girl cries out in pain but she grasps the idea and starts moving her leg. "Go on, pull, pull it up." Roy puts his hands under her shoulders and pulls upward as she twists her leg side to side. There is some movement, the grease is working and with a sudden jerk she is out and lying on top of Roy.

"Yeah!" cries Gene.

"My God!" says Roy as he senses the soft female form lying on top of him and the inevitable natural spark. "What are we gonna do with her?" asks Roy, enjoying this moment. He struggles up and takes her arm as if to stop her leaping off down the mountainside but she is motionless, her almond eyes stare out over the landscape as if expecting something. Roy and Gene can now really take her in. She's maybe eighteen or nineteen, wearing a deerskin dress which comes to her knees, a beautiful pendant around her neck, long, waist-length hair with braids, and to finish it off she's goddam beautiful.

"Well, may the Lord," says Gene. "She's somethin', awright."

"Zuni," says Roy. "I reckon she's a Zuni."

"What's she doin' here all by herself then," says Gene.

"Got lost mebbe," says Roy.

"They don't get lost," says Gene. "Hidin', mebbe. Let's take her to the camp."

"Okay, c'mon then," says Roy and he puts his arm around the girl's waist as if to help her, but the girl hops rapidly down the rocks, swift as a deer despite her bruised leg.

"Damn!" says Gene. "These people ..." They see her down at the bottom of the rocks where the horses are tethered. She stands there and looks up at them. "Goddam, she's waiting for us," says Gene. "How about that?"

"Mebbe we're worth waitin' for," says Roy. Gene laughs.

Back at the entrance to the camp, they approach her cautiously. Roy tries a few words in English including a "me Roy – he Gene" number. She doesn't say anything. She stands still, looking impassive and regal. Gene and Roy are at a loss as to what to do next and they feel slightly intimidated by her, as she gives off a certain power. They can't say what it is, but it's there. Suddenly the girl points to herself and makes some sounds that neither Roy nor Gene can understand. And then Roy gets it. "She's trying to tell us her name," he says. They listen hard as she repeats the sounds.

"Shi Shi," says Roy.

"No," says Gene. "Sounds like Rita."

"Could it be Sherita?" ponders Roy. Gene stares at the sand, listening. "Reckon it's Sunrita. Probably a Zuni name. Let's call her Sunrita. Kinda nice anyway, even if it's not right."

They say the name to the girl who recognizes their effort and nods in affirmation. Finally, Gene says, "Well, we rescued her but we gotta get goin'. I reckon her tribe will come and find her pretty damn soon."

The girl picks up a broken piece of tumbleweed and starts drawing in the sand. Roy and Gene don't get it at first but gradually it becomes clear. She draws a number of stick figures with marks over their heads. And then Roy bursts out, "I get it! Her tribe was attacked. She ran away – got away."

Gene stares down at the sand and whistles.

"Durn, Roy, I think ya got it. God, these people. Poor thing, guess we'd better take her with us. Let's give her some water."

They walk toward their small camp in the rocks, beckoning for the girl to follow. She trails behind them. Roy pulls out his canister of water, shaking it so that she is aware of what it contains, and offers it to her. She looks suspicious and briefly holds it upside down to let a few drops of water fall into the sand, and then raises the water to her lips and drinks.

"Well, I guess we should take her with us," says Gene. "Ain't no use in leavin' her out here with all the animals and such."

"Reckon mebbe you're right," says Roy. "Yep, better take her. Let's pack up and git goin'."

They stomp out the remains of the fire, lead their horses back out and pack their meager possessions onto the backs of the chestnut and piebald. They mount their horses while the girl stares at them. Then Roy looks at her and motions her to get up on the horse with him. She looks nervous. Roy puts out his hand to help her, but she puts one foot in the stirrup and in a fast, graceful move is behind him in the saddle.

"Lucky man," growls Gene, seeing his pardner with a young and beautiful female pressed up against him.

"Aw shucks," says Roy. "Just givin' her a ride."

"And then some," says Gene and spits down on a nearby saguaro cactus.

"Lets get a-headin'," says Roy, kicking his piebald in the ribs, and they all move forward.

Hours pass as they mosey on down the trail. Few words are

spoken, the girl is silent, but tears streak her face as she experiences grief for the death of her family, the attack and the horror of a few nights earlier. Her eyes rove across the horizon as if expecting a return of the enemy tribe. Roy feels her behind him, the softness of her body, the strong supple thighs pressing up against his. It's been a while and Roy tries to concentrate on the trail ahead, but his thoughts are becoming confused.

After a few hours they are hungry. It's time to stop, drink some water, eat something or maybe break open one of their precious cans if need be. They dismount and decide to make a fire. The need for black coffee is strong. Sunrita watches as Roy manfully strikes his flint to get the tumbleweed alight. It is slow, hard work even for a man with a lot of practice. She watches with an amused look on her face and then picks up a couple of twigs and begins rubbing them together in rapid motion. Smoke appears and then a small flame, she has made fire. She pushes the burning twig under the pile of tumbleweed and watches it set the dry plant ablaze.

"Well, goddam, Roy! She beat you to it," laughs Gene.

"Yeah," says Roy, "but we ain't got nuthin' to eat."

"What about the beans?" says Gene.

"Left 'em back at the camp," says Roy. "I wuz distracted."

"Goddam, Roy!" shouts Gene. "What's with you? We ain't gonna make it without food – tarnation."

Roy looks at the girl and asks, "What about her? She's from round here, mebbe she can get us some?" On an impulse they both look at Sunrita, rub their stomachs and point to their mouths. Sunrita simply nods and points to the knife on Roy's belt.

Roy is hesitant. "Give it to her, Roy," says Gene. "She knows what she's doin' out here."

"I dunno" says Roy, "this was my Granpappy's and it's kinda special … but … oh well. Maybe it'll be the difference between livin' and dyin'." He hands the knife to Sunrita, who takes it and in a flash is gone.

"I guess that's it," says Roy. "Ain't gonna see her agin', or my knife."

"Dunno," says Gene. "She ain't no ordinary injun – let's get some durn coffee." They sit in the desert sand and drink bitter black coffee, exchanging occasional grunts and homilies. Neither of them mentions Sunrita, as if they are avoiding the very fact of her.

Thirty minutes later she emerges from the sagebrush, knife in one hand and three jackrabbits in the other. "Goddam!" says Gene. "Look what she dun found. She's a hunter!" Sunrita barely looks at them but sits in the sand, skins and guts the three rabbits, runs a long stick through them and holds them over the fire. The delicious smell of roasting meat soon fills the nostrils of the cowboys and they start salivating. Sunrita judges the rabbits cooked and pulls them off the stick one at a time, handing one each to Roy and Gene and taking one for herself. The cowboys rip into the roasted flesh like it's the Last Supper, uttering unchristian oaths with mouthfuls of meat and juice dribbling down their stubbled chins. Roy tosses a small piece of bone over his shoulder for good luck and says, "Goddam, that was good, Sunrita. You sure can cook, honey."

Gene looks over, picks his teeth and grunts. "We gotta get goin', make some miles before sundown. How 'bout she rides with me?"

Roy gives Gene a slitty-eyed look and says, "I think she's fine with me, no problem. My horse – damn, what's his name?"

"Trigger," says Gene. "Git your mind straight."

"Oh yeah, Trigger can take it," says Roy.

"Yeah, well, Champion can take it, too. I insist."

"Well, geez!" says Roy. "If you really feel that way, I guess so …"

No more is said as they kick out the remains of the fire and mount the horses. Sunrita moves toward Roy, but Roy points her toward Gene and says, "Sorry, darlin', that man there." And he trots on out of their lunch spot looking kinda huffy. Gene follows with Sunrita and a grin on his face. They ride a few miles in silence, Gene enjoying it more than Roy.

Roy breaks the silence with, "Gotta pee – too much coffee." He comes to a stop, pats Trigger and jumps down into the sand and, as there is a female present, instead of pissing right there on the spot he walks into the bushes to begin a heavy and much-needed urination. Gene and Sunrita, sitting astride Champion, suddenly hear a scream from the bushes and what sounds like "Rattler!" Sunrita is down off the chestnut in a flash and into the bushes. Roy is standing there, his penis out, confronted by a rattler with a hissing head and arching back. With lightning speed Sunrita grabs a stone from the ground and hurls it with deadly accuracy at the snake, almost taking its head off. The defeated reptile slithers away into the scrub.

"Thank you, Sunrita! Thank you!" gasps Roy, forgetting that his manhood is still hanging limply outside his pants. Sunrita glances at him, laughs and goes back to Gene and Champion. They ride on until the sun lowers its fiery orange crown, the stars begin to glow and the desert turns purple. Roy and Gene grunt at each other and decide to stop for the night. There are no boulders this time, but they find a soft spot between some saguaro and haul their blankets off the horses along with their few meager utensils and supplies.

"Gettin' mighty low on water," says Gene and then, pushing his hand into a messy bag of what were their food supplies, looks up and says, "Still ain't got nuthin', mebbe two pieces o' bread. We're done for." They both look at Sunrita again.

Sunrita, sensing the situation, makes some noises in her own language and points at Roy's knife. Gene says, "Go on, let her have it, this whole place is like her house – she knows it better 'un us." Roy uneasily hands it over again, and Sunrita disappears into the surrounding darkness.

Roy and Gene struggle to get a little fire going and grunt about their predicament. "You said it," says Roy. "We gotta make it to Devil's Gulch tomorrow or we're done for – bad ending to this whole affair, durn it."

"Hey," remembers Gene, "ain't Devil's Gulch that town where Black Bart and his gang hole up?"

"Yeah, somewhere in the vicinity," says Gene. "Not in the actual town i'sself, don' believe, but he's a bad man. Sure killed a lot of innocent folk."

"Yeah, better watch our asses," says Roy. "Although I reckon I could outdraw him."

"That's crazy talk!" says Gene. "Ain't gonna end that way. Roy – d'ya reckon we'll make it there by tomorrow, or we gonna starve to death and die of thirst?" A rustling sound announces Sunrita's return from the dark, this time with a baby deer around her shoulders. She smiles at the cowboys. Once again, she skins and guts the animal, piles more fuel onto the fire and roasts the baby deer after first making signs to it and singing a few low, soft words.

"She's honouring the spirit of the animal," says Gene. "Ain't that somethin'?"

Once again, they eat in a spirit of communion and camaraderie. Sunrita seems to be slightly losing her reserve. Roy is moved by this moment and reaches for his guitar. He strums a few soft chords. Sunrita stares at him in amazement.

"Bet she ain't never heard nuthin' like that before," says Gene. "Go on, sing 'er a song."

Roy looks into Sunrita's eyes and thinks for a minute and then begins.

"Oh give me a home,
Where the Buffalo roam,
And the deer and the antelope play,
Where never is heard, a discouragin' word,
And the skies are not cloudy all daaaay."

And he puts as much feeling as he can into his guitar playing and singing. Gene is experiencing the same emotion toward the Indian girl. This female is something else, so different from the drunken coquettes that he and Roy meet in the rowdy saloons and parlours of the West. Gene wishes that he could do something to impress her, get himself in front of the guitar player. But he's lost for a way to compete with this; he ain't musical.

Roy continues singing and playing for a while, knowing that he is having an effect on the Zuni girl. His chords and voice drift out over the desert across the tops of the saguaro, across the ancient boulders, across the fragile nests of small birds and the deep burrows that hide the creatures of the desert, the silvery moon in rapport with the music, bathing it all in a soft luminous glow.

"What a night," says Roy.

"Yep. What a night," echoes Gene. They turn to thank Sunrita but she is not there. "Goddam, where'd she go?" says Gene. They search around for a while, but she is gone. Eventually they give up. "Injuns," says Gene. "What you gonna do?"

"Yep," says Roy, bitterly disappointed after thinking that he had met the love of his life. "Well, let's get some shut-eye," says Gene.

"Reckon so," says Roy. They get under their blankets, the only comfort against the cold, hard ground.

They sleep through the night, both of them dreaming about Sunrita. The dawn arrives. Their spot on the desert floor is slowly made bright by the sun's rays. They stir into wakefulness, glad to have made it through the night even if with troubled thoughts about the disappearance of Sunrita. But she is standing near and watching them, cradling a batch of eggs in her deerskin skirt. Roy and Gene become aware of her as she stands there motionless, practically blending in with the desert itself.

"Well, howdy, pardner," croaks Roy from between his blankets.

"Mighty good to see ya," croaks Gene. "What you got there?"

"She got eggs," says Roy. "Food. We can eat. Goddam amazin'!"

They get up from the ground smiling at the girl, who proffers the eggs. They both want to hug her, but it doesn't quite seem to be possible as both men are trying push to the favoured position. Sunrita is aware of it. It's no different in her own tribe – men. She places the eggs on the ground like an offering.

"Well, guess we better make us some breakfast," says Roy.

"Yep, now'd be the time," says Gene.

They break out a small pan, scrub it clean with sand, wipe it off with their shirt sleeves and put a drop of fat in it. All the while Sunrita has made the fire in rapid time, Zuni style.

"Goddam!" says Roy. "Wish I knew how to do that – 'mazin'."

Both men are smiling to themselves, thrilled that Sunrita has returned. They fry up the eggs in the pan and eat them with a few pieces of iron-hard bread that they have left. They offer the eggs to Sunrita who screws up her face in an enigmatic smile. Roy and Gene devour the eggs and chew on the crusts. Breakfast done, they pack up, get the horses ready and discuss the long, hard ride ahead of them to Devil's Gulch. Roy guesses that it's to the east and Gene to the west. They can't agree on it and they have no map, only a cowboy sense of direction.

It's a difficult decision. Secretly each of them wants to take off alone with Sunrita but they know it's risky to part ways, there's danger behind every saguaro and in every gulch, arroyo and dune. Eventually they grudgingly agree to take a middle route between south and south-west. Devil's Gulch has to be somewhere down that way.

They set out at a steady pace. Sunrita walks behind, sensing the tension between them. The day is long and hot, the sun beats down on the Sonoran Desert without mercy. They need water, the horses need water. "Goddammit, Gene!" says Roy. "I know'd this route was no good!"

"Shut up, Roy!" says Gene. "You don't know nuthin'."

"Know my throat feels like sand," says Roy. "And your way is gonna kill us."

"Why don't you ask the injun?" says Gene. "I can see where you're going with that."

"Okay, I will if that's what you want?" comes back Roy's parched reply. Roy reins Trigger to a stop and slides off his back. Sunrita stands there in the blazing sun as if this is just another day for her, another day in the desert. Roy points at his mouth and makes a few gasping sounds, then waves his water canister around showing that it is empty. Sunrita gets it and nods. She points at Trigger and then herself.

Roy looks at her and then Gene. Gene snorts and says, "She wants your horse, you fool, there's probably a goddam lake a mile away, only we don't know it." Sunrita walks over to Trigger and points to the saddle and then to the ground. Roy is confused. He looks over at Gene, who raises an eyebrow and stares with a shit-eating grin.

"She wants you to take the saddle off, you idiot, so she can steal your horse. What are you thinkin'?"

"Sure, I trust her one hunner per cent!" says Roy in defiance of Gene's sarcasm. He unhinges the saddle, stirrups and his pack of blankets and utensils that are loaded on Trigger's broad back. He hands the reins and his empty water flask to Sunrita, who takes them and in a swift, cat-like move is up on the horse's bare back. Trigger rears up magnificently, as if in harmony with his new mistress. She gives the cowboys an enigmatic look and gallops away at full speed.

"Jesus, she's somethin'!" drawls Gene.

"I reckon," says Roy. "Let's rest."

They tether Champion to a saguaro and then lie down in the sand under some sagebrush with their hats over their faces. They both immediately fall into a deep somnolent sleep, their snores merging with the buzzing silence of the surrounding desert. Time passes. Within the hour they wake to the sound of thudding hooves. It is Sunrita and Trigger. She holds the flask above her head and shakes it – the unmistakable sound of water. She slides down from the horse, pats him on the cheek like an intimate partner and proffers the flask to the two thirsty cowboys. Gene goes first, slugging down mouthful after mouthful. Roy follows, slaking his burning throat with gulps of icy water.

"Man, that's good!" says Roy. "Needed that. Where the heck she get it?"

"Dunno," shrugs Gene. "She's an injun. Okay, we gotta get to Devil's Gulch before sundown. But dammit, we're lost. As if lightning has struck, again they turn to Sunrita, who stands at Trigger's side. Roy looks at her, points at the sun and then makes a gesture in all directions, trying to signify that he and Gene are lost. Then he picks up a stick and draws a crude representation of men and buildings in the sand. Sunrita stares at it for a few moments and then points to the west.

"Goddam – amazin'! I know'd she'd know it!" shouts Gene. "See, I was right, Roooy! Let's go, amigo." He cackles and does a small dance.

They saddle up and start forward in a more westerly direction, following the path of the sun. Sunrita walks in front of them. From time to time she turns around and beckons. No doubt about it, she's in charge. The cowboys trot along behind her, happy to look at her young form as she moves at a fast, lithe pace.

They pull up through some small hills and finally get their first view of Devil's Gulch. To the cowboys it looks like heaven on earth, even though it's not much more than a one-street town with a post office, a bank and a few saloons. But both of them are filled with mixed emotions rather than relief at seeing their idea of civilization. Does this mean the end? No more Sunrita? What will she do? Will she take off into the hills? Should they take her into the town with them? They both want her as a wife, although marrying Indians is not too well looked on in these parts. Both of the cowboys think that he will be the one. She is extraordinary, probably the chief's daughter. They? He? Whoever … needs to look into this. Marrying into an Indian tribe is pretty durn complicated. But what about the attack? How many of her family or tribe are left? Their heads are spinning with these complications as they get closer to Devil's Gulch.

They are on the edge of town. "Sunrita," calls out Roy. "C'mon up here."

She turns and Roy, much to Gene's chagrin, waves to her. She gives a smile to Roy – he is the one calling her. She walks back and glides up into the saddle, this time in front of him. She takes the reins and Roy smiles. So be it. This woman will be his wife. Gene scowls and spits into the trail. They pass though the outskirts of Devil's Gulch and into Main Street. Right then Black Bart and his gang are in the midst of a hold-up at the Main Street bank. The sheriff and his posse arrive and begin firing their pistols.

Sunrita, Roy and Gene ride into a storm of bullets.

Black Bart is in the middle of the street with two guns blazing. He aims at the sheriff. A bullet hits the sheriff's badge and ricochets across the street to hit Sunrita in the chest. She falls to the ground. Roy and Gene jump down through a hail of gunfire.

# TREE

First you will locate a forest, preferably old growth – the wood will be drier, the trees having sung out all their sap with love songs to the moon. But on the other hand, if it's a sensitive eco issue, you will look for a young green forest, primal with the scent of a virgin.

You will want trees that are facing south by south-west, trees that have sunlight embedded in their cells, the universe in their being and music in their spreading branches.

Don't forget your chainsaw.

You will walk through a dark forest with slight apprehension, feeling like a murderer. Ignore this feeling. What you are about to do will lead to magnificence. An award! You are ready for anything. You will have a small compass, if you are doing this like your grandfather, but more likely in your case, a smartphone with GPS. You will have no memory of guidance by starlight, as it has been erased by never missing *American Idol*, not even once.

You will have no golden thread attaching you to your SUV back at the Walmart car park. (Can you believe they have a Walmart in the middle of nowhere?) But you will have a sense of mission, Gore-Tex boots, a Swiss army knife and all your senses as wide as the sky.

You've always been a loner.

It's who you are.

You will find yourself in this sylvan paradise, feeling rugged and *can do* because of one thing only – a humble wooden instrument called … the guitar. You are here because you want to start from the beginning. "A guitar begins as a tree." You repeat this to yourself as a mantra as you crush leaves and insects underfoot. You have lightly given voice to this line before – rather smugly or was it more Buddha-like? – as you intoned the phrase with a faint spiritual shyness and stared down into your martini glass, knowing that this folksy wisdom was actually blowing a few minds.

Your crowd – mostly thin-haired CEOs of private equity firms, with expensive foxy wives, Lamborghinis and bonus packages as big as the ocean – are all guitar geeks. You laugh together as you crack up about smoking weed and getting off on Hendrix or the Dead back in the day, the days before you all understood where the real gold lay. One or two of you can actually make a C chord on one of your phenomenally expensive vintage Les Pauls or Stratocasters. But you can usually silence them by sneaking into a relative minor and playing a blues cliché before, with a slight yawn, you pass the guitar off to a lesser talent. You are clearly of a different calibre when it comes to this stuff. You may casually drop into the conversation a word about your latest acquisition, a Gretsch White Falcon or a D'Angelico Excel, for instance. These remarks are usually greeted by what appears to be enthusiasm, but you sense an underlying hostility that is primal, a veiled rawness that is akin to having your woman be the object of another's lust.

This deep abiding love and sure hand with the instrument – along, of course, with your rep as a great outdoorsman, a rather cunning ability to sell short, corner various markets and speak Chinese – are what have led you, logically, to this point and these deep woods. YOU are going to build your own guitar, and not only that, you will find the tree, fell it and bring forth the planks from which your instrument will be constructed. That will put certain corporate pipsqueaks in their place.

You know that you have the soul of a luthier, you feel it, Spanish blood is coursing through your veins, it's undeniable. Thus, you are here. It is the clarion voice of destiny. You chuckle and absentmindedly kick a squirrel off the path and about twenty feet into the dense undergrowth.

You remind yourself that you must sense the tree, feel the tree offering itself to you, placing its life on the altar of your guitar-building ambitions. But you are a great spirit and therefore you will bow to the tree before taking it to the ground and ripping its heart out.

It's starting to get dark, but you need not feel anxious. You have the papers, a licence from the forestry commission (wonderful what slightly fudging the date of a major highway construction can do) and a sense of spiritual rightness.

It will be a great story, the felling of a mighty spruce, the float downriver, legs akimbo the trunk, timber yard stories, and then, of course, the ingenious design that followed all these exploits.

Suddenly you feel it, the call of the tree. You see it there in that grove. Magnificently stretching up toward the sky, it's calling you by name. You step forward, bow to it and raise your chainsaw.

You will have no trace of bitterness in your voice, or comments about the medical system, as you raise your martini glass to your lips and the entire room stares in amazement at the genius of your new, left-hand prosthetic.

# THE SIX-STRING METHOD

*Interview with Mikey Van Stoker*

*by Total Guitar Freak*

**TGF:** "So… when you are approaching the guitar solo in the middle of a song, how do you go about it, think about it, you know – effects, amps, strings and such?"

**MVS:** "The first step is intuitive, unwilled, unguarded, a gesture of surrender to the work. Yet it is, at the same time, utterly self-conscious and reflexive. Occasionally, I think of Olivier playing Richard the Third."

**TGF:** "Does that mean you pick out a certain type of amplifier for your electric guitar?"

**MVS:** "I hear the song and a colour comes to mind, therefore and obviously I look for an amplifier of that colour, although, that being said, colour may suggest questions, but it does not answer them. Blue remains blue."

**TGF:** "Speaking of the blues, are you trying to communicate ideas about psychological and emotional realities?"

**MVS:** "I prefer string gauges 12 through 46."

**TGF:** "What do you think about the scene today, the contemporary music scene? How does it speak to you?"

**MVS:** "Hell had to be invented, but paradise actually exists. It is blue in colour and may exist in a bedsit in West Kensington."

**TGF:** "Have you exploited the media for its capacity to create, not merely record, identity?"

**MVS:** "I leave all that to my publicist."

**TGF:** "Do you think that, in principle, tone is held in the mind of the player?"

**MVS:** "Many of my colleagues are investigating that very subject, but I consider it taboo and believe that it could be disastrous for my work."

**TGF:** "Do you think that Robert Johnson really did meet the Devil at the crossroads?"

**MVS:** "Hopefully one would always be at a spiritual crossroads. Art is created in agony. People want to see flowers, they make us forget the pain and anger of the present moment, but clearly RJ was in a different landscape."

**TGF:** "Do you think that you are a cultural symbol?"

**MVS:** "Only at the weekends."

**TGF:** "Do you believe in God?"

**MVS:** "I favour structure over entropy."

**TGF:** "What about the categorical miasmas you spoke of earlier?"

**MVS:** "Well you might continue to refer to them as the gulf wars."

**TGF:** "Are you like a compulsive Sisyphus pushing yourself and your ideas forevermore?"

**MVS:** "I sit in the shadows as the world advances toward me."

**TGF:** "What does your work mean?"

**MVS:** "Ha ha! I can only suggest that there are unfortunate consequences for reducing the variety of meaning available in a work of art to a single meaning. Do so at you own peril."

**TGF:** "Do you favour brass or glass bottlenecks?"

**MVS:** "As we all know by now, the meaning of cultural symbols is not fixed in time. Hence the circle of broken glass, the eternal zero of infinity turning back on itself. No beginning and no end, so when Sightless Red Grapefruit whips that glass up the neck of his National steel you know you're getting the whole story. *Comme ci, comme ça* ... no?"

**TGF:** "You speak of the blues, of course, but do you think that you are warping aspects of a minimalist vocabulary toward a metaphysical symbology?"

**MVS:** Speaking from a purely anthropological viewpoint, this question just shows you that the idea of art is strictly Western. It has no relevance outside of our culture. Can we have lunch now? No gluten."

# FLYING V

I t had only been a couple of them at the beginning. Two men leaning over the bar at the Flamingo, drinking beer and going through a review of the guitarist they were hearing that night and in particular which guitar model he was playing. But in a crowded scene like the Flamingo of that period their discussion was overheard by others, and words like *humbuckers, single coil, sunburst, headstock, Les Paul* and *Telecaster* had the effect on a certain type of man like the action of Cleopatra on Mark Antony.

The second time the two men met at the bar to resume their discussion, a third Flamingo regular joined in, to be followed on that night by a fourth, who also couldn't resist the temptation to voice an opinion about guitars. The conversations became more animated, and no matter which band was onstage pounding out a tight rhythm and blues number like 'Walkin' the Dog', they would talk heatedly and blissfully about their favourite guitars. The group expanded until there were seven of them sitting around a crowded table. To an observer staring from above, it would look like a black, mob-filled hole faintly illuminated by the flickering orange light that came from the stage. The night creatures of West End London, pill pushers, prostitutes, young men in Italian suits, their eyes bulging with the rush of purple hearts, men who had done time at Wormwood Scrubs, men who knew the Kray twins, all in contrast to the aficionados who sat at one side of the bar, dreamily expounding on every aspect of a guitar design they could think of. Leaning back on a stool and assuming a diffident pose, each one of them nursed a secret and intense delight about the chance to deliver his own feelings, his own exposition about the state of the guitar. Some of them were lonely bachelors, others were married, but with the ironic repartee and arguments about the merits of different guitars, they had become a fresh little community and there was comfort in that. Finally, one of them, John Hurley, suggested that they formalize these meetings, make it an official club and have somewhere regular to meet, and with minimal effort John Hurley fixed a place for a modest rental fee and they began meeting every Thursday night in a small room over a pub in West London. The star of their ardent conversation was, of course, the electric guitar, the six-string whining beast that lit them up, stirred their blood and gave meaning to their otherwise drab lives. But as their meetings began, and possibly because it was so loaded a subject, so dominant in their lives, they made the decision never to have an actual guitar present at the meetings, as it might interfere with the purity of their imagination. Nevertheless, the living presence of the guitar was there and it was deeply felt by all.

Over the course of their first few meetings they developed a few rituals, one being the five-minute guitar meditation. At the beginning of the meeting, for instance, someone might say, "'54 Stratocaster," and they would all go quiet as in their imagination the sound of the '54 Strat filled the room, possibly with each one of them hearing a different guitarist, a different tone, a famous or unknown song, a guitar lick, a chord. But whatever any one of them heard, it was being played on the iconic '54 Strat. Being Englishmen with tightly reined-in emotions, what each one of them heard in his private imagination wasn't usually discussed, but during that five-minute period there was a reverent silence. And although the grubby room over the English pub – with its dartboard on the wall, picture of the Queen and tatty Union Jack – would have seemed silent to the casual observer, the craniums of the Flying V Club members were filled with the twang and thrum of a sunburst Stratocaster, a reverential moment which ended, probably, with an imaginary chord or guitar lick inside each of the members' heads. In the case of John Hurley, the chairman and original founding member of the club, a Buddy Holly lick in the key of E major, the opening to 'That'll Be The Day'.

When it came to guitar stuff they never ran out of ideas or new channels to explore. In fact, they seemed to urge each other on to new heights. It was obsessive and compulsive and they all enjoyed it tremendously. So, though it was originally nothing but a few drinks at the bar after seeing early Fleetwood Mac, that casual encounter became a true dedication to the history and lore of the guitar and the birth of the Flying V Club. Within a few months they acquired a reputation, a small fame. People wanted to join, become members, and imploring letters arrived every week. Somehow, they had struck a nerve and they started to feel a sense of importance, a pride in their work, and they designed a small enamel badge to wear on their lapels. As they shut the doors to further membership and found comfort inside their own little enclave, the guitar world opened to them. They organized talks and forums about early resonator guitars, British solid-body guitars of the sixties, the rise of the Echoplex, the early days of Les Paul as Barbecue Red, the wonder works of Chet Atkins and his Nashville sound, and so on and so forth. Sometimes they got into the music itself – chord progression and stuff like that – but generally the talk reverted to the actual guitars. That was what they loved. Models, year of production, available colours, with or without a cutaway, style of tailpiece, tremolo bars, Gibson's jealous competition with Fender, the lesser-known companies that copied the works of Leo Fender. Sometimes the meetings turned into not much more than an incoherent babble that ended in shouting and, on one occasion, two members grappling on the floor, fiercely spitting out derisive comments about the right choice of whammy bar or solid bodies made from ash as opposed to poplar. But as time went on a more civilized competitive spirit emerged, although it was still there, with each one of them secretly nursing the desire to casually drop in some esoteric little gem of information, some little nugget of a hidden but vital historical fact that no one else knew. It was subtle, but there was a slight edge in the efforts to one-up each other, come up with the rare model, blow a few minds.

Gene Strimling, one of the early members, was particularly assertive in this sense. A bossy man who always had to have the last word, Strimling's proclamations tended to leave a bitter taste in the mouth of John Hurley. He decided to do something about it.

Hurley worked in advertising as a copywriter and was used to making things up, fabricating stories to fool people, showing how a certain cigarette would bring you a glamorous lifestyle, a Caribbean beach and a hot young wife. He thought of himself as a professional liar and, in more generous moments, as a weaver of dreams. But he didn't feel bad about it. He was supporting his family, was obsessed with guitars and was generally happy apart from the nagging fact that he would like to be a better guitarist. But the Strimling situation was getting to him, he needed to bring this arrogant snob down a peg or two, shut him up. He decided to play an elaborate hoax that would sort him out once and for all.

He knew that Strimling was a sucker for almost any rare or unheard of guitar, particularly if it had a blues connection. That was the one thing that would get him to go to the ends of the earth. It came to him in a dream. He saw a field worker in Mississippi, circa 1933. The man was standing in a rural area and holding a guitar. In the background were a shack and some cotton fields. In his dream Hurley thought he heard some original blues that sounded reminiscent of Robert Johnson. When he woke up next morning, he knew what to do. It would be just like creating an advertisement for one of the brands he was involved in. He needed a male model, a skilled photographer, a guitar and a letter. He knew many male model agencies and could run through them in his mind. The problem was that the models were all too good-looking, healthy, and ninety-nine per cent white.

The solution presented itself unexpectedly. Ray, the Jamaican janitor of his apartment building, knocked on his door one evening and presented Hurley with his umbrella, telling him that he had left it down in the lobby. A cartoon bubble appeared in Hurley's mind. Ray... of course, he could do it. Ray was around forty, a bit scrawny but good-looking in an old-fashioned way. He would be the mystery guitarist. The photograph would have to be a bit blurred, anyway. He was on good terms with Ray, always gave him a large Christmas bonus and a couple of other gifts during the year. This is how he got superior service. Later, he went downstairs to Ray's little office, greeted him and at first just had a casual chat about Chelsea's chances in the upcoming season. Then he asked Ray if he had ever done any modelling. Ray laughed out loud and said, "No, too ugly for that caper." Hurley asked Ray if he would pose in a couple of pictures for him. He was doing a new ad campaign for a vodka called 'Blues' that Ray would be perfect for, and it paid well. That got Ray's interest and he quickly agreed to do it. Hurley said he would set up the date and he would get back to him soon. He then called his photographer, Douglas Freeman, and outlined what he wanted to do and explained to him that it was a hoax. Freeman loved the idea and said he could shoot it on an old plate camera and that, with an added bit of laboratory magic, would give it the authentic look.

One week later Hurley turned up at Freeman's studio with Ray, who wore an old pair of rented dungarees, some sorry-looking boots and a faded denim shirt. To complete the picture, Hurley had brought along a battered vintage acoustic guitar. Ray stood in front of a plain grey backdrop and stared at the camera. Within a few minutes they had the photograph. Hurley praised Ray, who looked nonplussed but pleased to put some extra dough in his pocket. A few days later Freeman handed over the photograph to Hurley. He had superimposed a nondescript rural background behind Ray, complete with shack and cotton fields, and had given the whole thing a soft-focus look in grainy black and white.

"Masterpiece," smiled Hurley. "Just need to fuck it up a bit more." He creased the photograph on his kitchen table by folding and re-folding the photograph in different directions and finally tore a small piece off from the top left-hand corner. Then he put his mind to the letter. It had to have an authentic voice, to sound like some-one from Clarksdale, Mississippi had written it. He struggled to get the voice of the writer. It was difficult, his English grammar school education kept getting in the way, and then it hit him.

"Huckleberry Finn!" The voice of Huck Finn floated into his mind. He had always loved the book, read it when he was a kid and once again as a teenager. He took the book down from the shelf and read several passages. Inspired by Mark Twain, it suddenly flowed out of him, and rather smugly he thought, well, copywriting *is* what I do for a living. He was ready.

The plan was to have the photograph and letter arrive in an en-velope that was *actually* sent from Clarksdale, Mississippi. This was easy. He contacted his cousin Roddy, who worked in New York. He explained the whole thing to him and asked him if he could actu-ally drive down to Clarksdale and post this letter back from there so that the envelope would have the Clarksdale post office frank and postage stamp on it. Roddy was a guy with a sense of humour and he agreed to do it over a weekend later in the month, but he told Hurley it would cost him next time he was back in London. So Hurley put the letter and photograph inside another folder and posted it to his cousin at his New York City address.

A couple of weeks later Roddy called back and told him he had done it, driven down to Mississippi with his girlfriend and posted the letter from Clarksdale, and that he should be receiving it any day soon. The letter arrived a few days later and Hurley, holding his breath, stared at the envelope with its Clarksdale post office mark along with a USA postage stamp. He sliced it open with a guitar-shaped paperknife and there was his letter. He picked up his Gibson B-25 acoustic, hit a chord and let out a howl like a werewolf as if screamed by Muddy Waters to a blues club in South Side, Chicago. Everything was how he had imagined it and he could hardly wait for Thursday night and the next meeting of the Flying V Club.

Thursday night came and Hurley went to the club meeting as usual, making an effort to keep a smirk off his face. He was the current chairman, so as was the normal practice, he would make a few announcements at the beginning of the meeting. He stood on a small raised dais at the end of the room, cleared his throat and said, "Gentlemen, I have something unusual tonight. I have received a letter from the United States and I would like you to hear what it says." A murmur ran around the gathering as Hurley, in a pitiful effort to sound like a lady from the Mississippi, read out the letter:

"Deer Mister Hurley I heard about yor gitar club, even over heer in 'MERICA we knows about you. My cuzins follow all kinda stuff about gitar thangs, 'specially the blues music, which people seem to be likin' these days. I wanna tell you about ma great gran'pappy, they say he's the greatest of dem blues boys and the one that showed robert johnson how to play all that stuff. His name was Louis Hangdog Masters. Mos' people jus call him Hangdog or Dog, he died young, consumtshun they say but everwun wundrin' what happen to his gitar ... s'posed to be special like a magic gitar evri' bodi wants it – I think I knos wher 'tis an I kin git it if someone wanna pay for it – like I sed mi cuzin tol' me 'bout yu he be in a good skule and is mad on gitars – says it be uor hearitaje and we need to do somthin' bout it – the real truth he sez. Sorry bout ma spelin'

and poor ritin' – ain't dun skule yet
Tillie Henderson, Clarksdale, Mississippi
Ps git to Clarksdale and ask for Tillie."

There was a gasp from the Flying V Club members. Hurley then pulled out the photograph. He didn't say anything, just held it up for the members to see. One by one they all came up and stared at the photograph, muttering things about authenticity and saying they never heard about 'Hangdog' before. The whole meeting that night was a mess because no one could get over the bombshell that Hurley had dropped – that there might be a rare and precious historic guitar out there and it should be in the possession of the Flying V Club, particularly as they now fancied themselves to be a historical guitar society and the keepers of the flame.

Hurley kept a surreptitious eye on Strimling. He could see that he was agitated, burning even. Hurley gloated on the inside – the shark was going to take the bait. Sure enough, at the end of the meeting Strimling came up to him and said, "You know what, Hurley, I'll do it. I'll go over there and find that instrument. The woman has contacted us therefore it should be with us. It should be in our archive. Give me a copy of the letter." Hurley facetiously thanked Strimling for what he was about to undertake and agreed to get him a copy. He did this in the next few days and Strimling told him that he was going to fly to New York, rent a car and drive all the way to Clarksdale. He would enjoy the adventure, and he would come back with the guitar. After he left, Hurley was on the floor sick with laughter. Am I being cruel, he finally asked himself, or is pomposity getting a little prick?

The Flying V Club went back to its normal meetings but now there was an awareness that Strimling was in the Mississippi Delta on the quest to find what they regarded as the Holy Grail of guitars – a guitar that maybe had been in the hands of Robert Johnson, a guitar drenched with the blues and ringing with the aching cry of the oppressed. Good old Strimling, what a guy. If anyone could do it he could, they thought. Strimling began to acquire a new mantle and became a heroic legend with the members of the Flying V Club. They imagined him far from West London, crossing the Mississippi Delta in quest of the legendary guitar.

Letters began arriving from Strimling, including Polaroids of himself in the Delta. Like Hangdog, he was standing in a rural area but with the addition of a beautiful African American girl at his side. He said he was having a great time and had met the love of his life, and he was on the trail of the guitar. Hurley went into a mild state of shock. This was not even remotely going as he expected. He had predicted Strimling's return within the week, bitterly disappointed and empty-handed and then he, Hurley, could reveal the hoax and they would all have a giant laugh. But at the club, despite a feeling of wanting to scream that it was all a big joke, he had to go along with the lively conversation of the members who were deeply excited about Strimling's quest and the possibility of the fabled guitar arriving in London. Hurley had to force his mind shut to the reality of his own cleverly crafted set-up being sucked into a black hole. Instead of disappearing on the trail to nowhere, the hoaxee was having a great adventure, had risen in the esteem of the club members, was engaging in exotic sexual activity and seemed to be acquiring the status of a legend. He was getting up there with Stanley and Livingstone.

More letters came with talk about the Delta. More blues legends, more photographs of Strimling, his girl and several other happy-looking Mississippi folk. Finally, to finish it all off, the fateful letter arrived with a photograph of Strimling holding the guitar and pushing it toward the camera as if presenting the perfect undeniable evidence. It looked identical to the guitar that Hurley had faked up – a beaten-up old steel-string acoustic, the magic guitar responsible for so much of the blues they all revered. Hurley felt sick inside and grew a fierce new hatred toward Strimling.

Strimling announced in his final letter before leaving the Delta that he would be back next week and would be bringing the legendary guitar with him. Hurley experienced a feeling of having swallowed something rotten. How could this possibly be? He now felt like a fly trapped in Strimling's spider web. It seemed that Strimling had beaten him at his own game. He tossed and turned in his bed, internally screaming at the cul-de-sac of his own making.

Like a black flag of destiny, Thursday night came, and Hurley stood on the little dais disturbed by his own imagination and a prickling fear of Strimling's arrival. He tried a few desultory remarks about the agenda, but his tense anticipation for the Mississippi traveller confused him. Seven-thirty passed but there was no sign of Strimling. The atmosphere was electric. Hurley felt a strong urge to sob but straightened his tie and choked inwardly. The whole club stood in silence. At seven fifty-five the door creaked open and Strimling sauntered in as if he had never left. His hands were empty. He stood there for a minute gazing around the room at the gobsmacked members and then raised his arms and said, "Good evening, gentlemen. I don't have anything. I'm so sorry, what did you expect?"

He stared around the room at the now visibly sagging Flying V members. Hurley felt a huge surge of relief flood through his body. Saved, saved, he was saved. And then Strimling said, "Well, wait a minute, there is this." He turned back to the door and called out, "Cora, my love!" The door swung open again and a beautiful African-American girl swayed into the room carrying a battered guitar case. Hurley, flushing from the roots of his hair down to his Marks and Spencer socks, coughed, choked and stared in shock. Strimling looked across the room at him with a raised eyebrow. Hurley felt numb but, sensing all eyes on him and feeling the expectation, faintly beckoned Strimling up to the dais. The club burst into applause as Strimling crossed the room. He came up grinning, set the guitar case down and turned to the gaping members and said: "Gentlemen, sorry I'm late … flight delay. Please meet my wife, Cora Henderson, sister of Tillie, from Clarksdale, Mississippi. We were married there last week. I am now about to reveal to you an incredible piece of history."

Strimling gazed at the ceiling as a theatrical tear rolled from his eye and then he mumbled, "Sorry, gentlemen, this is a very emotional moment for me, but *this* …" and he pointed down at the old guitar case, "*this* is the guitar that was played by Louis 'Hangdog' Masters and by his young friend Robert Johnson. We will not have it long, as it's going to the British Museum as part of their collection ,but I want you to enjoy it tonight. Let's take a look…"

Hurley, overcome by a sensation of suffocation and drowning, crumpled to the floor as Strimling bent over and opened the guitar case.

# JOANNE STEPS UP

Joanne fancied the leader of Don't Give A Shit. 'The Shits', as they were known, were the rock band in her school. Teenage boys who sneered while they smashed their guitars and drums. The sound they made was that of a mad dog raging at a stranger.

Joanne had been to three of their shows and while her girlfriends dismissed them as true shit, she felt something she couldn't explain. She was hypnotized by the darkness and violence of their music.

Jason Schwarz was the leader of the band and was known as a mean motherfucker. Everybody was scared of him, including the other guys in his band. It was *his* band, everyone knew that. You didn't fuck with Schwarz. Joanne thought he was hot and wanted some of that shit, but then so did most of the girls in the school. She knew she had to come up with a plan to get him, but what? She knew she would look good with him, a hot blonde paired up with a dark-haired gypsy-looking guy. God, those other bitches would die.

Plan A. She could have sex with each guy in the band, slowly working her way toward Jason. But hmm, would that work? No, that was a dumb idea, even if possibly enjoyable along the way, sort of a power slut.

Plan B. She could offer to start a fan club for the band, maybe approach Jason with a half-assed fan club idea to get it going and see where it would lead, but then she thought he would immediately tell her to get the fuck out and slam the door in her face. That was lame.

Plan C. She could stalk him, but then stalking wasn't really her thing. Then it came to her that maybe the best approach would be casual, just be somewhere around him looking sexy and see if he hit on her. Yeah, let it come from him. She decided to try and find out stuff about him and his music. What about his guitar? What was it? It looked different somehow, but it must have a name. She needed to be more informed about their kind of music.

What was it? Death metal? Punk? Hard rock? She asked around among her girlfriends, who didn't have much of a clue. What sort of music is that, she asked uselessly, what do they call it? She knew it was some sort of heavy metal thing but that if she was going to get Schwarz she needed to know more. During a school break she called her friend Xiomara, because apparently she had been to a Shits show and was into the heavy stuff. Xiomara picked up the call and, after some brief gossip, said that she couldn't give her the exact answer to the questions, but she knew a guy who could. His name was Alex Crowley. He was deeply into this kind of music, sort of a nerd, but would probably tell Joanne everything she wanted to know. Joanne thanked Xiomara and wrote down his number. A few minutes later she called. A croaky voice answered and said, "Geek Embassy".

"Oh, sorry," said Joanne, "I was trying to call Alex."

"This is Alex," the voice responded.

"Oh, excuse me," said Joanne, "I was confused."

"I gave you a confusing response?" asked the voice.

"Well, yeah," said Joanne. "Um … my friend Xiomara said that you were an expert on heavy metal music and that you could answer a few questions for me. I'm … um … writing an essay about it."

"Yeah, probably could," said Alex, "but we would have to meet so I can ascertain where your knowledge is at. There's a lot to learn. Come here on Friday night at 9pm."

Brief thoughts of axe murderers, serial rapists, stalkers and freaks zipped through Joanne's mind, but she heard herself saying "Okay, yes, I'll be there – thanks!" as she scrawled his address on the bathroom mirror in pink lipstick. She called Xiomara back.

"Is this guy okay?" she asked.

"Sure. He's kind of weird," said Xiomara, "but not dangerous. Some of the kids say he's a genius."

Joanne put the phone down, excited and also wondering why she was doing this all for the pursuit of Jason Schwarz, but like – whatever …

Friday night arrived. Joanne tried on several outfits for her meeting with Alex Crowley, finally deciding to play it casual in blue jeans and a loose cream shirt that said, *Feeling lucky, cowboy?* She wasn't after this guy, he was just a signpost by the road on her way to JS. That hunk. She took her dad's Chevy out of the garage – he was away in Vegas and her mom was on a hot date with a guy half her age. She could do what she liked.

Alex Crowley lived on the other side of town, the upper-class side, if there was such a thing in Rainbow Valley, but she knew her way around and arrived at the address in a fast twenty minutes. The house was imposing, a Victorian Gothic pile not unlike the house in … "Christ!" said Joanne, pushing the stick shift into park. "Norman Bates. Good luck, girl." She had a nasty vision of her own grisly death and the strident local newspaper headlines:

'TEEN LOSES HEAD IN UNSOLVED MURDER'

'WOMAN DECAPITATED'

'HEADLESS TORSO FOUND IN RAINBOW VALLEY, KILLER LOOSE'

She got out of the car, locked it, put the keys in her pocket and walked up the path to the front door. She gave a timid knock on the heavy oak and heard a shuffling of feet. The door creaked open and a lady, probably from Central America, stood there in the gloom and said, "Yes?"

"I'm here to see Alex," said Joanne.

"Mr Alex!" the maid yelled out. Joanne heard a muffled response from somewhere below the stairs. The maid said, "Come, I take you."

Joanne followed behind her and they went through a side door in the hallway and down a flight of stairs into the basement of the house. They came to another door bearing a strange hieroglyph. The maid knocked and a voice yelled out, "Here be dragons." The maid pushed open the door and Joanne walked into what looked like a wizard's lair, an underground room filled with exotica: Viking helmets, masks, spears, shields, fur, animal skins, wood carvings and strange figures in welded metal. Joanne gasped at this alternative reality.

Alex Crowley sat hunched over a computer screen, furiously working the keyboard. He was small and troll-like, with a fuzzy little beard, sideburns and thick black hair that careened down past his shoulders. He was dressed entirely in black and had a heavy gold chain around his neck that held a small red skull with obsidian eyes.

"Wow!" said Joanne.

"That's one response," said Alex, rising up from his computer desk. "Everything in here can be explained in depth. What would you like to know? Want a soda? Maria, bring us two cokes, uh, *por favor*."

Maria bowed to Alex and backed out of the room.

"Sit down," said Alex. Joanne sat on a plump black sofa with arms that ended with some sort of animal heads that looked like gryphons, if she remembered her mythology class correctly.

"How can I help you?" asked Alex, now standing over her.

"Well, I want to find out more about heavy metal music, if possible?" said Joanne. "I'm just a beginner."

"That's a good place to be," came the reply. "It means you are a virgin."

Joanne blushed and stared at the floor, instantly re-enacting a scene of three years past with her cousin Billy.

"Do you want to play it or be an expert, know the subgenres and their glorious history, take a walk on the wild side?"

"Yeah, that's what I want to know," said Joanne.

"Where do you want to start?" he said.

"I don't know, I just … "

"Okay. Somewhere in the middle like grindcore and we can work our way back through black metal, Christian metal, doom metal, drone metal, sludge metal, deathgrind, goregrind and maybe talk about some of the bands like Brutal Truth, Pagan Metal or Ultimo Mondo Cannibale. What do you think?"

"Wow!" said Joanne, "I didn't realize …"

"What, you didn't know there was so much?" asked Alex, putting his right hand on a gryphon's head. "It's a force, and eventually it will take over the world. It's inevitable, man. May the force be with you." And he cackled madly at his own joke.

"Let's start with simple heavy metal tonight for our first session."

Joanne gulped again. "First session?"

"Ever play guitar?" he asked.

"No, not yet," said Joanne.

"It's the best way to learn about this shit," said Alex as he pulled out a freaky-looking guitar from its case and picked up a cable already plugged into a small amp at the side of the couch. "Okay, listen to this, it's a C chord. Almost never used in any kind of metal, in fact mostly avoided." He whacked the strings and a roaring sound burst from the small guitar amplifier.

"Wow!" said Joanne.

"You say that a lot," said Alex. "What did you feel from that?"

"Um … er, good," said Joanne.

"Good?" said Alex. "That's a bit vague. It didn't rock your world? We call it the tickler, it's like an hors d'oeuvre, something to wake up the palate, get the taste buds rolling. Try this."

He flipped a couple of switches on the guitar and struck another chord in a different position. The sound was somehow darker and more menacing. Something stirred in Joanne.

"Well?" said Alex, staring at Joanne. Joanne knew that she had to come up with something different, a bit more intelligent than *Wow!*

"It's darker, more evil," she ventured.

"Good," said Alex, "you are starting to be aware. Do you know why it sounds *evil*, as you put it?"

"Well, no, I …" She paused, struggling to make an equation between words and the churning in the pit of her stomach. "Um… it's…"

"It's because I'm adding a flat 5th to a major chord. Do you know what that is?"

"Not really," said Joanne, sinking deeper into the black couch.

"In the Middle Ages they called it the *diabolus in musica* – the devil in music, so when you call it evil you are right on. Maybe you have a feel for this. Listen, first this, an E major."

He struck the chord and released a triumphant major sound and then he grunted "And now I put this in," and he added a b flat on the third string of his guitar, creating a nasty dissonance within the chord.

"Get it?" he yelled, and then he started zooming all over the guitar in a fast sixteenth-note metal rhythm, jockeying between E major and B flat major in a set of rapid variations. Joanne sat up straight, consumed with desire and heat.

Alex finally stopped and, with a strange sound to his voice muttered, "tritonus tritonus tritonus." Then he looked at her and said, "Do you want to play with the devil?"

"Yes," said Joanne huskily, and moved forward.

# MAESTRO

from *Classical Music World*

A grey-haired and earnest-looking man, Thomas J Hobbes, knocks on the door of a sumptuous London hotel suite. There is no answer. The silence from the deeply carpeted hallway is deafening.

He leans toward the door and faintly hears the sound of classical guitar arpeggios from the interior. He knocks again and coughs nervously. The door suddenly swings opens to reveal a midget-sized woman with a stern look on her face. She stares at the man intently, as if examining him for concealed weapons.

"Thomas J Hobbes, Senora Segue," stammers the tall man. "I am here to interview Senor Segue for *Classical Music World*. May I come in?"

"*Si*," yawns Senora Segue and then belts out, "Augusto, it's the man from the magazine."

The guitar arpeggios stop abruptly. There's a clunk of something wooden being set down and a long, drawn-out sigh. Augusto Segue enters the drawing room wearing a silk dressing gown and smoking a pipe.

He nods at the interviewer and with the pipe in his mouth manages a small "… *Si?*"

"Good afternoon, Maestro," says Thomas J Hobbes, almost bowing in front of the short Spaniard. "I'm here to interview you for *Classical Music World* magazine in celebration of your fifty years in the recording business."

"Do you mean fifty years of artistry in making music or giving a hand in the production of plastic?"

"Um," coughs Hobbes and makes some minute adjustments to

his tie. "I mean..."

"Fifty years of shit," snarls the maestro. "Sit down."

Thomas J Hobbes collapses onto a nearby divan. "May I begin?" he asks, unpacking a small tape recorder.

"What's that?" snarls Segue.

"It's a recorder for the interview, so I don't forget anything."

"Put that shit away," says Segue, "and memorize as I have done for the last fifty years. What's wrong with you?"

"Yes, Maestro, as you please."

Hobbes wishes he was at Regent's Park zoo but nervously continues. "So, um... if I may, let me ask you the first question. I'll begin by asking you of your perspective on your place in the guitar spectrum."

**Segue:** "Plectrum? I don't use those disgusting things."

**Hobbes:** "No, Maestro, sorry, er, *spectrum*."

**Segue:** "SPECTRUM. Why didn't you say that? What are you talking about? There is only me, nothing significant before and certainly nothing since. Please..."

**Hobbes:** "I see. Um, well, do you acknowledge maybe Miguel Llobet, Tárrega, Carcassi, Sor, Dowland?"

**Segue**: "They're just a bunch of pluckers. What interest are they? I make my own music from true composers. The music of Segue has nothing to do with this penny-ante history you are coming up with. Where did you go to school?"

**Hobbes:** "Uh... Scrawley Grammar. You don't think then that they made any contributions to the development of the instrument?"

**Segue:** "There's only one contributor and you are speaking with him right now."

**Hobbes:** "Well... do you then see yourself in a role of saving the guitar?"

**Segue:** "What was there to save? A corpse? I gave this thing the breath of life, threw it a flotation device, gave it wings. Haven't I proved that with fifty years of golden recordings?"

**Hobbes:** "Indeed, indeed. Well, do you see any future for the instrument? Do you not think there are some young players coming up now that may take on the mantle you bequeath them?"

**Segue:** "I'm not bequeathing my mantle to any of those little rats."

**Hobbes:** "Really? But you trained some of them yourself."

**Segue:** "I only did it for the money – none of them has any talent."

**Hobbes:** "Well, alright, let's move on. You play music of a certain distinction; let's call it romantic music redolent of an older world. Since we have endured two world wars in this century the prevailing thought is that there is no longer a place for romanticism. How do you see it faring in modern times in light of people like Stockhausen, Ligeti or John Cage, for example?"

**Segue:** "Who and what the hell are you talking about? I play God's music, he speaks through my hands. It's the only thing worth listening to and anyone who disagrees can step outside with me."

**Hobbes:** "You don't think music should express alienation, disenchantment, any sort of reaction about the millions that died in the war? The Holocaust?"

**Segue:** "How the hell would I know? I was living on another continent far from all that. I was playing sweet and lovely music, being an entertainer, for God's sake."

**Hobbes:** "Well, let's talk about your marvellous guitar, the Hooser."

**Segue:** "It's not the guitar that's marvellous, it's me. Don't you get it? That little German wretch has been trying to make a decent guitar for the last fifty years. I don't travel with my best instrument for obvious reasons. This thing is just a working tool. I don't care if it gets broken. Smash it for all I care."

**Hobbes:** "Yes, well, do you think that there is a place for violence in music? Some young people today smash up their guitars as a protest against the prevailing social order."

**Segue:** "I set the prevailing social order years ago, so if these hoodlums are smashing up their guitars, then let them. It's painful to hear the horrible noise they make. Anyway, it's they who need to be smashed."

**Hobbes:** "So you don't believe that young talent should be encouraged?

**Segue:** "Well, we are not talking about talent, are we? Just animals with criminal intent."

**Hobbes:** "Do you think music has a future …?"

**Segue:** "Without me? Certainly not."

# VAMPIRES

I suppose I could be an asshole, thought Sullivan, as he took in the three guys who had come to interview him wearing T-shirts covered in skulls, bats, visions of hell, crucifixions, screaming faces and vampires. Judas Priest, Def Leppard, Iron Maiden. He swallowed some more bubbly water and thought this entire thing, this look, sums up everything I have tried not to be – the vicious gang mentality, Satan, the apocalypse, the demon spawn, the fucking end of the world. Why the fuck do they want to interview me? I'm not heavy. Christ, I feel like I'm in Transylvania. Not even a hint of irony. Maybe they are true believers, hearing the message, and I'm deaf. Forty years later and they are still rocking out to ancient heavy metal, the sounds of doom – 'No one knew who they were or what they were doin' ...' So much for Spinal Tap, I thought that had put an end to all this. I suppose there's nothing wrong with it as long as no one gets hurt ... Oh, c'mon man, give 'em a break, they're alright, quite polite actually. Those bands are alright, probably great in their genre, could probably show me a thing or two. But what do I have to say to this lot? Which one is going to interview me? I can hear it now: "Why do you use this amp, what do you think about using Gibson frets on a Stratocaster, blah blah blah." I try to write lyrics with humour, allusions, irony, and play weird notes on the guitar, so why the interest? All the bloody hits, I suppose. Is it possible to have an ironic demon of hell? I've never heard of it, maybe I haven't paid proper attention – Gothic shmothic, 'eavy schmevy! Those T-shirts are completely lacking in irony. I should start a band called Irony Maiden – ha ha, just thought of that, like it – but that music, I don't find it sexy, there's not a lot of blues going on with that stuff.

Fuck doing this interview.

Oh, shut up, deal with it, they are here to make you look good.

Be gracious, you asshole. Be nice, for fuck's sake ...

One of the men leaned over to Sullivan, his hair dangling in Sullivan's Perrier.

"Mr Sullivan, my name is Ivan. I want to introduce you to our interviewer, Natasha. We are ready if you are."

"Natasha?" said Sullivan, startled by hearing the name and that the interviewer was not with one of the goths surrounding him. "Well, okay, sure, I'm ready."

Ivan stood up and looked across the restaurant and made a beckoning motion with his tattooed index finger. A beautiful sophisticated-looking young woman glided across the room and sat down at Sullivan's table.

"Pleased to meet you," she said in a soft purr. "I would like to talk to you today, not about your guitar playing, which the whole world knows and is a given, but about your lyrics. Your use of irony, metaphor, metonymy, synecdoche. The elective affinity and the objective corollary. In general, the poetic world view that has been so influential on us, including my brothers here. We want to thank you for making our lives better and ask you, really ... where does it come from?"

"Let's start with 'Arctic Heart' ..."

# THE RED GUITAR

S he had seen them the last time that they were here in her country. She loved their music, with its jagged edges and impossible melodies. It thrilled her and made her a little bit crazy, especially when the March winds blew through the open windows of her grandmother's house, bringing the smell of sand, salt and oranges that always rose like a spell at that time of the year. Then, she would sit by the open window and play the guitar music of Villa-Lobos to the sea. She would play fiercely to see if she could whip the waves into a frenzy. Etude 11, with its fierce jungle arpeggios, was good for that. Sometimes, when the sea was calmer she would use the lapping of the waves on the beach as a metronome and play slow, languid melodies of her own. Then she would grow sleepy and go upstairs to lie naked on her little bed at the back of the house, the guitar beside her.

She dreamed and, as always, images of them came to her, flying guitars and songs with choruses that repeated and looped in her head like a bird in the rainforest. She knew everything about them, their names, the food they liked, their favourite colours, who they were influenced by, even the names of their parents. Their life was her life. Next week they would be here again, and she had thought it all through – the plan. The design was perfect, and she would become part of the group in her own unique way.

The concert was sold out and raged for three hours as the group strutted, paraded and taunted the crowd with their guitars. She pushed to the front of the stage and wept with the other girls at the beautiful sounds that passed from their guitar amplifiers out over their heads in great waves. The concert came to an end and she slowly walked from the hall, stunned, silent. She always came alone to their concerts, it was too deep and spiritual for her to be able to talk to anyone else, she felt that she alone among all the other young girls in the audience was the one who understood them. Her best friend Laura, for example, chattered like a parrot the whole time, so this night she moved away from her friend and stood alone to take their pulse and vibration into her body and mind.

It didn't matter which one it was, but it would be one of them: Nick, Sam, Johnny, Jet or Carl. She walked slowly out of the hall, the spell of their music ringing like a church bell inside her head. It would take them time to get back to the hotel. At this moment, for instance, they would be in their dressing room drying the sweat off their faces and bodies, lighting cigarettes and making jokes. She walked across the botanical gardens and into the lobby of the hotel where she had booked a room the day before, and where they were staying.

She went to her room, took off the clothes she had worn to the concert and stepped into the shower, singing fragments of their songs as she soaped herself to a new radiance. After drying and perfuming she slipped a red silk dress over her head which accented the curves of her youthful body. Humming the beautiful melody of 'Danza Paraguaya' by Barrios, she stared into the mirror and brushed her long dark hair. Who could resist her? She had to admit even to herself that she was a beauty, the green eyes with their central flecks of gold, the silky olive skin. Her grandmother would look at her and shake her head and mutter something about being even more dangerous than her foolish mother. She had the power to destroy men with these gifts but she also knew that this God-given beauty was a weapon and must be used with care.

Naked under the red silk, she felt ripe like a fruit that is ready to fall. She slipped on the slingback stilettos, picked up the small jewelled handbag that her grandmother had given her and left the room.

At the bar she sat on a high stool and sipped a Belvedere, the only cocktail name she knew. In the red silk dress she seemed sophisticated enough to be there and no one questioned her. Maybe the men in the bar were staring at her for different reasons, but she met their looks with an even gaze which made them look away, even more inflamed.

The door swung open and they came in and saw her. "My God,"

an English voice croaked. She smiled at them, martini in hand, heart beating. Jet, the guitarist, came over to her. "Hello, what's your name? I'm Jet. Would you like a drink?"

"I have one," she said, feeling slightly drunk.

"Okay, well, how about another one? What's that?"

"A Belvedere. Okay."

She let him talk to her for a while and she replied to all of his questions with a sweetness that seduced like a beautiful flower in the presence of a bee. He asked her if she would like to have one more Belvedere in his room upstairs, emphasizing that he had a very nice suite with a view of the sea.

They entered the room, which was filled with the soft light of the southern sky. She could hear the sea in the distance. He moved his guitar off the side of the bed and then tried to embrace her, pressing his mouth passionately against hers. Her lips parted and their tongues entwined like roses. She felt his hands on her body, as the red silk rose up her thighs like a butterfly. He groaned and she thought, he's lucky, he can't believe this is happening, but I chose him.

"Just a minute ..." He broke off and disappeared into the bathroom. She let her dress fall to the floor and then bent over and unlocked his guitar case. It was a red Stratocaster – she sat on the bed and pressed it into her body. This magic machine that had given her wings so many times, the red lacquer against her golden skin. She placed the headstock between her breasts and the body between her legs.

The bathroom door opened, he came out and stopped dead when he saw her. He smiled and moved to the bed, kissing her with the guitar between them. As they began an endless kiss, he twanged the strings and stroked a nipple, and a laugh like a silver dove escaped her throat. Their lovemaking was deep and long, as she reached to him with her entire being and engulfed him like an ocean around a small sea creature. The music of his group echoed in her head like a great chord. He was lost in her. He felt jungles, mountains and rivers passing through him. This exotic beauty was the pinnacle of all his effort – her being seemed to be the sum total of all that he was trying to express on his guitar, but somehow she, this, was it, the exquisite essence, somewhere beyond music. His head filled with the scent of her skin, the scent of her hair, the smell of the sea and rain. Outside a macaw sang into the dark heat.

Their lovemaking subsided and became gentle waves kissing the sand. He passed into a deep sleep. She rose and picked up the red Stratocaster and sat on the edge of the bed cradling it in her arms, and although the solid-body guitar without its amp sounded thin and muted, she leaned over his sleeping form and played the savage Villa-Lobos' Etude 11.

She slipped on the red silk dress and left the room.

# THE MEETING

The church hall is close to my home, not more than a few narrow streets away. The building rises from the surrounding shacks like a grey rose. One weekend a month I go there with my stringed instrument and sit in the centre below the dome with its purple and blue light. I sit with sinewy old men and we pluck and strum together to make a mighty soul-raising cacophony. Most of us know the old songs. They take us back and enable us to go forward. We play as if we have always been together. Our gnarled fingers press on frets and strings as if they were caressing flower petals. Somewhere outside in the street there are children, and their screams and yells seem to fit hand in glove with our old-time rhythms. Some of our men stamp and shout as our leader flourishes the headstock of his Mandorla. Our music is a prayer. Secret words pass between us to revive those who are falling. Someone turns the large electric fan up to three. We are happy. We are as one again; the gods are smiling. As we come to the end we are elevated, raised as if borne on wings. The outside is numinous. Our old leather instrument cases gently bang against our legs as we disappear into the streets of our city.

# HILL OF BEANS

In my small bar in Akahashi Prefecture things are generally quiet, not much going on. A few faithful customers most nights, usually lonely men with nothing to do except order a beer and stare at it. They're probably fried after a long day in the corporate tower. Sometimes a single woman or girl comes in, but the men don't usually hit on them. Everybody just drinks and stays in his own space. It suits me. I am not the extrovert type. I like pulling the beers and mixing the occasional cocktail, a Tom Collins, a dry martini, a whiskey sour. I dream about America in the fifties: long-finned Cadillacs, Los Angeles, men wearing suits and hats, and palm trees hovering over wide boulevards. I have a fascination with that period and its expression in film noir.

Sometimes I think that's what made me open this bar, because it gives me a place to play the music I like, mostly jazz – in fact, really jazz guitar, like Kenny Burrell's *On View at the Five Spot Cafe* (killer album), *The Incredible Jazz Guitar of Wes Montgomery*, or *Jimmy Raney Visits Paris*. Actually, those are my top three. I play them over and over. It's weird that no one seems to mind hearing this stuff almost every night. Sometimes I think I'm a kind of jazz DJ, but that's just my fantasy, it doesn't mean anything. But to give myself credit, the customers keep coming back and I think it has something to do with the music. For instance, I notice a slight change of the room's vibes when Kenny Burrell's version of 'Lover Man' plays, with its liquid and heart-stopping phrases. I can't help smiling at that, it's like we're sharing a moment. But I suppose that's what music is or should be: a voice that brings us together for a moment.

One night a beautiful woman came into the bar on her own. She was immaculately dressed – probably all Issey Miyake or Yohji, I'm not sure, I don't keep up with these things – but she was elegant, poised and obviously very desirable from a certain point of view.

I had never seen her before, but I was intrigued, she looked a cut above our normal customers. She didn't look like someone who had to work for a living. In film noir talk, she looked like a classy dame. I mentally pulled my lips back in a Bogart grimace and ran the immortal lines in my head: "Of all the gin joints, in all of the towns in all of the world, why did you have to walk into mine?"

I wanted to lean across the bar and call out to an imaginary Sam and say I told you never to play that and then she would walk over to imaginary Sam and say "Play it again, Sam …", but in fact she walked straight up to the bar and sat on a bar stool opposite where I was polishing a few glasses and said, "So … you like Kenny Burrell?"

My mind was blown. I couldn't believe what I had just heard from this beauty. "Yeah," I replied, still polishing a glass. "Sure do, sure do." She nodded, took a drag on her Pall Mall and said, "What's the name of this joint?"

"Hill of Beans – it's my place," I muttered back, affecting what I thought was a cool, world-weary persona à la Bogart.

"That's perfect. And you are?"

"Rick," I said as I placed a polished glass back on the shelf. Then, looking at me with a kind of Mona Lisa smile and elegantly putting out her cigarette in a nearby ashtray, she said, "People who don't drink are afraid of revealing themselves."

I got the line, held a glass up to the light and drawled, "The problem with the world is that everyone is a few drinks behind."

She took a slug from her Tom Collins, came back with, "I gave up drinking once. It was the worst afternoon of my life," and she smiled at me.

I was so excited I had to make an effort not to tremble. My God, she was into Bogey and she looked like a Tokyo version of Lauren Bacall. She was also into Kenny Burrell. How could this be? And to finish me off she remarked, "'Lover Man' – *On View at the Five Spot Cafe*. Kenny was really into it that night."

I stared at her dumfounded and just said, "You're good. You're very good."

She looked back at me and said, "There's more, there's a whole lot more. Let's see … Do you know Kurosawa's *Drunken Angel*?"

At this I almost broke the glass in my hand. I was a huge

Kurosawa fan, especially the post-war movies of the fifties, with *Drunken Angel* being my favourite.

She spoke again. "How hip was that thing he did with the guitar – you know, the bum down by the river playing the simple version of a folk song on his guitar, then the head gangster turns up after four years in jail, rips the guitar out of the bum's hand and plays the same piece, but with all the beautiful harmonies. Kurosawa just tosses that in, but it's magic. What a genius."

I was absolutely in love now. I knew she was the woman I had been waiting for all of my life. Still trying not to lose my cool I said, "I've been looking for someone a long time. I didn't know her name or where she lived. I'd never seen her before."

She smiled at me in a heart-melting way and finished the line: "A girl was killed, and because of that, I found what I was looking for. Now I know your name, where you live, and how you look."

I went silent for a moment, looked down the bar and then came back with, "You're a good man, sister."

She smiled and said, "Hit me again but more Tom and less Collins."

I took a chance on breaking the spell and asked, "What's your name?" and then I added, "sister."

"Ilsa Lund," she said, brushing a delicate strand of hair from her brow. I could only reply, "Of all the gin joints, in all the towns, in all the world, you had to walk into mine."

And she came back with, "I was born when you kissed me. I died when you left me. I lived a few weeks while you loved me."

As she said this, a tear rolled down my cheek because I felt so vulnerable and so in love – and because saying Bogart's lines moved me as much as they always have. How can anyone get past the Bogart of *In a Lonely Place*?

She looked up at me and in her eye I saw a tear like a tiny crystal. She put her hand on mine and stared down into her glass.

"Rick," she said.

"Ilsa," I said.

# BAKLAVA BLUES

"... No, they don't understand. What I'm doing is playing in a tradition. It's an expression of something else, something deeper. If I have to play pop music, then I quit. Let's go and get some baklava. One last hit?"

The two young guitarists both took a last hit of the almost expired joint and stood up. Ernie, the blues traditionalist, walked into his bathroom and flushed the remaining stub down the toilet.

They emerged from Ernie's Earl's Court bedsit into a cold, grey London morning. Merging with the crowd of depressed-looking workers, they walked in the direction of Earl's Court tube station. As they headed toward the entrance of the Underground, Ronnie took up the conversation again.

"Yeah, but Ernie – all that distortion? Doesn't it drive you crazy? It sounds like your fuckin' amp speakers are ripped to shreds. How can you stand it?"

"Yeah, Ronnie." Ernie let out a deep smokers' cough. "But that's the point, man. It's the sound of despair. You know, misery, the cry of the oppressed."

"Jesus, Ernie, it sounds like you were born to play the blues." Ronnie stared at his friend as if seeing him for the first time.

"Yeah, man, really, perhaps I was. I dunno where it comes from, but this is what I gotta do. No choice, born for it," said Ernie, loftily looking at the Earl's Court tube sign overhead as if it was a benediction.

"Even if it sounds like shit?" Ronnie doubled over laughing.

"Yeah, well, what you gotta understand is that these people *were* living lives of shit. That's where the music comes from, it comes from pain," said Ernie, looking over at Ronnie with a stern expression.

"Well, maybe they just couldn't afford decent amplifiers."

"Yeah, well, even on acoustic they sounded the same way," retorted Ernie. "Ever listen to Skip James?"

Ronnie was silent for a moment and then muttered, "Really? That's amazing. Actually, why do they call it the blues rather than, say, the reds or the oranges or the greens? I don't get it."

"Hmmm, yes, that's worth looking into," mused Ernie. "Someone somewhere must have said it for the first time. Yeah, I'd better research that. Fuck…"

"Maybe it was Louis Armstrong?" ventured Ronnie.

"No, I don't think it was him. Too late in the early period. Anyway, that's jazz shit. By that time the purity was already being lost."

"Really? What about all those Armstrong tunes? You know – 'West End Blues', 'Yellow Dog Blues', 'Potato Head Blues', 'The Wolverine Blues', 'Jazz Me Blues' … loads of blues."

"Well, clearly he knew what he was doing. He was just selling off the blues to white people. Didn't know you were so into the Armstrong shit."

"Yeah, well, amongst other things. But let me ask you something,"

"Oh, hang on," broke in Ernie, "here's the baklava place."

They pushed the door open and entered a small dark shop with a few tables and chairs. At one side was a glass case filled with pastries and baklava. A man wearing a fez and a tight red waistcoat beamed over the cabinet in their direction.

"Morning, Ahmed," called out Ernie, smiling across the room at the waiter.

"Good morning, sir. Sabrina, please help the gentlemen."

A luscious, dark-haired girl in a belly dancer's costume swayed out from behind the counter and came over to them.

"Good morning, God," she said to Ernie, her ruby-red lips somehow making the sentence into a kiss. "Do you want to sit here?"

"Yes, this is good," breathed Ernie.

"What would you like," murmured Sabrina huskily, her full young breasts inches from Ernie's face.

"Two baklavas and two Turkish coffees," croaked Ernie, his face about half an inch from her left nipple.

"Okay, I'll come in a minute." She smiled and turned away.

"Jesus," moaned Ronnie, "she's fucking incredible."

"Why do you think I come here?" asked Ernie, lighting up a Gaulois. "I hate baklava. She comes to every one of my gigs."

"No, you're fucking joking. What, with the Rhythm Breakers? You haven't…"

A smug look passed across Ernie's face as he stubbed out a cigarette in the ashtray.

"Told you, man. You gotta play the blues."

# CONVERSATION

"**Y**ou just lie there not speaking. I know this one, silence as a tactic. We've been through this before. I know your moves. The stillness, the corpse – lying there playing dead, lifeless. If that's how you feel I'm not going to get anywhere near you, I won't even touch you. Yes, you – the bringer of life, the high priestess, the spell caster, the dream maker, the voice of night. You can be on your own if you want. Why are you ignoring me today? We work together, play together, co-exist in physical and mental union. I know I can make you scream, make you crazy, make you laugh, make you sob, but you know what? We have a true marriage. Glory and shit, that's what we've been through, shit and glory – and nothing has broken us up. Sure, I'm a jealous guy and I don't like anyone else to touch you and, I can assure you, others have come and gone but... you are the one, my true love. I am one hundred per cent faithful and always will be. We have been there for each other through grief and ecstasy. 'Til death do us part.

Do you remember that basement we inhabited for a while?

God, what a rat's nest that was, but we stuck it out, got through it, paid the rent and finally got out of there. Look where we are now, who would have ever thought it? You and me! Together we became famous, loved and admired. It's hard to believe when you think back to where we were. Could you have done that with someone else? Could I have done it without you? I don't think so. We were meant for each other, we were each other's destiny. We have had a life. My God, we've seen the whole world from shit hotels to grand hotels, countries on the edge of war, countries that threw money at us, presidents and even generals that have kissed you gently. I know we fight, but we feel each other – I feel you when I'm away from you. We've had a few laughs, haven't we? What a life. One to look back on with pleasure and thanks for getting through it together. I look back at the old photographs now and laugh – crazy times, crazy people, memories galore of a life that brought out the best in each other. I don't know what's going on today, but I'm feeling that I have to start all over with you. I know what you like – the gentle touch, tenderness, my hands moving up and down your body, your curvy waist until you begin murmuring and we come back together. You know you are beautiful. I always tell you so, I always acknowledge that. That is something you can be secure in. You are one of a kind – a rare beauty, in fact – but is that a reason to just lie there in your bed not saying a word? I hardly think so. You know I love you. Do you want a cup of tea? What is it? Was I too rough the other night? Did I make you sing too loud, did I go too hard? I didn't mean to break anything or hurt you. Come on, baby, let's do something…"

Sullivan leaned over and gently pulled the guitar up from its plush red case and into his arms.

# A JOINT IN WEST KENSINGTON

"Yeah, well, it's like the Devil at the crossroads, innit?" Phil leaned down to the Axminster and picked up a Rizla paper. "Not too much tobacco," sighed Pete, from the other side of the room. "I'm too young for cancer."

"Yeah, one more nail," said Phil. "We all gotta go sometime. Don't worry, mate, I'm the best roller in West London. This is Lebanese Red. Better than Temple Ball, if you ask me."

"Phil," said Pete. "Do you want to go to Kathmandu? You know, take the trip? S'posed to be amazin'."

"Like I wuz sayin'," Phil gasped and let out a long stream of Lebanese Red. "Danger. He's gotta make a choice, the right moral choice. Fucked if 'ee does, fucked if 'ee don't."

"Kathmandu," mused Pete. "Crossroads of Asia..."

"It's either work with the best drummer in London – Wurzel – even if he has had it off with your old lady, or lose a lot of fans and get a worse bloody skin basher."

"Maybe Danger should have it off with Wurzel's girlfriend?" ventured Pete. "You know, even the playing field like..."

"Well, that's a thought," coughed Phil, through a thick haze of smoke. "Wouldn't mind a go at that m'self. God, those legs! What is she anyway... Vietnamese? 'Ere, grab 'old of this." He passed the spliff over to Pete.

"Vietnamese-French with some Indian thrown in there somewhere." Pete took a long toke on the Lebanese Red and exhaled a blue cloud into the room and then, coughing ferociously, squeaked out, "She's fuckin' beautiful ... What the fuck's she doing with Wurzel?" He sputtered and choked his way through these words like a dying man and then rolled over onto the carpet like a frog taking its last few breaths. "Fuck me!" he finally managed after a few minutes.

"You awright, mate?" asked Phil, staring down from the great height of the tatty old couch, his fingers nimbly rolling another fat joint.

"Yeah – just fuckin' dyin'," gasped Pete.

"Wot, again?" Phil started laughing at his own brilliant humour and then also began heaving and wheezing, until finally he stopped by pushing a tatty sofa cushion into his face. He pulled his face out from the tat and finally gasped, "Christ, I think some cunt done us with this lot. This ain't Red, don't know what the fuck this shit is, but… Christ…"

"I think I'm in a bardo," coughed Pete.

"What the fuck's that?" said Phil. "A fish and chip shop?"

"Don't be a cunt," croaked Pete. "You know, a fuckin' bardo like that Leary bloke goes on about, after yer dead and all that bollocks."

"I'm in West Kensington, Pete," Phil whispered with exaggerated elegance to his friend, waving the joint in the air. "You aw'right, mate?"

"Course I'm fuckin' aw'right." Pete got to his feet and did a Pete Townshend windmill. "How does that look?" he shouted and with an Elvis sneer on his face dropped to his knees in imitation of the King, then rose and did a funky twirl à la James Brown… Mid twirl there was a knock on the door.

"Christ!" said Phil. "I think it's the bleedin' landlords. Quick, hide the dope."

Pete dived back into the shag carpet looking for the little plastic baggie that held their Lebanese Red. "Fuck," said Pete, "it's here somewhere."

"It's in your hand, you bloody idiot," snarled Phil. "Shove it under the sofa, quick!"

The door thundered again…

"Coming," Phil cooed out in a high falsetto.

He opened the door. Two men stood there in pinstriped suits and bowler hats. It was Brown and Sterling, their landlords.

"Evening, gentlemen." Mr Brown spoke first, looking around the room with a slight look of dismay which crossed with a smirk on the word "gentlemen". Cigarette butts, torn posters, underwear, a guitar with a few strings missing and a dozen empty beer bottles greeted Mr Brown's eyes as they roamed around the room in utter horror. It was more of a gypsy encampment than the smart London West End rental unit that Brown and Sterling had expected. And the strange smell in the room ... what was that?

Mr Sterling cleared his throat in an upper-class way and, staring at Phil and Pete with what he intended to be a steely-eyed gaze, piped, "You boys are three months behind with your payments. What do you intend to do about it?" And then he added "– eh?" as if adding a threat. The 'eh' made his Adam's apple pop out like a Gaudi gargoyle and Phil and Pete, stoned to the max, started giggling.

Mr Sterling went red in the face and struggled to come up with another line, slightly intimidated as he was by these louts.

"Now, look here ..." he spluttered.

"Sorry, Mr Brown, I mean Sterling," coughed Phil, trying to suppress his giggling fit. "It's just that ..."

"We ain't got no money," hooted Pete and they both rolled over sideways laughing into the mouldy shag.

Mr Brown, the larger of the two, advanced one step into the room and immediately regretted it as his leather shoe by Lobb (fine custom footwear for gentlemen) trod in something squishy.

"Ugh!" he said. "Disgusting. What is that?"

"Fish and chips?" ventured Pete cautiously.

"What the hell is that doing down there on my carpet?" barked Mr Brown.

"I left it there for the cat," said Pete.

"You are not allowed to have a cat," snarled Mr Sterling, loosening his tie, "or animals, animals of any kind ..."

"What is this?" yelled Mr Brown. "A bloody zoo?"

"Yeah, sort of," said Phil.

"Right," said Mr Brown and Mr Sterling virtually in unison. "You are ...? I don't know ... just get out! Not tomorrow or the tomorrow after that either. Right now ..."

Phil took a hit on his relit joint and drawled:

*"Tomorrow, and tomorrow, and tomorrow,*
*Creeps in this petty pace from day to day,*
*To the last syllable of recorded time;*

*And all our yesterdays have lighted fools*
*The way to dusty death. Out, out, brief candle!*
*Life's but a walking shadow, a poor player,*
*That struts and frets his hour upon the stage,*
*And then is heard no more. It is a tale*
*Told by an idiot, full of sound and fury,*
*Signifying nothing."*

Brown and Sterling looked over at Phil in amazement.

"But how could you know that? That's Shakespeare," croaked Mr Brown.

"Yes, looks can be deceiving, old chap," said Phil, whose voice had now somehow changed from Brit working class to a rather posh Oxbridge.

"What doesn't kill us makes us stronger, I'm sure you've heard that one before and maybe it is the case here. You see, chaps, we are at the leading edge of the revolution. The leaderless society. Peter and I are trying an experiment in social behaviour. We are neuro-nauts. The reason we are here in this overpriced shithole in West Kensington rented from two crooks – namely you – is in an effort to challenge what we know as the of dance of illusion. Maya, as the Hindus call it..."

"What rubbish," barked Mr Sterling. "You've taken too many drugs that's all, why are you pretending to be something that you are not...?"

"I think you are missing the point and that is the point. This is 1967 and the world is about to change. We are shedding a skin."

"Yes, very well," uttered Mr Brown, "but you still owe us a con-siderable amount of rent."

"Well," said Phil leaning forward, "how about you take a hit on this beautiful smooth Lebanese Red and then I will introduce you to Aisha."

"Who the hell is Aisha?" groaned Mr Sterling in despair, shaking a piece of cod off his shoe.

"She is one of our family, probably the most beautiful woman you will ever see in your life." Pete sang out graciously across the room.

"Well, I want to see her, how could she put up with the likes of you?"

"Well, normally she lives with me in my Scottish castle," drawled Phil, "But obviously, as you can see, we are in London performing, we are a living theatre. Our professional name is 'The Seven Stages', is that not apparent?"

"No, it's not bloody apparent! Scottish castle?" snarled Mr Brown. "What are you talking about?"

"He is a Laird," Pete said pleasantly from the deep recess of the couch. "The Laird of Craigellachie, it's a beautiful castle."

"Gimme that bloody cigarette," said Mr Brown. "I'll show you it's all fake."

"Colin, be careful," said Mr Sterling anxiously.

"Of course, my dear chap," said Phil, passing the large burning joint to Mr Brown.

Mr Brown took the joint from Phil and took a huge sucking hit.

"Easy on, monsieur," said Phil. "You are going to get ahead of us all. You'll be the first one through the doors of perception, bon voyage …"

Mr Brown, now red-faced and doubled over, somehow passed what was left of the joint to Mr Sterling, who, looking pale and intimidated by all of this strangeness, shrugged and said with a weak sort of defiance, "Why not? It's nothing, I know it's nothing. Neuronauts be damned!" He inhaled a lungful of Temple Ball and then choked out, "Christ, what is this stuff? It's disgusting!"

"Give it a few minutes, you might find it beautiful," smiled Phil. "Pax vobiscum, my friend." He began rolling another joint and gently called out, "Aisha darling, would you like to join us …?"

A door at the back of the room opened and a stunningly beautiful girl walked in.

"How did it go, darling? asked Phil, looking up at her.

"It was very good tonight my love, pure Beckett. You and Peter have really got the hang of those characters. I can't believe these two landlords turned up, they put it at another level and you both still so in character."

"Absolutely bloody brill! We are still rolling, by the way."

"Well, good," said Phil. "It's good to have all this on film. It will be historical one day."

"What about these two blighters?" said Aisha, gesturing at the two men in suits who were lying on the floor gazing at her as if she was a goddess from another planet.

"Why don't you dance for them, darling?" said Phil. "I think they would enjoy that. Maybe drop some clothing on the way …?"

"Really, darling… Well, I will if you want me to."

"Well, don't get too carried away, sweetheart, you know how jealous I am, but do give them at least their rent money's worth."

"Alright, my love," said Aisha. "Peter darling, please put on that Ravi Shankar record."

Pete crawled across the room to the stereo unit, pulled a long-playing vinyl record out of its sleeve and put it on the turntable. The music started playing. Long sitar drones emanated from the walnut cabinet speakers, the tablas joined in and a sinuous raga rhythm filled the room. "I love this one," sighed Aisha as she began unbuttoning her blouse. "Such beautiful playing."

Brown and Sterling gazed up at her from the floor, their eyes glassy, bewitched by the lovely vision gliding around in front of them. Neither of them could speak as this lovely girl revealed most but not all of her lithe and perfect body. She looked down at them, laughed and did a lascivious little twirl of her hips. Brown finally croaked out, "My God!" and looking over at Sterling wheezed, "Robin, old boy, are you alright?"

"I have never been so happy," panted Robin. "Sterling, this is wonderful. I love everything. I love the world, I love you. Love, Love, Love…"

Phil picked up the acoustic guitar that was leaning against the wall and began playing a finger-picking pattern, then softly began singing Donovan's 'Jersey Thursday'.

"In the tiny piece of coloured glass, my love was born, and reds and golds and yellows, were the colours in the dawn. Night brought on its purple cloak, of velvet to the sky, and the girls go willing spinning, on Jersey Thursday."

Mr Sterling and Mr Brown, full of love, smiled up beatifically from the floor.

"This is marvellous," said Phil, teasing a few more silvery harmonics from the Martin. "This a great note to end on. These are happy men and I rather think it's time for us to leave this love fest."

And while Colin Brown and Robin Sterling rolled around on the carpet dazed and happy, Phil, Pete and Aisha packed up a few things, took the film camera from its niche up on the wall and departed, but not before Phil dropped a large handful of bank notes at the feet of Mr Brown.

# DISCIPLINE

"What I want in this band is chaos, structured chaos. To get chaos to sound right you need discipline. Discipline is a code of behaviour, a hewing to the line, the abandoning of stray impulse, a regimen, a drill, a direction, a marshalling of the senses in service to the gods, yes, that is what I said … the gods. Without discipline there is only suffering … misery. So … when we do this stuff, imagine you are giving birth, and I mean the real thing, not a bloody Caesarean. Any of you moo cows up for that?"

Rupert leaned back on his stool and gave the band a beady-eyed stare. "You see, you lot want bloody heaven on earth, but you are not willing to sacrifice for it. How do you think they got to the top of Mount bloody Everest? By eating cream puffs all day? Thinking about French girls in bikinis? No, they had bloody discipline. From discipline you get sinew, muscle, mental focus, power. And with that come all the rewards that you are looking for and, correct me if I'm wrong … 'rumpy-pumpy', 'a bit of 'how's your father'', 'doing the nasty', 'making the beast with two backs', 'a helpless rutting' … Yes? So, if you want to 'take old one-eye to the optometrist', let's try to play our music as if we are not in kindergarten sitting on a toadstool but in the presence of the gods, sharp and dangerous as a freshly honed sword. If you do what I say, the maidens will arrive."

"Now let's try 'Bleak Night of the Death Hawk' again, it's only in seventeen-four, any dummy could get that. You should be doing this in your sleep and, come to think of it, do try to stay awake this time … okay? One two three four five six seven eight nine ten eleven twelve thirteen fourteen fifteen sixteen and yeah …"

With a huge groan sounding like a falling tree, the band crashed into life: 'Finks', the drummer, thrashing wildly on his ride cymbal and desperately mouthing the seventeen-four time signature. 'Screw', the second guitarist, holding long fuzzbox chords so that he would not have to attempt counting anything. 'Lick', the keyboardist merely fucking around with wheezy little sounds that didn't make much difference to anything, and 'Plonk', the bass player, just hitting a doomy bass note whenever it occurred to him.

In the middle of all this energy sat Rupert, who stared outward, never looked at his guitar and yet rattled off the polymetric guitar figure as if he was knitting a cardigan for his granny. About fifteen minutes later the whole band let out something like a death rattle and it all came to an end.

Five whole minutes went by in deadly silence as Rupert looked around the room and gave each player his own brand of death stare. Then he chuckled and said, "Okay, girls, come in …" The door remained shut – no girls.

Finally, Rupert broke the void-like silence by looking over at Finks and said, "Finks, do you think that the drums are really the right instrument for you?" Finks, sweating and swigging a bottle of lemonade, gurgled, "Was alright, wasn't it? I thought I …"

Rupert moved on to Plonk. "Plonk, what's that thing made of? Sheet metal? Balsa wood? Cardboard? You might get something for it down at the pawnshop, think about it."

"Lick, have you ever thought about taking up the keyboards? Might be a good career for you, don't let it slip away. Screw, ever think about helping the elderly?" Rupert continued with this line for a few more minutes as he effortlessly played the seventeen-four riff independent of all his speech.

Then, as if talking to himself, he intoned the word "Master" and repeated it in an endless loop for what, to the rest of the band, seemed an eternity, an eternity of hell and then, as if channelling a different spirit, moaned, "I can't do this any more, I can't do this any more, I can't do this any more." He chanted this over and over, like a voodoo mantra. The faces of the band were by now ghostly white as they witnessed their leader going off the deep end, the next American tour cancelled, without a gig, never mind the maidens.

Suddenly Rupert looked up and started the seventeen-four riff up again. He looked over at Finks the drummer and with a drill sergeant's voice shouted, "Play with me, Finks, and try to hit the fucking one! Accent the one so you bloody well know where you are and give us all a fighting chance." Finks picked up his sticks and started tapping tentatively along with Rupert.

"Don't be a bloody coward!" roared Rupert across the room. "Take fucking charge." Finks moved over to the ride cymbal and tried to be confident, sensitive and macho all at once, which was a bit demanding, but he seemed to be getting it right. Was he actually catching the one? Was he beginning to feel the beginning of a pulse in this monstrous concoction?

"Plonk, where are you?" screamed Rupert. Plonk woke to life, looked over at Finks and by sheer luck caught the downbeat as Finks mouthed the count in his direction.

"Okay, Screw! Lick!" Rupert yelled across the sonic roar. "Play some real fucking chords now, let's go." As a man, Lick and Screw whacked out two giant atonal chords that sealed it all together like a gargantuan silken canopy. A gargantuan silken canopy that made it all good, that made it like heaven, like paradise, like love...

The five musicians flew on this way for another thirty minutes as if winging their way over a mighty ocean. No one lost their way, no one fell overboard, all were purely in the present. Time had been stopped, magic had said Hello and the clouds had parted.

Finally, Rupert looked up from his guitar and spoke quietly. "Gentleman, we have a beginning. We open at Madison Square Garden next Tuesday. Maidens will appear..."

# THE GREAT MACKLEBY

"Of course, the effect he had on guitar playing worldwide was historic, galvanizing, nuclear – like the Chicxulub asteroid that struck earth sixty-six million years ago. Nothing was the same afterwards. It was devastatin' – a point zero if you will. We still feel the shock waves the noo ... that was his effect ... power ... mystery ..."

A short, stocky Scotsman with a waist-length beard, a kilt and sturdy hiking boots leads a small group of people through a dank subterranean corridor. Along the wall are paintings of a wild-looking man with a long mane of hair streaming behind him as if in a gale-force wind. His fingers, six of them on his right hand, grip a guitar neck in a formidably long, stretched-out shape, impossible to replicate with a mere five-fingered hand.

This is Mackleby. The legendary and infamous guitarist who emerged from, and then disappeared back into, the mists of the Scottish Highlands. The mystery and enigma of Mackleby continues to expand and grow more vivid with each passing day. No one has ever heard him play ...? Have they ...?

"Now we're coming to the cosmic cloud chamber, so I'd like ye to speak in whispers and listen carefully," intones McDougal. "If you listen carefully you can hear the vibrations – the upper harmonics of 'Martian Desolation', they're still here in these very walls – och aye the noo."

The group behind McDougal – a motley crew of American tourists from Ohio, a few Japanese loaded with cameras, one or two Germans and thirty-four Dutch people – quieten down and stare at the walls in silence. And then it comes, or maybe it doesn't. A faint whirring sound, almost like the rotor blades of a chopper roaring over the moors on a search and rescue mission, and then, slowly, almost imperceptibly, a high keening note – almost the cry of a gull or a petrel hawk soaring over the cliffs of the Outer Hebrides, its small, beady eyes scanning the churning foam below that smashes violently into the wet black stone at the edge of the vertiginous cliffs.

Or is it a guitar…?

There is a reverent hush in the chamber. The tourists are gob-smacked into a stunned silence. Is it possible? Can music live on like this – a ghost in the ether, how could this be?

McDougal turns to face them, tears running down his cheeks. "Och," he murmurs and stares down at his North Face hiking boots. "Och…" and then, gruffly, "Questions the noo…?"

"Where he play last time?" a rotund Japanese lady pipes up.

"No one knows for sure," answers McDougal through his beard. "Maybe a cave at the base of Ben Nevis or Ben Macdui, it's a great mystery."

"No one was there?" an elderly blues fan ventures from the back of the small crowd.

"Did ya know him?" an American voice asks.

"Know him?" spits McDougal, "how can you know anyone? Know…? Know…? Did you not hear it? There's your know the noo."

"Jeez – sorry," whispers the American.

"What about his style? Where did that come from?" garbles a Dutch person.

"Aach!" McDougal hawks a loogie into a nearby brass spittoon. "Don't insult a god ye Sassenach – I'll have yer guts f'garters!"

"Was he influenced by quantum physics?" a bronzed German tourist asks in a loud lederhosen voice.

"He was fully quantum," sprays McDougal. "Ken y' no hear that? He could make himself disappear – dissemble hisself at will. Vaporize his corporeal flesh into pure harmonics, merge with the sky… the infinite…"

"I'm Florence from Cincinnati," a large, bosomy lady suddenly booms out. "I want to know where he played, his age when he disappeared? Why *did* he vanish and what about his music? Did he use a Floyd Rose Tremolo or a standard Stratocaster whammy bar? Who was his roadie? His technical assistant…?"

McDougal turns a whiter shade of pale.

"Roadie ... roadie ... !!?"

McDougal shakes in his kilt, his skin turns white, his nose grows purple. "Ye think that a god needs assistance? Yer not fit to be in this chamber."

The lady from Cincinnati visibly deflates in front of this tartan force. McDougal appears to stamp his feet on the flagstones in a primal rage.

"Let me explicate the workings of mysterious forces, other than the likes of ye would know about," snarls McDougal. "Yer not meant to understand everything in this life – some things ye have to take on faith, like he was there but not there, if ye see my meaning. It might depend where you're standing and if you were actually watching or listening. But the music lives – in us – it *is* us ... it's ... it's ... It contains all of history and the destiny of man ... the likes of ye call that guitar playing? I don't think it's something we can understand, it's beyond our ken. But only – in our decrepitude – acknowledge ... that he was here, and he is still here if you open your eyes. This was his message. It's all a load of ..."

McDougal turns his back to the tourists. He bends over, lets out a loud howl and raises his kilt to reveal and finally dispel any questions about what Scotsmen hide under there.

# HOOKED

You look up at the guitar suspended high on the wall of the guitar shop. You feel its call and imagine its ringing steel-string chords, a low-throated E minor, a rich and joyful D, an E major, second inversion high up on the neck across the first four strings where it stretches from the ninth to the twelfth fret. You would strike the low open E string and feel its sonorous bass chime in your gut.

*– her eye, her mouth*

You would brush the natural harmonics at the twelfth, seventh and fifth frets, tease out their ghostly chimes, their high taunting cries.

*– mouth – lips*

You might run your fingers over a C# minor where it takes its position in the centre of the neck like a gate that swings open to a previously hidden sound meadow and where a gathering of open unfretted strings ring against each other, a choir that sings all the sadness inside this guitar, the ruined life of its maker, the departed woman, the empty bed,

*– the brief tear-stained note*

and from this central position on the fourth fret the C# minor reaches down to the great E major guitar chord and on to the declarative A major, crowing and certain,

*– someone else*

and you might follow that with its own relative sixth, the obsidian F# minor that once struck shape shifts to the B triad on the fourth fret,

*– realization*

where its innocent trio led by the sly D# pushes against the eleventh of the open first string, the bright and silvery E.

You gaze at this jewel hanging from a hook in the wall, a symbol of future lost. A face floats ghost-like from the unplucked strings, a pre-echo of unheard songs.

*She left you for a drummer.*

# KITTY

I got on a bus with my guitar. I didn't have a case for it. It was a German guitar called a Voss. It was a beautiful honey-gold and on the shabby local bus it looked like an exotic being from another planet. I was sixteen, without a guitar case and no means of transport other than the local bus. I was also wearing a bow tie with a white shirt that my dad had given me. The collar was really loose around my neck and hung like a white circle of dog collar, an inch free of my neck. Over that I wore a two-sizes-too-big dinner jacket with a mismatched pair of grey slacks held up with an old leather belt, also of my dad's. I had to bang a couple of more holes in it with a hammer and a six-inch nail so I could get it tight enough to stop the slacks falling around my ankles. A couple of people on the bus asked me how I was doing with the banjo. It was humiliating and I smiled and cursed them through gritted teeth.

"Where's the case for yer banjo?" one old geezer asked.

"Cat pissed in it," I replied, looking out of the window. I had a gig in a local hotel down on the seafront. The hotel had decided that they needed to have a guitar in the band to make the place seem more up to date, something lively between the dreary old foxtrots and waltzes. I was thrilled to have the gig because it made me feel grown up, like a professional. The other musicians in the band were more than twice my age, to a man they were exceptional musicians and sex mad with it. They all played jazz but had to perform at way below their actual capability in this hotel band. It was great for me because they all liked me and were willing to teach me things about music that were far beyond my years. They also shared very sick humour, especially about women and sex. Most of the time I didn't know what they were talking about but laughed anyway, as if in sheer derision of anyone who was a virgin.

As we were the band, and therefore employees of the hotel, we were only allowed to enter through the back door, the employees' entrance. We had to take our breaks in the kitchen and were told never to mingle with the hotel guests. Most of this was treated with a fair degree of irony by my band mates, but they kept it to themselves when Cyril was around.

Cyril was the so-called band leader. It was his job, and he called the shots. He literally called out foxtrots, waltzes or polkas on the bandstand as he saw fit. I thought his bass playing was shit, the most simplistic one note per bar that he could get away with. Seeing this old git standing there and smiling greasily at the patrons as they crept around the dance floor made me want to turn my amp volume to the highest and blow the old fucker off the bandstand. But I got to play a bit. Mike the drummer would start into a mild rock 'n' roll feel and I would have a go bending the strings and putting a bit of blues edge onto the chandeliered dance floor. I was the young guitarist, and the young teenage kids would come close to the bandstand to take a look. I didn't mind, in fact I liked it, and there was some flirtatious eye contact. Cyril, who drove me home each night, warned me to stop staring at the girls. Mrs Goldthwaite, the hotel owner possessed of a physique that resembled the hotel, stood at the edge of the dance floor each night with a hawk-eyed stare, ready to seize on any small act of misbehaviour that strayed from her ironclad rules.

She had already said something to Cyril about me. Cringer that he was, and threatened as he was, he told me to keep my eyes down and stop bloody staring. I tried to cool it for a while, but it was useless and one night a very pretty female patron dropped a note by my music stand with a message to meet her out on the cliffs. I couldn't wait for the night to be over, and once we had got through 'Hava Nagila' I packed up rapidly, left through the servants' entrance and headed out toward the cliffs, where the message said she would be waiting in the bus shelter. It was late August and the weather was blustery, with air that felt humid and close, as if it was about to burst into tears. But I headed toward the bus shelter at warp speed, in high anticipation, and there she was, smiling and amused at her own daring because someone like me was strictly off-limits. But we started chatting in the shelter as the wind picked up and the universe spread its wings around us. It was a lovely magical feeling with the warm summer air, a few spatters of raindrops and the two of us teenagers in a moment of clandestine *amor*. She was dark haired, full-lipped and moving against me as the wind gusted across our backs, and as we kissed and fumbled, our mouths locked together in a prolonged duet that seemed to last forever, I couldn't believe it. It was so exciting, so dreamlike. The night came on with more urgency and whipped at our clothes as our passion burned in the neon light of the corporation streetlamps.

Kitty's bra fell to the ground on the floor of the shelter, and then flew like a kite and down the path where it impaled itself on a rhododendron bush. Kitty shrieked "My bra!" and then pushed her tongue into my mouth. I was thinking about dm7 in the fifth position, imagining its move to some sort of G7th as I desperately tried to hold myself in check. Kitty's supple flesh moved under me like a snake in the Garden of Eden. The wind howled and the sea below roared like a mad dog.

Everything was in motion, driven by the engine of a southeaster. Clouds raced across the sky, old ice cream wrappers flew from the litter bins, trees and bushes whirled in a mad dervish dance, and finally a copy of yesterday's *Daily Mail* wrapped itself around my head. Kitty and I, locked in a deep snog, sputtered into uncontrollable laughter and fell apart on the bench. Kitty finally sat up giggling and made some clothing adjustments. She looked at me and said, "Well, gotta go, maybe see you tomorrow, Romeo." She disappeared into the night and the thick sheet of rain that now sobbed itself down from the August sky. I chased after her tripping and staggering in the watery onslaught, but she was gone, lost in the storm.

The next night Cyril fired me.

# THE BALLAD OF DJANGO AND PABLO

In 1929 two young men in Paris, both hard up and without a sou to their names, moved into a room together at the top of a house in the Rue du Bac. Some people passing by looked upward and grunted, which was a nasty expression for the poor and bohemian.

One of the two was a guitarist, the other a painter. The guitarist's name was Reinhardt, the painter's Picasso. Within their small circle they were known as Django and Pablo. Pablo and Django! Those names rolled off the tongue like silvery dewdrops. They became popular just because of their names. Django played fast gypsy music with a lot of wrong notes. Pablo began painting backwards so that everybody laughed and fell over on the boulevard. Pablo was so funny.

One day, September 27, they were up in their garret where Pablo was sloshing paint about in a way that Django couldn't understand, but to be good company he played his guitar along with the rhythm of Pablo's brushstrokes. It was a good atmosphere. Suddenly Pablo turned to Django and asked, "Hey, what is that crazy music? It's so sad. It makes me sad but happy at the same time. I can't explain ..."

"Zis za blooze from America. Louis Armstrong," said Django in bad French.

"I like it," came back Pablo. "I am in a blue period myself."

"*Oui*," said Django, bending a string and swallowing a mouthful of vino tinto, "*Nous sommes le bleus.*"

"*Oui*," said Pablo. "*Nous sommes* and I don't have any other colour in my paintbox – no money, so *comme ci, comme ça*," and they both laughed merrily.

"What are you painting there?" asked Django, striking a D9th chord at the fifth fret.

"Oh, just some women, I don't know, *comme ci, comme ça.*"

"It looks like a bad dream," said Django, and struck a strange chord with a lot of peculiar notes in an attempt to parallel Pablo's painting efforts. Pablo, startled by the atonal harmony, made a conventional brushstroke. "Must be that crazy left hand," he thought.

"I must think up a name for it," said Pablo.

"I know," said Django. "How about 'Guernica'?"

"Hmm," mused Pablo, "I don't think so, but I will try and use it somewhere."

"Okay," said Django, "how about 'Les Demoiselle d'Avignon'?"

"*Oui – pas mal …*" said Pablo. "How did you come up with that?"

Django stared at his plectrum for about thirty seconds and then said, "Well, I know some girls in the town. We should go down there sometime."

"That sounds good," said Pablo, rubbing a crusty bread roll through the paint to get what he called his breaded effect.

"But," said Django, suddenly knitting his brow, "I have to say Pablo, *et excuse-moi,* I am only a Belgian Gypsy who grew up in abject poverty, but my women in Avignon are a lot better looking than those in your painting."

"Oh, I just paint 'em like this so I'll know 'em when I see 'em and then I can avoid 'em. Simple trick."

"*Oui,*" said Django, "it's like getting all the bad notes out of the way."

"I've been with an awful lot of bad notes," said Pablo and they both laughed until tears ran down their faces.

# THE DAVES

His face, like a dark circle, would appear in the lustrous brown and gold of its surface, his outline really not much more than a shadowy silhouette, subtle but just enough for them to identify him as the master of this fabulous instrument, this six-stringed wonder, this wooden angel that would sing to the stars as his hand teased the most beautiful and intriguing chords from its vortex of strings and frets. Females would swoon and offer themselves to him, swear undying love as his hands traversed the neck, conjuring one piece of magic after the other, a dazzling succession of harmonies that fell from the luminous sky of his guitar. They would call him a boy wonder as his hands, his spirit, flew across the strings, their faces smiling almost laughing at the effortless wizardry. "How do you do that? That's impossible. Oh, it's lovely," they would all cry. The word would travel, the world would come, the wound forgotten.

Sean leaned back on the couch lost in his own reverie and then came to with a jolt as a bus screeched to a halt on the street outside. He remembered where he was and stared up at the wall filled with glitzy posters, pictures and notices of money and all sorts of tawdry commercial success. Yes, the famous grungy studio where hits are made blah blah blah, well it's not the bloody Taj Mahal, is it? he thought, in an effort to quell his nervousness.

He gave a sigh and looked down at his battered guitar case. So what then, he questioned himself. Did any of this matter, did it matter that one day no one would remember him, his name nothing but a rained-out smudge on some half-buried gravestone? The world would continue, life would race on without him, his music forgotten. But music, it doesn't die does it – it moves on forever into the universe, travelling in waves into the far reaches of ... whatever.

There was no death, just a changing of forms, he would have left an imprint, he would always be here as unceasing energy, like Hendrix.

Sean stared at the wall. Unceasing energy? I'm here to do an audition, to bare my soul to a bunch of strangers in a crap situation. Who cares? All I do is practise, it doesn't mean anything – well, I like it – but nothing means anything, anyway. I've got to stop reading Nietzsche, all that Swiss-German alpine crap is doing my head in. I might as well move to Denmark and sit in a hut. Why am I here? I'm not good enough for this band, no … no … I am, I am, I am … I really cannot …

His thoughts were banging around in his head like a warped tape loop. Like so much mental furniture rolling down the steps at Tottenham Court Road tube station at rush hour.

The number thirty-seven bus started up outside the window and hauled itself away from the curb. Should have got on it, he thought, get out of this situation. He felt the familiar safety of his bedroom, his mother calling him, his record player, his vinyl collection, his dog.

His hands felt the guitar pick in his pocket, his fingers curled around the heart-shaped piece of celluloid for comfort and he prayed that it would all come together. I'm good he thought, I'm good, don't worry mate it will be fine. He glanced up at the gold records high on the office wall. They seemed like exotic suns, shining in some far distant universe and now glinting and smug they taunted him, a symbol of everything that seemed out of reach.

"This is the big time," they said in whiny, gold record voices. "What are you doing here sonny boy? You'll never sell a million." How did it ever happen? How could you ever get to that shiny place? The millions of sales, fame; all of that stuff. All he knew was how to practise the guitar, play it endlessly into the night until his fingers were raw. Over and over and over, working his way through the maze of frets and strings, the long stretchy chords, the natural harmonics, the chord progressions, which notes sounded good on them and which didn't. Right notes, wrong notes, and then there was a thing called feeling. How did you get that? Only by listening like a maniac and playing along for thousands of hours. Well, I've done that, he told himself. I've done that, so this is the test, they are looking for a guitarist, maybe I'm the one, what if I'm better than them? Their stuff is pretty simple, nothing I can't play. I wonder if they're good enough for me? I better play a bit. He opened the guitar case and pulled out his old Telecaster. He immediately felt better with the guitar in his hands, and started running chords and licks and getting into a nice musical space in his head.

A beautiful girl appeared in the doorway. She leaned her lissome shape against the door frame, looked down at a piece of paper and smiled at him, "Wow, that sounds good," she said.

"Hi Sean, I'm Shana." Her radiant smile floated across the room and kissed him on the nose, where it popped like a soft soap bubble and washed over him in a gentle little wave. "Sean and Shana – pretty crazy, huh?" She let out a silvery little laugh and smiled at him again.

"Hi," he croaked, feeling dizzy and dazzled by the way she had just connected their names. He managed a garbled sentence, "Guitar. I mean me, I play it."

"Yes, I didn't think that was a trombone between your legs," replied Shana, wiping him out with another sparkling smile.

"The boys are in there, they're all dying to meet you. I must say you look the part. Are you ready Sean? Are you ready to rock …?"

"Mmmm," he croaked.

"C'mon then," said Shana, "let's do it."

She remained in the doorway as he awkwardly brushed by her, feeling her heat, her youth and the overpowering sensation that he needed to kiss her lips, her perfumed body and her sweet fingers as they touched him lightly on the elbow and she whispered, "You'll be great."

Sean, now floating on air and with a candle flickering in his heart, gestured to her to lead the way and blushingly followed into a small room where three sulky and shabby-looking guys were hanging around by the drum kit.

"Here's Sean," said Shana brightly.

One of the guys moved his ass off the drum rostrum and extended a hand to him, "Ello mate, I'm Dave."

Dave was tall with slicked-back hair and Buddy Holly glasses. It was a look. Sean shook his hand nervously thinking – right … Dave, Dave.

The drummer came from around his kit and said, "Hi Sean, I'm Dave." Sean felt a mounting confusion. As this confusion flooded through him, the bass player, tall and blond like a Californian surfer, appeared in front of him and said, "Hey man, I'm Dave, good to meet ya." Something clicked in Sean's brain – right, r-i-i- i-i-i-ght that was them, this was them – this is them, the band – The Daves. Of course … he knew that. That's why he was here, he was here to audition for THE DAVES. He smiled in a general sort of way as if acknowledging the coolness of the idea, the name – whatever – they were at the top of the heap. It was intimidating and then it came to him. WIND THEM UP …

"How are you feeling today?" asked Dave with the Buddy Holly glasses.

"Oh, I dunno, like an insect – like that giant bug, you know, in *Metamorphosis* – Kafka?" said Sean.

"Yeah," replied Dave. "I know the feeling. Where did you learn to play?"

"Mostly in Eastern Europe, Turkey, Romania, places like that."

"How come?" asked Dave. "That's pretty unusual."

"My dad owns a Greek shipping line," answered Sean, fingering his guitar pick. "I was all over the place."

"Let's see yer axe," said Buddy Holly Dave. "Yeah sure," responded Sean, who opened his guitar case and pulled out his battered Telecaster.

"Nice," said Dave, "looks like it's seen some action."

"Yeah, it's a shit guitar, but I get by on it," said Sean.

"You're a funny guy," said Dave. "Do you know any of our stuff?"

"Yeah, I do," said Sean, seeing Shana out of the corner of his eye, and melting at the thought of her and how she had put their names together – like they were an item, a couple.

I'll play for her, he thought. I've got to get this, if only to see her again. Shana smiled perfectly and gave him a thumbs-up.

"Why don't you plug into that Twin Reverb there," said Dave, twirling a mic in his hand. "Let's see what ya got. How about we try something like … hmmm … do you know 'Devil Heart'?"

"Can you hum it to me?" asked Sean, quickly adding, "No, just joking, I know it went to Number Four."

"Actually, Number One" said Dave, "for eight weeks straight."

"Yeah, quite good, quite good," said Sean, quickly striking an E7th to make sure the amp was working. "It's in A flat, right?"

"No, we always do it in G, that's the right key for my voice."

"Okey-dokey," said Sean. "I guess I can move the whole thing down one fret – why not?"

Then he held up his guitar to the three Daves with his hand on the third fret, and asked innocently, "Is this G?"

"Okay," said Dave, grinning as if he was now on to Sean. He looked over at the drummer and said, "Okay Dave, count us in."

Dave behind the drum kit smacked out a 1-2-3-4 with his drum sticks and they roared into 'Devil Heart'.

Sean knew this one inside out, it was a big hit and he'd played it before on some gigs.

He felt good. The drummer rocked, the amp sounded good and in the middle of the song he ripped out a guitar solo even better than the original. Oh yes, this was it, he felt like he had been in this band all his life. He was hitting it all the way, the whole thing, as if they had always played together and then, right as he was really climaxing in his solo, his top string broke with a shrill twang. Incredible! and Fuck! flashed through Sean's mind, but undaunted he poured his whole being into the last chorus of the song as a naked Shana flicked through his brain, and they crashed into the final dirty chords. The cymbals faded to silence, the guitar chords turned into a low buzz and the last bass note disappeared like a raven in the night. Nobody spoke until finally Dave the singer looked over at him with a raised eyebrow, and with the reverb from the micro-phone ringing and repeating "Dave … Dave, Dave, Dave …"

# THE PEARL-HANDLED KNIFE

He pulled the guitar up from the little curling waves as they broke on the sand. Early morning, the sun beat like a knife on his back. He shook the salt water off the guitar as best he could and saw the falling rivulets as tears.

He choked out "guitar..." and fell forward on the sand.

Blackness.

Later he opened his eyes, crawled up the sloping sand and pulled himself into the small shade of a rock.

He put his hand on the guitar for comfort and coughed some salt water into the sand.

He slept again and dreamed of his wife Sen Nguyen. She appeared to him, whispering something he couldn't understand – maybe it was Vietnamese, probably something comforting. She smiled and faded.

He slept again and then woke with a start, shivering in the sun. Nothing had changed, the little waves were lapping on the shore, the sun was high overhead, the rock still full of heat. He picked up his guitar and played a chord, but it was out of tune and full of se water. He let out a long breath and stared at the placid ocean. Then Sen came into his mind and he sobbed.

He walked down to the beach. It just looked like a beach, nothing had drifted up to the shore, no sign of human life, just a few shells. The palms whispered in a fresh breeze from the east and clouds appeared. He looked up into the sky – no birds. He imagined it on the BBC news: "A cruise ship has disappeared somewhere in the Philippines, at this point it has not been found. There is radio silence, no emergency signal was recorded."

He sat there staring into space as the sun climbed toward its highest point. The waves curled over his feet and he remembered being a kid on the beach at Shell Bay in Dorset – lovely days plunging in waves and munching on cheese sandwiches. He was thirsty, throat dry and as if in hallucination he saw himself down on the sand, his tongue hanging out, a word balloon popping out of his head. He shook his head to dispel the stupid image and decided to move. He got up and muttered, "follow the sun." He cast a look at the rock as if wishing it goodbye and leaned down to touch what was now his only possession in the world, his little Yamaha guitar. In normal circumstances he would never leave it, but that was ridiculous *here*, in this place, this situation. Who was there to steal it? But he placed his hand on it as if in assurance and set off along the beach toward the west end of the bay. He trudged on for a couple of miles, staying down at the surf's edge. The interior, a thick jungle of palms a hundred feet back from the water's edge, now appeared to him as hideous and dangerous, harbouring God knows what. He shivered at the sight of it. As he walked West he saw hills rising above the tree line. He took that as a good sign – he could get up there and make a fire. But with what? came the following thought, and why would he make a fire anyway…? He began scrambling up the slopes, pulling on vines and small bushes to ascend. He finally reached the top, which had a small grassy plateau as if it was meant to be a lookout point. He looked back and down at the bay behind him and the view prompted something inside to tear open like a glacier ripping apart – the horror of thick swamping water, a pale hand in the dark, the black speeding terror of the vessel going down, her, she… He had grabbed her hand and thrown himself out of their cabin as a huge flood of water rushed down the galley. He lost his grip on her. And for an interminable few minutes he was drowning, being battered, hurled into hard objects and finally a feeling of a lightness, of floating, of being carried by a new current as the fast-drowning ship released him into the surrounding ocean. He struggled in the waves searching for his wife, but the sea seemed to mock him as if it had never happened. It came to him now that it was the guitar that saved him. It had given him buoyancy and pulled him upward and away from the fast-sinking ship. A miracle, or just dumb luck?

He lay face down in the grass, stunned. Misery poured through him with no relief from the blue sea, cloudless sky and lush tropical vegetation.

He lay there motionless while the sun moved through the sky and small waves emptied themselves on the shoreline below. Through a half-closed eye he watched a black ant slowly move across the dirt in front of his face. It carried a small thin straw in its jaw and seemed to have a destination. Up tiny crests and indentations the ant moved forward. He watched its progress and then felt saddened as the small piece of straw became snagged on another piece of fallen vegetation. The ant re-attached itself to the straw and, struggling, freed it and continued its progress.

"It's going somewhere," said Heath out loud. "It's going home, it's going home." He rolled over onto his back and stared up at the sky.

And then he seemed to hear voices, military voices, questioning, commanding voices and orders, and with what strength he had left he sat up straight, knowing what he had to do. He was a marine. He was trained for all survival situations. He must survive, that was his duty. He got to his feet and looked about almost automatically for the necessities of survival. They would be proud of him and how he could handle even a situation like this. He wrestled with a sob in his throat. The events roared through his head like a bad film, like some mad test. Here he was on an island in the Philippine Sea with nothing, his wife gone. His mate gone. It was only him now.

The sun beat down on his head making him feel sick. He uselessly bent two fallen palm fronds together into a sun hat. Then, returning to some vague *Robinson Crusoe* idea in his head, said to himself "Well this will be the signal point," and almost jumped at the sound of his own voice. He felt a need to return to his rock on the beach and his guitar. The descent was faster, but with his arms scratched in a few places he finally hit the beach again. He walked to the water's edge and sat there for a few minutes, letting the salt water wash over him. It felt good at first but then he started to shiver and felt cold again. He pulled himself up and continued walking back to the rock and his guitar, which was about another fifteen minutes of walking. The rock came into view, but where was his guitar? He felt dizzy, as if he was hallucinating. He had left it there leaning on the rock. It wasn't there now. He looked in amazement and disappointment. Had an animal taken it? How could this be?

He finally got to the rock and slumped against it. Where was it
– his guitar? Then he heard a sound from somewhere in the trees
behind him. It came again – and he knew it for a guitar string. He
got to his feet and listened with great intent. It came again and now
started repeating – one note over and over, like a detuned E string.
Incredible he thought, another human? Another human? I'm not
alone … and stifling a cry of joy and desperation he cautiously crept
through the trees and bushes toward the sound and emerged into a
small clearing. A small Asian man was sitting there, leaning against
a tree, the guitar in his arms. He was thumbing the top string. He
looked up and smiled. Heath, to his own surprise smiled back. And
then the man got up and came over to where Heath stood immobi-
lized. He was laughing, and so Heath started laughing too, and they
laughed together as if they were both sharing the same great joke.

After a while their laughter subsided and a different look came
over the man's face as he picked up the guitar and beckoned Heath
to follow him. The small Asian set a rapid pace and Heath struggled to keep up. It came to Heath that the man was Japanese but
what were those clothes he was wearing? Torn and ragged as they
were they looked like some sort of military uniform. They moved
on through the dense trees for what to Heath seemed like hours,
although it was probably only one. Disoriented as he was, Heath
stayed close behind the man and his guitar because it seemed the
only logical thing to do. We must be going somewhere he thought,
maybe there are others, maybe I will be out of all this in a few days.
Then he thought of his wife again, and life without her. His parents
appeared in his mind, his mother and father full of the good old
words, "Buck up love. Come on, you can do it – brave soldiers never
cry." The melody of 'Land of Hope and Glory' came into his head
and then the words and melody of 'Jerusalem' as if he was back in
school; "And did those feet in ancient time, walk upon England's
pastures green …" Well, here he was in a dense Philippine jungle
following a stranger dressed in tattered rags. He wrestled with a
laughing sob in his throat as again the nightmare ran through his
head like a bad cartoon. He cursed himself, he cursed the path that
he could barely make out in the penumbral light. He cursed his
luck. He should never have listened to Reggie. They had been in

the marines together. After demobilization Reggie left for southeast Asia, saying he loved it and it would be home to him and his Thai girlfriend for the rest of his life. And he, Heath, returned to England and Lewisham where he soon met Sen, one of the first Vietnamese immigrants after the war. They had married and settled down. What possessed him to listen to mad Reggie and the idea of a late honeymoon cruise in these seas in Reggie's old junker of a boat? He should have seen it coming. Reggie always liked risk.

"This old tub will live forever," he had boasted, slugging back another beer.

The absurdity and the cruelty of the situation hit him and now he burst out laughing – it was all so terrible. The Japanese, without looking back, joined in laughing again and crazy as it was, they seemed to be forging a bond – they were in this together. They arrived at an open space of flatland, the jungle now behind them, and he saw a small shelter constructed from a few poles and a stack of palm fronds. Close by were the remnants of a fire with a log at one side. Clearly this was the home of his new friend. They approached the front of this humble structure and the Japanese turned to Heath, bowed and extended his hand in the direction of the shelter. He said something in his own language. He must be saying welcome to my humble abode, thought Heath, it would be fitting. He gave a small bow back, pointed to his own chest and said "Heath." The Japanese, apparently comprehending his meaning, jabbed himself in the chest and said "Yushimi", then repeated it and gave a small bow. Heath looked at him and croaked back the name. Yushimi gestured toward the shelter and bent down to enter the frail structure. It was difficult to see much in the closing light, but Heath made out a tiny photograph in a silver frame, a thin mattress – obviously Yushimi's bed – and a pearl-handled knife at the place where a pillow might be. Alongside that lay a rifle with a leather shoulder strap. Heath made some encouraging noises as if impressed. The Japanese smiled and then pointed to his mouth and rubbed his stomach. Heath nodded, realizing that he meant food as he gestured to the log at the edge of the fire, inviting Heath to sit. He then disappeared back into his shelter and came back with various items that looked like some sort of meat and green plants. How is he doing this wondered Heath, how long has he been here and what is that shirt he is wearing? While he was thinking about all of this, Heath picked up his guitar from where Yushimi had left it leaning on the log. He strummed the open strings and the guitar responded with a sour, rasping tone. He looked up and saw Yushimi staring at him. He smiled back and Yushimi pointed at the guitar and made some grunting sounds that sounded like approval, then turned back to his small fire and cooking.

Heath sat on the log, watched and felt as if he was in some sort of fantasy, suffering a surreal hallucination attended by brief shocks that shuddered through his body. The Japanese just seemed to accept his arrival without question. The heat of the fire passed across his face and the rancid smell of the wet jungle undergrowth entered his bloodstream as if claiming him captive.

Yushimi made grunting noises as he pulled food from the fire and piled it onto a small metal plate, which he handed to Heath. Heath nodded at him and took some of the meat in his hand and quickly pushed it into his mouth. The flavour overwhelmed him and had an immediate, emotional effect. He ate rapidly, scooping the contents into his mouth until it was gone. Yushimi looked over and grinned at him as if to acknowledge that food was a good idea and then said something in Japanese as he pointed back at the pot on the fire. Heath took it that he was being offered more and passed his plate back. As he did so he noticed what appeared to be some sort of seal stamped on the side of the plate. It was in Japanese characters and official-looking, he supposed that it was some sort of legal stamp that indicated that the plate was the property of … what? who? Yushimi piled more of the meat onto the metal plate and Heath ravenously swallowed it all again. His host sat opposite, staring at him and slowly ate his food with what looked like a hand-carved pair of chopsticks. He pointed at the guitar and motioned for Heath to play it. Heath picked up the small instrument and brushed his fingers over the strings again. It was hopelessly out of tune. He began twisting the tuning pegs, bringing the strings back to pitch and uttering a small prayer that they wouldn't break. Slowly and with great delicacy, he raised the slack strings up to what he thought was close to standard pitch, even if a little flat and then finally struck an E major. It rang out through the trees and Yushimi's face lit up in a huge smile. Heath felt encouraged and thankful that the guitar was still capable of music. He played a series of chords: E, D, C, B7th, Gb minor, A minor and then from A minor he tremblingly played 'Greensleeves', a song that he had known since he was a kid. Hearing it now, with its quintessential Englishness against the backdrop of a thick jungle, brought a choking sob to his throat. He then sang two Beatles songs thinking that Yushimi might recognize them, but when he looked over at him his face seemed to be frozen with shock. Heath guessed that he was experiencing some sort of emotion but, in a Japanese way, locked it down. He wondered again who is this man, are there more like him, why is he here on this island? In these mountains?

He looked over at Yushimi and made a gesture with his arms as if to encircle the surroundings and then pointed at him with up-turned hands as if to ask "Why are you here?"

Yushimi looked at Heath and nodded. Heath sensed that he had understood the gesture and felt a peculiar relief – all was going to become clear, there would be a way out of here, he would get back to England, he would go home. And then *she* rose in his mind again and washed away any feeling of restoration or hope; instead, he felt desolate, ridiculous and alone. Maybe he would die here.

Yushimi stood, picked up a stick that lay nearby and began making marks in the sand. Heath stared at the marks as they became more and more elaborate and began to understand that it was a drawing. It was crude, but Heath made out that the marks were pictures of aircraft and beneath the planes were several round circles. He began to realize in a dazed way that Yushimi was trying to depict some sort of enemy, for he now made guttural noises as if in imitation of explosions and bombs going off. He then pointed up at the sky with raised arms as if firing a rifle, continuing to make deep throaty noises as he fingered an imaginary trigger.

An incredulous thought sparked in Heath's brain and he started laughing. It couldn't be ... could it? An impossible thought. The war had ended twenty-nine years ago. Was this lone Japanese man still fighting? Lost here in the jungle alone, isolated and unaware ...? How could this possibly be? It was unbelievable, but it explained the tattered uniform, the stamp on the metal plate, the rifle, the knife.

"No, No!" Heath almost shouted at Yushimi. "Over. Over – no more."

But Yushimi didn't seem to understand what Heath was saying, and kept looking at the sky with anger on his face. Heath was at a loss as to how to explain it. He grabbed the stick from Yushimi's hand and brushed away the marks. He then drew a sun and its rays, and as an afterthought a couple of flowers, before finally drawing a smile on the circle that represented the sun. He looked over and said, "Finished, finished; no more – happy." Yushimi stared back with an impassive look on his face. He doesn't believe me thought Heath – incredible. Then Yushimi put his head against his hands in a gesture of sleep. Yes, thought Heath, sleep, this will take time. The Japanese gestured toward the shelter. They went inside and from somewhere Yushimi pulled out a decent-sized piece of cloth and invited Heath to lay on it. Heath practically fell down with gratitude and exhaustion. He quickly sank into a deep, dreamless sleep as if in a black void. And then, breaking through the black tide of sleep he felt a strange, pricking sensation as if a small fish were biting him. He opened his eyes and stared in horror at Yushimi, who was above him, the pearl-handled knife at his throat.

# ICE BLONDE

"Thanks mate," said Sullivan.

He slammed the door of the UberX and crossed the pavement quickly to slip into the semi-darkness of Oh My Sole, an overpriced little seafood restaurant in Knightsbridge.

Everything was coloured white and blue, with walls, dishes and tablecloths all displaying various slimy sea things – fins, tentacles, shells, clumps of seaweed and a couple of lascivious-looking mermaids bathing in foam. He sat there for a minute looking around the room, wondering what it would be like to have sex with a mermaid, and then stared at the menu and thought, think I'll get a burger, this place is crap. Barclay was late, but then he usually was. A woman brushed by his table on the way to hers, leaving a subtle hint of exquisite perfume, skin and the scent of sex. He saw the beautiful ice-blonde hair tumbling down her back, the slender waist, the dancer's glide and in a second the most ancient of impulses arose inside. He hadn't seen her face but surely … She melted into a chair at a table near a window facing him. He breathed deeply. She was classically beautiful – Russian? Scandinavian? – and she brought her desirability to a pitch with a silky black skirt that slid high up on her perfectly shaped right thigh as she crossed her legs and stared out at the street.

My God, she's perfect, he thought, but she's waiting for someone – lucky bastard, whoever he is – probably James fucking Bond. The waiter delicately put a glass of water on the table, waved a menu like it was a handkerchief and asked if he could get him started with a drinky-poo. Sullivan stared up through his Oliver Peoples shades and in his best Glaswegian roadie voice said, "Och nae, better not – mebbe a wee drinkie later pal – thanks, ah'm waitin' for Rob Roy." The waiter looked confused and twirled away to another customer.

Sullivan continued staring at her, trying to guess her name. Brigitte? No. Laura, maybe? Ivanka? Could it be Katya? A whole slew of Slavic-sounding names fluttered through his brain.

He started imagining a life with her. She would be sweet and funny, always gorgeous – even in the mornings as she yawned her way out of bed with her tousled hair and oversized men's pyjamas, on her way to a modelling engagement for *Vogue*.

She would be playful in a Nordic way, slaloming down mountainsides in tight ski pants, throwing snowballs, racing on a toboggan, conjuring up magical stews from reindeer meat or freshly speared salmon. No doubt she also played the cello. He saw her perfect thighs wrapped around the deep-brown body as it resonated and sent a bowed C# minor triad into her. He felt the pulsing ache of desire and wished he was a cello or a chess master or possibly a theoretical physicist.

Should he just go over there and introduce himself? Say hello? Maybe she'd recognize him – it would depend if she was into music or not, maybe she was strictly classical, no interest in rock or pop, even if his face was plastered on every bus in London at the moment. I can't blow this, he thought, got to be casual, got to be smooth, no pressure, no double entendres, charming that's the word, charming … Jesus, she's fantastic. I'll just make my way over there – absolutely incognito – no one will notice me. The restaurant dining room was packed tight with full tables and happy diners. Sullivan rose to his feet. He was wearing a Jean Paul Gaultier black leather jacket, bright red Comme des Garçons pants and an Alexander McQueen pirate scarf around his neck, all topped off with those silver reflective Oliver Peoples shades.

Then providence took a hand, and a young woman got up from her seat and approached his table clutching a pen and a piece of paper and with profuse apologies asked him for an autograph. He gladly signed, smiled at the young woman and said, "Anita – alright there you go sweetheart, good luck." She was followed by a couple of teenagers who left their parents' table and came over with the same request. He did it again and then, as he narrowly avoided putting his elbow in the bowl of an elderly lady's clam chowder, a middle-aged married couple materialized muttering that they didn't usually do this sort of thing but, by God, what a chance, and could he possibly sign their restaurant napkin – they'd driven down from Hatfield – what a night. He scrawled on their paper napkins and then looked up to see that Ivanka-Katya-Brigitte was looking across at him with interest. He caught her eye and his heart thumped out a paradiddle as they faintly smiled at one another. But his cover was blown. Damn, he thought. So much for incog-bloody-nito. Well, better make the most of it. And smiling at people, he began signing his way through a sea of napkins, showing that he was a decent bloke after all and not just an ultra-famous rock star wanker. All eyes were on him now, fascinated by his slow progress as iPhones were raised when he stopped in front of another old lady who was handing him a greasy napkin to sign. Sullivan stared down at her old crone face.

"Pleased to meet you," he said. "What's your name?"

"Eunice – it's me birf-day," shouted the old lady.

"Oh lovely," said Sullivan, "how old are you?"

"'Undred and fuckin'-six," the old lady croaked back. "Can I 'ave yur jacket?"

"Well of course," said Sullivan, "it's your birthday – here you go!" He slipped out of the Jean Paul and handed it to her.

"'Ere 'ave a drink," said the old lady, and she pushed a glass of champagne into his hand. "Get it down ya – go on!" Now aware that the whole restaurant was watching him and expecting a bit of rock star stuff, he raised his glass and bowed to the goggle-eyed ensemble and said, "Okay, well here's to your health," and slugged the whole glass down in one gulp. A small cheer went round the restaurant. Seeing an opportunity, the restaurant management seized the moment and turned off 'Sea Pictures' by Elgar, cranked up the speaker system and let rip with 'She's Everything' his latest hit single, and the entire place burst into applause. Now stripped of his black leather, which had revealed he was wearing only a tawdry Lemmy's Motörhead T-shirt underneath, Sullivan continued inching his way between the tables in pure rock star agony. Faint smears of clam chowder now streaked his T-shirt and a lobster claw had attached to his belt buckle as he made his way through the tightly packed tables. His head spinning with cheap champagne, he knew his cool was blown and he wished he was dead. About a million years later, feeling like he had just traversed all the labyrinths of the ancient world and feeling horribly famous to boot, he arrived at her table. The entire restaurant – diners, waiters, busboys – all stared hungrily.

The rock star and the hot babe.

It was so obvious that they were a couple, a beautiful couple in fact, meat for the front page of *The Sun*. Forks suspended in mid-air in front of open mouths and English dental work as the whole mob of diners eyeballed this modern-day Adam and Eve, imagining them doing the nasty later on tonight.

He stood there for a few seconds as the perfect opening line "I just came in for some fish and chips" tried to escape from his brain, but now slightly scrambled by the trek across the dining room, it came out as "I just came in for love some chish and fips you." He looked at her with a shrug and a grin as if to say, "Well, what can you do?" and leaned into the table toward her. She gazed up into his face, her lovely eyes reflecting the dazzling blues and whites of the dining room and then brightly popped out, "Oh, here's Barclay."

Sullivan turned and saw that his bloody manager was advancing across the restaurant toward them.

He cursed inwardly. I don't bloody believe it. *Him?* He tried to maintain a cool composure. He turned back to Eve and said, "Oh, you know him? That's my manager. He works for me."

Eve looked up at him, a look of conflict on her perfect face.

# SHE'S EVERYTHING

t wasn't as if she was feeling that great anyway, but then she entered the room where the whole lot of them – all those bloody relatives – the aunts, uncles, nieces, nephews, in-laws, were sitting together like so many sheep, all staring at the telly and fiddling with Christmas crackers. They all turned toward her yelling her name in unison through the suffocating stink of smoke, beer and cheap perfume which pitched into her throat with an added hint of something electrical, maybe the faulty electric fire with its four devilish red bars burning the air near the Christmas tree.

It was all of them and it was nasty. She saw the Christmas tree catch fire, the paper angels and golden horse ornaments burst into flame, the house become an inferno as she got out and they all died in the furious blaze, she the only survivor, front page of the tabloids.

She saw her cousin Billy leering at her and refocused. But this moment, with its claustrophobic fug, made being with her family feel like she was locked in a broom closet dosed with Old Spice, her own life stuck in a tight dark corner. Got to get out.

They could all die in here, thought Dot as she stared back at their grinning faces and dodgy dental work. She was late coming down from her room, like a film star or something.

She briefly flashed on her crumpled bed upstairs and wished she was back there instead of having to face this lot. She gave a half-hearted grimace back at the staring pink blobs and managed a faint "Appy Xmas."

"Appy Xmas Dot!" they yelled back. They were already half pissed. It was more like a pub than her mum's best room. She sat down on the sofa next to her Aunt Vi and buttoned the top of her jeans.

"'Ere, got something for you Dot," said her aunt, and she passed over a badly wrapped present in sloppy brown paper, tied with some knotty white cord.

"Go on – 'ave a look," said Vi.

"Thanks Vi, that's sweet," she mumbled with little enthusiasm. Dot pulled the wrapping apart and took out the present. It was a stuffed parrot – red, yellow, blue and green.

"I thought it's just what you needed right now," said Vi, swirling her glass of mother's ruin and laughing. "Seein' as you ain't got a boyfriend no more."

The mini-mob began laughing and cackling ("Dot and her bloody boyfriends"). She stared at them with what she fancied to be a face of ice. It shut them down a bit and the crude laughter subsided into a low sniggering. They all knew about Dot's latest break-up this week. It was Kevin last week, it was Robbie this week, next week it would be Mike, Martin or Joey right after that – girl gets around.

"Well let's see if it can fly," she said, and hurled the parrot into the air where it somersaulted a few times, got caught in the paper chains and crashed down onto her Uncle Bill's lap, knocking his beer to the floor.

"Gawd now look at what y'done," said Terri, her mum. "Ruined the carpet – bloody 'ell – gotta be more careful Dorothy!"

"I like 'im," Jimmy, her nephew, piped up from somewhere down on the carpet, placing the parrot on the top of his head.

"Thanks Sully," said Dot. They all called the kid Sul or Sully, what with his surname being Sullivan from the Irish side of the family.

"C'mon Sul," she said, "let's go upstairs and play guitar together, leave this lot to get pissed."

"You only just got 'ere!" said her dad, struggling on the sofa with a plate of Spanakopita.

"Yeah!" said nine-year-old Sul, "Thanks Aunty Dot."

She stood up and moved to the doorway, Sul got up and followed her.

"Shall I bring the parrot?" asked Sul.

"Yeah bring 'im," replied Dot, and they both headed up stairs to her room.

In the bedroom, they plonked down on the bed, and Sully asked, "Where's the guitars?"

"Under the bed," said Dot as tears welled up in her eyes.

"Aunty Dot, what's the matter?" said little Sully. "It's Christmas – don't cry." He reached under the bed and pulled out two small guitars.

"This lot don't get me," said Dot through muffled sobs. "They just think I'm boy mad, but that's not it, it's 'cos I'm crazy about music, all these guys I go out with are musicians, I just like pickin' their brains, that's all. I learn stuff, it's not all about snoggin'. Sorry Sul, you're a bit young for all this – what do you want to do today?"

"I got a new song," said the boy. "I wrote it last night!"

"Christ you're only nine and writing songs already – you're a bloody marvel. Go on then, give it a go." She sat up on her bed and wiped away a tear.

"Okay," said Sully, and he strummed an E chord. "'S'called 'She's Everything'."

He strummed the guitar for a minute and then with his young but perfectly pitched voice, broke into a bittersweet little melody over the chords. It was basically a two-part A-B construction with a verse and a chorus that used the phrase 'She's Everything' four times in a row, ending on a relative minor chord with the words "to me". He sang the whole song staring out of the window as if the world was watching, and came to the end with a natural rallentando as the song hit its final chord.

"God that's wonderful Sully," said Dot, her hand over her mouth. "I can't believe it, you're a bloody star – it's so natural for you, you're better than any of those idiots I hang out with. Let's start a band. I'm twice your age and half as good – but Jesus, you are a talent…"

Dot fell back on the bed and said, "God – music – it's everything – there's nothin' that comes close. C'mon show me those chords, let's do it together. Christ, that was a Christmas present."

"Yeah, Merry Christmas Aunty," said Sully, smiling over the top of his guitar.

# ROLL OF HONOUR

The publishers gratefully acknowledge the contribution of everyone listed below, whose generous support helped bring this project to fruition.

Armand J.
  Abbondanza, Jr.
Jason Addesso
Bruce T. Adelman
Moises Alanis
Chandra Alderman
Rodrigo Altaf
Paula Amato
Anders Andersen
Colin Anderton
Andrea
Leslie Anne
Antoni
Andrew Antropow
Roger Ash
Mirza Asif
Kristian Aspelin
Michael Atkinson
Steve Avery
Sascha Bahr
Jack Baillieux
Brian Baker
Joanne Baker
Per Balazsi
Jeremy Balcirak
David Bales
Michael Ball
Nick Banschbach
Frank Bardessono
Lou Barnett
Seth Baugh
Peter Bayliss

Uwe Becker
Jimmy Bejarano
Donald Bennett II
Anthony Bentley
George Berberian
Brian Bernitt
Susan Bett
Jim Bing
Karsten Bohmann-
  Hesse
Carlo Bolchini
David Bonechi
Sara Borella
Damien Boudreau
Gary J. Boulanger
Brandon Bowers
Paul J. Brennan
Marianne Bressanelli
Jeb Brethauer
Andrew Brignell
Anna Brown
Gary Brownrigg
Mike Bryant
Jeff Buda
Kathy Burville
Bytor
Rob Cable
Alvan Caby
Stephane Caille
Monica Chavez
  Cajiao
Matthew Nicholas

Callaghan
Brett Cantrell
Derek Cantrell
Bradley Carr
David Carroll
Simon Castellan
Andrea Andy
  Cesarini
Cesar Chavez
Brian Chenault
Valerie Cholet
Dean Coffman
David Cohen
Gareth Cole
Scott Collins
Guido Colombo
Eric Columber
Barry W Combs
Alison Cooper
Brian Cope
Jonathan Copley
Roi Croasdale
Dr Chris Crockford
Kimbley Crouthers
Michael James
  Curran
Paul Curtiz
Jeffrey D. Kent
Gabriel da Silva
  Coelho
Alicia Danielle
  Thomas

Sarah Dardick
Sarah Dardick
Melinda Darling
The David Family
Janet Davison
Andrew de Araujo
Steve Dean
Ellie Dees
Andrea DeJong
Marie-José Dekkers
Jamie Jr. DeMelo
Des
Grace Dillon
Joseph DiMattio
Brown Dithrich
Matt Doan
Vin Downes
Francis Dowson
Jean-Paul Draper
Anne-Jelmer Drent
William Drewry
Matt Dudenhoeffer
DumDumBoy
Alan Edwards
Ron Egatz
Matthew Eison
Matthew Eison
Jason Elliot
Søren Elnef
Andreas Engel
Fred van Engelen
Jacques Engler
Paul D. Englund
Dirk Fabritz
Giorgio Fairsoni
George Farley
Chris Ferraro
Sharon M. Fetter

Maciej Fleischer
Chris Foster
Ben Fothergill
John Fowler
Andreas Franke
Sarah Freeman
Rob Gagnon
Gian Luca Gaiba
James W. E. Gale.
Alexander Gallo
  and Juliet Lawn
Frédéric Galvani
Hooman Ganjavi
Brian Garza
Malachy L. Gately
Petrina Anna
  Gattuso Copes
Andrew Geisler
Kurt Gensert
Megan Geraghty
Janne Gezelius
Jeremiah A. Gilbert
Karen Gilmore
Tony Gleed
Bobby Górka
Rich Gorzynski
Lee Graham
David J. Grden
Julia Green
Joseph J. Grinvalsky
Addy de Groot
Albert Gualtieri
Luigi Guastella
Jean-Yves Guyon
Rich Haddad
Matt Hadden
Linda Haley
Brooke Hamilton

Kenny Hamilton
Yuji Hanashima
David Hannah
Steve Hansen
Ben Hardy
Cheryl T. Hardy
Andrew Hartley
Ian Hartley
Jon C. Henderson
Charles
  Heppenstall
Carl "Egg"
  Hernandez
Marc Herold
Scott Hessel
Darren Higham
Hiroyuki
Rüdiger Höckel
Dieter Hoffmann
Hans Hofmeier
Maureen Hollowell
David Hooper
Vanessa Hooper
Matthew Howard
Gareth Hughes
Pauline Hunt
Travis Husband
Anthony M.
  Iannuzzi
Rick & Dorie Ijams
John Jackson
Dagon James
Martyn Jeffery
Inge Brede
  Johannessen
Shaun Johnsen
Keith Johnson
James Johnston

Rick Jones
Scott Jones
Steve Judd
Andy Jurik
Junko Kambara
Chie Kanaya
Raj Kapila
Damara Kaplan
Thomas Kasten
Miki Katz
Hiroyuki
  Kawaguchi
Joseph Kelly
Jeff Kendrick
Klark Kent
Angie 'Kay' Kessler
Phil King
A Kingsman
Jeremy Kinn
Deborah Anne
  Kinsella
William Kirkwood
Rob Kiszko
Andy Kneale
Diego Kovadloff
Sam Krahe
Michael J. Krantz
Dave Krawczyk
Thomas Kronik
Nick LaBran
Karim Laiquddin
Lair
Jay Lalor
Edwin Lammers
Andy Lancelot
Nicola Lane
Tripp Lanier
Laurent

Sean Lawler
Michael Lee Nelson
Simon Lehva
Steve Leicester
Elisa Leon
Jens Licht
Keith Liddle
Boris Lidukhover
Niclas Liebling
Louis Lima
Eric Lindsey
Philip Lindsten
Martin Lister
Jonathan Livesley
Anna Livia
Roy Long
Bruno Duarte
  Lopes
Lux Lopgil
Nancy Loughlin
Art Love
Paul Love
Andy Lovegrove
  (twelveof)
Danny M.
Louis Magnifico
Michael Malchioni
Peter Man
Our Man Will
Stephen Manning
Raj Manoharan
Marta Maraboli
Jack Markey
Rob Marshall
Sarah Masiero
Claudio Massara
Jay Matsueda
Félix Matte

Roberto Mauri
Matthew Mayer
Gerrie McCall
Declan McCarthy
Debbie McCarthy
  Sutton
Mark McCloskey
Wayne McCrory
John McEwan
Danny McGuinness
D. S. McIntosh
Colin McKay
Mercère
Brad C. Mettler
Ian Miller
Larry Miller
Angelo Mimmo
Paul Minett
Barry Mingard
David Mischoulon
Andrew Mitchell
Mark J. Moerman
Chris Molinelli
Allison & Austin
  Moore
Simon Moore
Marco Morana
Leigh Moyser
Volkwin Müller
Albert Mur Tejeda
Gergely Nagy
Joh Nakahara
Slava Nekrasov
Mjyke Nelson
Ashley Newnam
Erik Nielsen
Peter Noon
Kenn Norman

Darren J. Norton
Danny O'Donnell
Des O'Mahony
Yosh Okabe
Mark Oliff
Omegaman
(and the rest of
Synchronicity III)
Jude One Eight
Sandor Ostlund
Mrs Saskia P.
Alan Page
Sanjay Paranandi
Bill Parish
Peter R. Patrylo
Lyn Richards
Pawlowski
Clay Pendergrass
Omaha Perez
Luca Perissinotti
Lucy Perry
Ben Peters
Petrina & Jason
Rachael Pfuetze
Kate Pierpont
David Pinder
Michele Piumini
Christa Planko
Doug Pollock
Joseph Pombo
Ian Pordon
Brenden Portolese
Joel Pospychala
James Powell
Alex Pritsker
Gina Puga
Richard Pydiah
Jan Quinlan

Paul Rab
Z. Ranch
Mark Randall
Josh Ray Barrett
Thom Rayne
Davis Reed
Philip Reeves
Jon Regen
Jeremy Reid
Randy Reid
Stefan Reijenga
Victor Reynaga
Steve Reynolds
Al Ribickas
Beth Anne Riches
Kyle Rile Watson
Peter Jason Riley
Peter Alan Roberts
Jodi Robinson
Luis F. Rocha
Josh Romaine
Ryan Romano
Rochelle Romo
Adam Rosen
Ira Rosenblatt
Rebecca Rothrock
(Roxy)
Wizard of Roz
Rousian
Lisa Roy
Nigel Rozier
Eric Rusack
Marjorie Ryan
Nikki S.
Maurizio Saccani
Alex Sadowsky
Donato Salamina
Miles Salisbury

Bud Salter
Jonathan Samway
Massimiliano Sani
Antti Sannela
Famiglia Santillo
Paul Savin
Jennifer Schiavo
Alessio Schiavone
Tjitze Schiphof
Luuk Schroijen
Wendy Schulz
Matty Scrape
Quintin Sean
Grubb
Frank Sell
Pocket Sengupta
Puneet Sethi
Michelle Sheridan
Stephen Short
Alfonso Siino
Johnny Silva
Christopher Simar
Jeffery Simpkins
Mike Simpson
Ed Skero
Mark Smartnick
Andrew P. Smith
Angela Lynn Smith
Chris Gateshead,
Queens
Hall, Twickenham
& Manchester
Smith
Darryl Houston
Smith
Jan Smith
Jason Somerville
Rich Southgate

Chris Spalding
John Stenlake
Tom Stenström
Mike Stephens
Scott Stevenson
Bill Stone
Kara V. Strickland
DJ Driko Suave
David Suber
Chris Sudall
John Summers
Anja Suontausta
Rodney Suttles
Jason Swierski
Matthew Symes
Jerry Szczybura
Tagyerit
Ehab M. Taha
Suguru Tanaka
Kevin Tanswell
Dayna Giselle
 Tausig
Bob Taylor
Timothy Taylor
James Tees Wood
Jack Thetgyi
Julian Thomas
Stephen Thorpe
Nigel Tolley
Darin Toohey
Sherri Toy
Tjarda Tromp
Yves Tubiana
Andy Tuck
Kerry Tucker
Anna Maria
 Tulimiero
Duncan Tyler

Paul Ullmann
Rev. Lindasusan V.
 Ulrich
Inge van den Burg
Glenn van Dijk
Erik van Maren
Vania
Koko Vayedjian
Jessica Vickers
Lionel Villanueva
Roberto Viscardi
Joe Vitoulis
Steve W. Dickson
Martin Walker
John Walliser
Peter Walmod
Jay Walsh
Susan Walsh
James Warman
Michael Weatherly
Mark West
Phil West
Whitt
Sheila Wiggins
John Daniel
 Wilkinson
Darren P. Wilson
Zachary Wilson
Max L. Wisley
Jonathan Wright
Robert Wright
Dave Yackaboskie
Ryan Yamorsky
Kris Yanalitis
David R. Young
Yoyoronnie
Korlath Zalan
J.E. Zerpa

rocket88books.com